Anthony Gilbert and The Murder Room

>>> This title is part of The Murder Room, our series dedicated to making available out-of-print or hard-to-find titles by classic crime writers.

Crime fiction has always held up a mirror to society. The Victorians were fascinated by sensational murder and the emerging science of detection; now we are obsessed with the forensic detail of violent death. And no other genre has so captivated and enthralled readers.

Vast troves of classic crime writing have for a long time been unavailable to all but the most dedicated frequenters of second-hand bookshops. The advent of digital publishing means that we are now able to bring you the backlists of a huge range of titles by classic and contemporary crime writers, some of which have been out of print for decades.

From the genteel amateur private eyes of the Golden Age and the femmes fatales of pulp fiction, to the morally ambiguous hard-boiled detectives of mid twentieth-century America and their descendants who walk our twenty-first century streets, The Murder Room has it all. **>>>**

The Murder Room
Where Criminal Minds Meet

themurderroom.com

Anthony Gilbert (1899–1973)

Anthony Gilbert was the pen name of Lucy Beatrice Malleson. Born in London, she spent all her life there, and her affection for the city is clear from the strong sense of character and place in evidence in her work. She published 69 crime novels, 51 of which featured her best known character, Arthur Crook, a vulgar London lawyer totally (and deliberately) unlike the aristocratic detectives, such as Lord Peter Wimsey, who dominated the mystery field at the time. She also wrote more than 25 radio plays, which were broadcast in Great Britain and overseas. Her thriller *The Woman in Red* (1941) was broadcast in the United States by CBS and made into a film in 1945 under the title *My Name is Julia Ross*. She was an early member of the British Detection Club, which, along with Dorothy L. Sayers, she prevented from disintegrating during World War II. Malleson published her autobiography, *Three-a-Penny*, in 1940, and wrote numerous short stories, which were published in several anthologies and in such periodicals as *Ellery Queen's Mystery Magazine* and *The Saint*. The short story 'You Can't Hang Twice' received a Queens award in 1946. She never married, and evidence of her feminism is elegantly expressed in much of her work.

By Anthony Gilbert

Scott Egerton series

Tragedy at Freyne (1927)

The Murder of Mrs
  Davenport (1928)

Death at Four Corners (1929)

The Mystery of the Open
  Window (1929)

The Night of the Fog (1930)

The Body on the Beam (1932)

The Long Shadow (1932)

The Musical Comedy
  Crime (1933)

An Old Lady Dies (1934)

The Man Who Was Too
  Clever (1935)

Mr Crook Murder
  Mystery series

Murder by Experts (1936)

The Man Who Wasn't
  There (1937)

Murder Has No Tongue (1937)

Treason in My Breast (1938)

The Bell of Death (1939)

Dear Dead Woman (1940)

 aka *Death Takes a Redhead*

The Vanishing Corpse (1941)

 aka *She Vanished in the Dawn*

The Woman in Red (1941)

 aka *The Mystery of the*
  Woman in Red

Death in the Blackout (1942)

 aka *The Case of the Tea-*
  Cosy's Aunt

Something Nasty in the
  Woodshed (1942)

 aka *Mystery in the Woodshed*

The Mouse Who Wouldn't
  Play Ball (1943)

 aka *30 Days to Live*

He Came by Night (1944)

 aka *Death at the Door*

The Scarlet Button (1944)

 aka *Murder Is Cheap*

A Spy for Mr Crook (1944)

The Black Stage (1945)

 aka *Murder Cheats the Bride*

Don't Open the Door (1945)

 aka *Death Lifts the Latch*

Lift Up the Lid (1945)

 aka *The Innocent Bottle*

The Spinster's Secret (1946)

 aka *By Hook or by Crook*

Death in the Wrong Room
  (1947)

Die in the Dark (1947)

 aka *The Missing Widow*

Death Knocks Three Times
  (1949)

Murder Comes Home (1950)

A Nice Cup of Tea (1950)

 aka *The Wrong Body*

Lady-Killer (1951)

Miss Pinnegar Disappears (1952)
 aka *A Case for Mr Crook*

Footsteps Behind Me (1953)
 aka *Black Death*

Snake in the Grass (1954)
 aka *Death Won't Wait*

Is She Dead Too? (1955)
 aka *A Question of Murder*

And Death Came Too (1956)

Riddle of a Lady (1956)

Give Death a Name (1957)

Death Against the Clock (1958)

Death Takes a Wife (1959)
 aka *Death Casts a Long Shadow*

Third Crime Lucky (1959)
 aka *Prelude to Murder*

Out for the Kill (1960)

She Shall Die (1961)
 aka *After the Verdict*

Uncertain Death (1961)

No Dust in the Attic (1962)

Ring for a Noose (1963)

The Fingerprint (1964)

The Voice (1964)
 aka *Knock, Knock! Who's There?*

Passenger to Nowhere (1965)

The Looking Glass Murder (1966)

The Visitor (1967)

Night Encounter (1968)
 aka *Murder Anonymous*

Missing from Her Home (1969)

Death Wears a Mask (1970)
 aka *Mr Crook Lifts the Mask*

Murder is a Waiting Game (1972)

Tenant for the Tomb (1971)

A Nice Little Killing (1974)

Standalone Novels

The Case Against Andrew Fane (1931)

Death in Fancy Dress (1933)

The Man in the Button Boots (1934)

Courtier to Death (1936)
 aka *The Dover Train Mystery*

The Clock in the Hatbox (1939)

Miss Pinnegar Disappears

Anthony Gilbert

An Orion book

Copyright © Lucy Beatrice Malleson 1952

The right of Lucy Beatrice Malleson to be identified as the author of this work has been asserted in accordance with the Copyright, Designs and Patents Act 1988.

This edition published by
The Orion Publishing Group Ltd
Orion House
5 Upper St Martin's Lane
London WC2H 9EA

An Hachette UK company
A CIP catalogue record for this book is available from the British Library

ISBN 978 1 4719 0998 6

www.orionbooks.co.uk

To
Edmund Crispin.
You're exceedingly polite.
And I think it only right
To return the compliment.
          – Gilbert

CHAPTER I

THE PUTNEY-BOUND BUS was in such a hurry that the conductor rang an impatient bell before the last of his intending fares could mount the step. Although she uttered a protest he paid no heed, and the great red monster sailed scornfully away into the chilly spring morning. It was Sunday, and a grey haze, promising later rain, overhung the sky; the wind was cold and Miss Pinnegar was well past her first youth. She drew an unfashionable tweed coat more closely round her shoulders and pursed up her long unpainted mouth.

"Most inconsiderate," she said to no one in particular, since, so far as she knew, she was alone. Certainly there wasn't a soul in sight. She was the more startled, therefore, when a cheerful voice observed, " Spoken like a lady," and a small conveyance, by courtesy a car, drew up at the Request Stop. A burly man with a red face, and eyebrows and hair as red as a fox, seemed to be bursting out of it.

"Going my way?" asked this vision.

Toad of Toad Hall, decided Miss Pinnegar, who had been puzzled for a moment by a deceptive familiarity. But Toad fallen on evil days. Indeed, the car looked as though it had been knocked up out of biscuit-tins painted a vivid scarlet.

"Allenfield Mansions, Merlin Road, near South Kensington Station," said she. The driver leaned forward and wrestled with the door of the car.

"Don't often open it," he explained. "Me, I just step over the side, and—well, most dames are so choosey. It's a Hawk or a Hillman for them every time. But, to my way of thinking, a car's a car if it gets you from one place to the next."

As she stepped in and drew her long grey skirt clear of the wheel, the man went on, "Crook's the name, Arthur Crook. Well, what do you know?" For, to his amazement, this drab-looking female turned to him with a smile that completely transfigured her long plain face. Like a noble and ancient horse, he thought. But a Derby winner, in her time.

1

" Mr. Crook ? I've heard so much of you, though I've never had the pleasure of meeting you before."

Crook looked more gratified than you would have thought possible. " Any time I can be of service," he insinuated.

" Quite a number of my patients, when I was theatre sister at St. Margaret-by-the-Docks, had reason to bless your name. Such charming people, but a law unto themselves."

" Good luck to 'em," said Crook heartily. " Always defeats me why we bow down to whatever the johnnies in the talking shop tell us is good for us. Some of the laws I'd make 'ud surprise 'em, and who's to say they wouldn't be as good as theirs ? "

" There are penalties in living in a community," agreed Miss Pinnegar. " But the advantages far outweigh them."

" Made a bit of a change, haven't you ? " suggested Crook in his outspoken fashion. " I mean—St. Margaret-by-the-Docks to S.W.7. Still, I'll say you've earned a bit of a rest. Can't have been a picnic down there during the war."

" It was where I preferred to be," returned Miss Pinnegar serenely. " I am one of those fortunate people who have been enabled to earn a living by doing the work they best enjoy."

" Same here," said Crook heartily.

" Oh, yes, I've always realised that," agreed his companion. " I have always thought of you as Robin Hood in modern dress."

Crook nearly fell out of the Scourge. " Sure you're not mixing me up with someone else ? " he suggested anxiously.

An onlooker would have sworn there was affection in Miss Pinnegar's smile. " I doubt if that happens very often. But I am quite sure that you must have had to—er—soak a great many Peters to pay your bare expenses in connection with many of my Pauls."

Crook waved a huge hand with the effect of swinging the world a trinket at his wrist. " Pleasure's mine. Don't say another word about it. I never could see," he added confidingly, " why people should be paid a packet just for havin' a good time. Makes you into a sort of gigolo, would you say ? " He really sounded quite anxious.

The notion of Crook as a gigolo was so entertaining that Miss Pinnegar laughed outright. " I think not. Nevertheless, I couldn't agree with you more, as my young nurses would

2

say. I have never seen the justice of giving the luxuries of this world to the people who have the greatest of all blessings, the work they themselves have chosen. Cabinet Ministers, writers, bishops, actors, why should THEY have the large incomes, the foreign holidays, the expensive cars ? Their work and its contacts, with a sufficiency for their upkeep, should be a reward in itself. We shall never persuade people to abandon materialist standards until our leaders give them an example."

" Attlee must love you," said Crook dryly, swinging the Scourge neatly round a corner and depositing Miss Pinnegar in front of a block of pleasant but old-fashioned flats. " How does all this strike you after the docks ? "

" You really wish to know ? Yes, I can see you do. Then I feel like a rabbit in a comfortable hutch. I am grateful for shelter and a steady diet, but there are necessarily times when I remember my days as a wild rabbit, if I may be permitted the expression."

" Jake by me," murmured Crook, who was watching her fascinated. " Any of the wild 'uns ever find their way down here ? "

" Not very many, of course. Well, they have their own lives, into which, for a time, I intruded. Now someone has taken my place, and they have—readjusted—themselves. Besides, Florence, my maid, isn't precisely welcoming. She regards a cage as the anteroom to Paradise."

" She come from the docks, too ? "

" She was with me at St. Margaret's during the war. At her own request she joined me when I retired, as seemed to me fitting, in 1945. A bomb destroyed the settlement house and—I was foolish enough to get in the way of some of the débris with the result, as perhaps you saw when I was attempting to board the bus just now, that I am not quite so—er—nippy on my pins as I once was. Nor do I visit them, since I should feel myself in the position of a mother-in-law foisting herself on her son's household. *Autres temps, autres mœurs.* And I am very fortunate to have a cage at all," she added, stepping out of the car. " A man to whom I was able to render a little service some years ago promised to find me accommodation when the time came to retire, and as that coincided with a small flat falling vacant here, it seemed to me that for once I must give Providence best. And, really, it's very pleasant to be able to read and go about and listen to music. Until now I've never had the leisure."

Crook looked at her with an expression of unusual shrewdness on his big pug face. " Don't tell me you haven't rumbled that one," he said. " Leisure's like a mirage. Lovely when it ain't there. When you are—it's a desert. Right ? "

Miss Pinnegar put out her hand. " How did you discover that ? I should never have expected you to have sufficient leisure."

Crook, unaware that he was hanging on to her hand in its narrow shabby glove like a dipsomaniac clutching a bottle, said earnestly, " Went down to the country once." He said it as Pluto might have spoken of his descent into hell or Lazarus into the grave. " Landlord would insist on doin' some redecorating—makin' leeways with some of Hitler's mess. ' Don't mind me,' I told him. ' My shoulders are broad. If a bit of the ceiling falls on me I shan't notice.' But no, he wouldn't listen to reason. Saw a chance of getting something from the Government. Not that I blame him, mind you, but what a way to spend it ! Well, there I was like a snail without its shell, so I went down to see if the country's all it's cracked up to be. I tell you one thing, if I'd had to live there when I was a young shaver you wouldn't have found me fighting for England's green and pleasant land in 1914. Talk about quiet ! Never a minute's peace. Always a horse shoving its great head over a fence and blowing at you as you walk down a lane, or a cow telling you what it thought of you, and lucky for me, I dare say, I don't understand cows' language—and the birds nattering like a lot of M.P.s. Luckily, I fell over a body in a church and by the time that little bit of trouble had been cleared up my landlord had spent his pittance and I could come back to S.W.5." He dropped her hand at last and felt in the pocket of his bright-brown waistcoat. " Take this," he offered, handing her a card. " Not in the way of business, you understand, but—well, it might come in handy. I mean, there don't seem much sense in you and me meeting at the bus-stop if that's going to be the end of it."

Miss Pinnegar took the card and put it inside her large, shabby handbag. " You won't misunderstand me if I say I hope I shan't require to refer to it again."

4

Crook grinned. " I'll be surprised," he said, and stepped back into the Scourge.

Florence looked at her employer with astonishment. " You didn't get off the bus," she said accusingly. " I was watching."

" A man very kindly gave me a lift in his car," said Miss Pinnegar.

Florence instantly looked suspicious. " What did he want ? "

" One of the few advantages of being obviously elderly and poor is that you never need ask yourself that question," said Miss Pinnegar serenely. " As a matter of fact, it was Mr. Crook."

Florence's reaction was instantaneous. " Crook ? No, not that one. See here, Miss Pinnegar, you don't want to get yourself mixed up with that kind of person any more. You've left the Settlement behind you. Anyone might think you'd be glad."

" Anyone might be wrong. You don't imagine I like being old and useless, do you ? "

She went away into her room to remove her hat and gloves—it was Sunday morning and she had just returned from church—reflecting that if there's no cloud without a silver lining equally there is no rose without a thorn. Florence was loyal, hard-working and honest. Yet, when Miss Pinnegar was asked, " What is she like ? " all she could ever think of to reply was, " She has very high principles and varicose veins."

Florence had never approved of Miss Pinnegar's reckless-ness at the Settlement, the way she went about all hours of the day and night quite alone, not even armed with an umbrella. She was silly about her possessions, too. " If anyone wants something of mine so badly they're prepared to steal it, then they are welcome to have it," she would say. " They will, in any case."

It was due to Florence that so few of the St. Margaret's folk came visiting at Allenfield Mansions. Miss Pinnegar recalled one young woman turning up beaming with an enormous baby in her arms. " I never heard you were married," said Florence, looking at the baby as if she expected it to drip all over everything within five seconds.

" Well, I never heard that myself," agreed the besotted mother.

" He does you great credit," intervened Miss Pinnegar, who for all her own high principles was deplorably lax about other people's. " A wonderful child."

" The Lord sends them, they say," remarked the Wonder's mother. " No sense blaming me if sometimes He sends one to the wrong address. Best take it up with them Up There." She grinned mischievously at the shocked Florence.

Miss Pinnegar's recollections were interrupted by Florence's voice at the door. " Your breakfast's getting ruined," she announced disapprovingly. " Seeing you only have it once a week you might as well eat it hot."

Miss Pinnegar came out wearing the sort of smile Florence had learned to distrust. It meant she was waiting an opportunity to open the door of her nice refined cage and pop back among the savages in the undergrowth. That was how Florence always thought of them.

As it happened, events distracted Miss Pinnegar's attention during the next few weeks and it was early summer before she had any reason to look for Mr. Crook's card. She was temporarily in sole possession of her flat, Florence (" the silly girl," said Miss Pinnegar indulgently) having attempted to board a bus at the lights a few days previously.

" This vanity of yours that makes you determined to present a record of never absent, never late in your threescore years and ten is your undoing," said Miss Pinnegar unsympathetically.

The conductor, appearing like a bad fairy from the upper deck, bawled, " Carngetonere," and when Florence said defiantly, " You can't stop me, there's room inside," he put out a large hand and, according to her story, deliberately pushed her off the platform. His version was that, flustered at being baulked, she missed her footing. At all events, she fell flat in the gutter and discovered to her fury that she couldn't get up again. A few sightseers, mildly entertained by the incident, stood on the kerb and watched her struggling like a fly that has fallen on its back. One said, " Dunno 'ow she does it this time of day. They don't open for 'alf an hour." Eventually, a philanthropist telephoned for an ambulance and Florence, still protesting furiously, was carted off to the hospital. Here it was discovered that she'd broken two small bones in her leg and she was told she wouldn't be able to get about for a month at least, and lucky if it wasn't six weeks.

" What's Miss Pinnegar going to do without me ? " she demanded. " Get into trouble, I shouldn't wonder. They ought to hold that man for attempted murder. In the old days I could have sued the company. Now it's the Government nobody gets their rights."

Miss Pinnegar, pouring dubious oil on the seething waters, pointed out that in the old days she'd have had to pay for hospital treatment, whereas now she got it free.

" Free ? " snorted Florence. " I pay my stamp, don't I ? "

" I pay it," returned Miss Pinnegar calmly.

" That's right, rub it in I'm past sixty. But I can do a day's work with any of the youngsters and don't you forget it."

" Now do look on the bright side," Miss Pinnegar urged, looking remarkably untroubled by this minor disturbance in her own routine. " You're always telling me how tired you are. Now you can have a nice rest."

" What she really means," observed one young nurse to another (" No sympathy at all," complained Florence bitterly), " is that she can have a rest. I dare say even St. George didn't mind saying good-bye to the dragon now and again."

Miss Pinnegar came back to what she irreverently called Broomstick Country to find a visitor on her doorstep. This was a small black kitten mewing persistently and lashing a tail about as thick as a piece of tape. " You were all I needed to complete the picture," Miss Pinnegar told it, taking it in with her as a matter of course. Forty years of discovering strangers on her step had made this random hospitality second nature to her. She set her long, serviceable umbrella in its stand, reflecting that in these days of Hoovers, broomsticks were really out of fashion and an umbrella of this type was an excellent substitute. She poured out some milk for the cat, which proceeded to make itself at home immediately. " How very considerate of Providence," Miss Pinnegar reflected. " I'm so unaccustomed to my own company I might have felt a little lonely while Florence is away. Nobody can be lonely with an animal on the premises."

It was a week later that her second and far less welcome visitor put in an appearance on a grey blustery evening in May. It had been raining all day as it did mostly during the early summer of that year, and Miss Pinnegar shivered with appreciation beside her warm electric fire. The curtains were drawn, her supper things neatly washed and stacked, she had heard the news. The usual trouble in Paris, Korea and Persia; a front-bench Minister had influenza; a Harley Street doctor had had his car, containing some dangerous drugs, stolen from a cul-de-sac while he dined near by; 200 employees of a nationalised industry had staged an unofficial strike. . . . Miss Pinnegar put out her hand and switched off the programme. Nothing new, she reflected. At nine-thirty there was to be a concert by her favourite pianist, that would effectually wash the grit of this troublesome information from her mind.

It was shortly after ten-thirty and she had put on the kettle for her final cup of tea when the front-door bell rang. The management of Allenfield Mansions was wholly in accord with the authorities as to the importance of saving electricity and the hall and landing lights gave only the dimmest of illumination, and even that would go off at eleven o'clock when the front doors were locked. The tenants were provided with front door keys, but the management didn't encourage visitors after 11 p.m.

" Dear me," reflected Miss Pinnegar. " Now who can that be ? Miss Michael perhaps come to borrow something." Miss Michael was the tenant of the flat across the landing, who perpetually found herself short of small necessaries. Not that Miss Pinnegar really believed her housekeeping to be so deficient, but she was a woman of few acquaintances and she liked to find excuses for hovering on the verge of other people's lives, even, reflected Miss Pinnegar, lives as uneventful as my own. Still, it was late for Miss Michael.

When she opened the door she realised it wasn't her fellow-tenant, for the woman on the mat had something she doubtless called a hat on her head. She took a step forward as if to enter the flat without invitation and instinctively Miss Pinnegar closed the gap with her own lean form.

" Miss Pinnegar," said the stranger, not in an inquiring but in a flat assertive tone.

" Yes," said the spinster. " Do I know you ? "

" You ought to," was the grim reply.

A suspicion so monstrous that it could scarcely be entertained flashed into Miss Pinnegar's mind. As her visitor took a step forward she instinctively retreated, so that the light from the little hall fell on the newcomer's features. Miss Pinnegar flung up her hand, looking remarkably like a scrawny angel guarding the Gates of Eden.

" No," she said in a low tone. " No, you can't come in here. You're dead."

" Looks like it, doesn't it ? " retorted the other. " And how you wish it was true."

" You've been dead for ten years," amplified Miss Pinnegar, still refusing admission. " I saw the certificate myself."

" Ah, but you didn't see the body. And that's what matters. Well, aren't you going to ask me in ? Your own nephew's wife ? Anyone would think you weren't glad to see me."

" Anyone would be right," returned Miss Pinnegar grimly. All the same, she stood back and allowed her visitor to enter.

" Anyone with you ? " demanded the woman.

Miss Pinnegar shook her head. " My maid is in hospital."

" Come up in the world, haven't you ? A posh flat and a maid."

Miss Pinnegar winced. " What do you want ? "

" Perhaps I'd like some news of my husband."

" I hardly think so. After all, you've displayed no interest in him for ten years. I should find it very difficult to believe you were developing scruples at this time of day, Violet."

" Might pay you to keep in with me," said the woman called Violet in threatening tones. " I could do your precious Geoffrey quite a lot of harm."

" You haven't changed an iota," was Miss Pinnegar's dry comment. " You've never done him anything else since the day you seduced him when he was a boy of twenty."

" Here, language," protested Violet furiously. " It takes two to make a get-together. Not that you could be expected to know that. All you vinegar virgins are alike." She glanced round her. " Very cosy." Then her glance fell on the kitten, christened Grimalkin, and known as Grim, who here

9

appeared from beneath the fold of a curtain and stood directly in front of the visitor, arching his back, bristling his minute whiskers and slowly lashing his tail. His mouth opened to reveal tiny pointed teeth, his eyes flashed.

Violet retreated a step. " I'm not coming any farther till you put that cat in the kitchen," she announced. " I don't like them. They give me the creeps."

" The abhorrence appears to be mutual," said Miss Pinnegar. She bent down and scooped Grim into her arms. " I must remind you, however, that Grimalkin is here by invitation and in his own right, while you are here by neither."

" Rights ? " sneered Violet. " Forgotten, haven't you, I'm still Geoffrey's wife, if he is living with that concubine of his."

Miss Pinnegar dropped the kitten into a chair and deliberately slapped Violet's face.

" I will not have that kind of language under my roof. If you wish to go I am not detaining you."

" It's a pity some of your dock rats who thought of you as a cut between Florence Nightingale and Lady Galahad can't see you now," exclaimed Violet viciously. " That's assault."

" The telephone is beside you. You can summon a policeman if you wish." She was watching Violet as she spoke and she saw the look of terror and dismay that flashed across her face. " So that's why she's here," she reflected. " I might have guessed. In some sort of trouble and come to me because she knows my hands are tied. Whatever she's done I can't give her up to the authorities, for Geoffrey's sake." Racked with anxiety though she was, she maintained a surface serenity.

" Do I take it that you don't propose to avail yourself of my offer ? I thought as much. Very well. You had better sit down and we will talk things over. What trouble are you in now ? "

" Don't talk to me as if I was one of your girls you'd taken off the streets. Don't forget I'm your precious nephew's wife, whether you like it or not. I've got the right to demand your help. . . ."

" You have no rights," returned Miss Pinnegar in a voice that would have turned the cream sour, had there been any on the premises. " Get that into your head at once. Nobody in this world has rights, except children and those who are physically or mentally incapable. Moral deficients are in a different category. Do I take it you are seeking sanctuary from the authorities ? "

" If you mean, have the police got anything on me, no, they haven't."

" Then perhaps you are having a little difficulty with your landlady," suggested Miss Pinnegar in the same acid-honey tones.

" I haven't come here to beg," shouted Violet. " I don't need to. Come to that I'm probably a lot better off than you."

" That would be perfectly simple even for a person like yourself. I can't help thinking, all the same, that you have come to ask some favour. If this were merely a social call you would hardly arrive so late in the evening."

" I thought," said Violet sulkily, " you might put me up for a day or two. Lucky for me your skivvy's away."

" You really believed I should offer you hospitality ? What a preposterous notion. I notice, by the way, you have brought no luggage with you."

" Well, no." Violet paused but Miss Pinnegar gave her no lead. You wouldn't have guessed that her heart was beating fit to choke her. The resurrection after more than ten years of this vulgar woman who had done her best to ruin Geoffrey Pinnegar's life was the worst shock she could have received.

" Perhaps," she said after a moment, " you could explain a little. When my nephew married Marcia Edwardes five years ago he had every reason to believe himself a widower. Your death in an air-raid had been reported and confirmed so far as confirmation was possible, when so little evidence was forthcoming. A direct hit on the F.A.P. . . ."

" I know all about that." Violet laughed harshly. She was a woman of about thirty-five now, with nothing left of the plump deceptive prettiness she had had ten years earlier. But then she had never had anything but a surface charm Geoffrey had been too young, too inexperienced, too infatuated to fathom. There was no trace of that charm left now. She had grown rather fat, with a stupid, malevolent, heavily made-up face and unexpectedly shrewd eyes. Rat's

11

eyes, Miss Pinnegar called them. She was fashionably but not suitably dressed, and Miss Pinnegar's fastidious spirit was shocked by the untidy, not to say dirty, condition of clothes that had once been of excellent material and cut. A button was missing from the dark green coat and a second hung by a thread; there was a run in her nylon stockings and the ridiculous hat she wore had a long slender feather broken at the tip. Her shoes weren't well polished, there was a hole in one glove, and her expensive crocodile handbag had a smeared surface. "Well?" said Violet in loud defensive tones. " You'll know me again, won't you?"

"You haven't changed much," said Miss Pinnegar pitilessly. " You were always a sloven, but when you were younger you had other qualities that distracted the eye from your shortcomings. You don't appear to have the wit to realise that as you get older you cannot afford to let your appearance go."

Violet gasped. " There's a case of the pot calling the kettle black," she exclaimed. " You're no oil-painting yourself."

" I didn't ask you here in order to exchange vulgarities," said Miss Pinnegar coolly, her heart beating more irregularly than before behind her meagre black bodice. " Kindly state your business and go. And if," she added, " you have come for Geoffrey's address, you are wasting your time."

" I can get that through the proper channels," retorted Violet. " I know he's in the army. All the same, you may not be so keen for me to go when you know what my business is."

" I'm yearning for you to come to the point," said Miss Pinnegar.

But Violet still hesitated. At last she said, " Well, it's a man." Miss Pinnegar's expression of distaste increased. " I'm in danger," pursued Violet desperately. " He—he wouldn't think twice about getting rid of me if he could."

" He has my sympathy," said Miss Pinnegar almost cordially. " Perhaps we could come to some arrangement. A married man, I presume?"

" Oh, come off it," shouted Violet. " That was half the trouble from the start, you and Geoffrey always being so high-toned and lah-di-dah, using words I couldn't understand, always showing me how common you thought I was.

It wasn't my fault I didn't go to your old Roedean or Oxford University, like Geoff."

" I trust," said Miss Pinnegar, who hadn't been named the Battleaxe for nothing, " you're not going to suggest I am responsible for a time when I was happily unaware of your existence ? You were twenty-five at least when I first set eyes on you on the ill-fated day Geoffrey introduced you as his wife. If I had known only a little earlier I would have stopped the marriage, but the harm was done. It was too late to point out that you were five years his senior and by no means inexperienced."

" And of course he didn't know a thing," sneered Violet.

" He knew so little that he was caught by the oldest trick in the world. I don't believe you ever thought for a moment there was going to be a child."

" Well, there would have been," said Violet sullenly, " only seeing how things were turning out and you being about as friendly as an iceberg, I took steps——"

" So you couldn't even go through with that ? "

" Easy for you to talk." Violet flashed. " You try having a baby with a war on and your husband leaving you practically on the altar steps. . . ."

" He went to fight for his country."

" I know, I know, he was a hero. Well, I can tell you it's not much fun being a hero's wife."

" You weren't one for long. You were reported missing without trace in 1940, and leave to presume death was given the following year. Everything pointed to your having lost your life in the raid on the first-aid post. Two survivors remembered seeing you sign on, and the bomb came down half an hour later. There were a great many casualties, many of whom were unidentifiable. If you weren't killed, then you can't have been on duty."

" Well, I wasn't. I should have thought even you would have got around to that by now. We weren't all as keen to be heroes as you and Geoffrey. It's all a matter of temperament. I know some people liked the bombs, they gave them no end of a kick, made them feel how goddamned wonderful they were. Well, I wasn't like that. I hated them. They scared me stiff. Every time I heard the siren go I began to shake all over. I didn't stay on duty because I wasn't fit for that sort of work, they'd no right to put me into it. . . ."

" In that case I wonder you remained in London. You admit yourself you'd no ties to keep you. You might have gone to the country; there was plenty of useful work to be done in the reception areas."

Violet stared. " You must be bats. Me go to the country ? I'd as lief throw myself into the sea. I'd have gone crackers, nothing but old maids and kids and their mothers. Anyway, that night I was with someone who didn't like the bombs any more than I did. Mind you, he wasn't a shirker, he worked in London all day. . . ."

" And retreated to a safe area after dark ? "

" What if he did ? He was doing work of national importance. It wasn't going to help anyone if he was killed. He was married to one of these women that liked feeling important and getting into uniform and bossing people about. She used to be out night after night, shelters and all that. It wasn't much of a home for him to come back to after a long day's work, so he got this little place outside and he had his car, of course, being someone important in the Government, and one night he asked me if I'd like to go with him. Well, I needed my sleep like anyone else, but I knew what Lady Muckamuck at the post would say if I asked her, so I just signed on and then slipped out the back way to where George was waiting, and lucky for me I did. A bomb blew the place sky-high not an hour afterwards."

" If the bomb had come a little later someone might have noticed you had deserted," commented Miss Pinnegar. " As it was, there weren't many survivors and it was taken for granted you were part of the—er—human débris that resulted. But why didn't you report yourself next morning ? "

" I came up," said Violet sulkily, " and the whole place was cordoned off. There was a policeman each end and a lot of women in W.V.S. uniforms making notes and being nosy, so I just said I'd had a friend and I gave my name as hers, see, and they were very sorry they were afraid there weren't many saved and this name wasn't among them. They asked me if I could identify any of her belongings, and they showed me a ring. Funny how little things like that escaped the blitz, isn't it ? And I remember when I got there I went along to wash. Well, I wanted some excuse for getting off, see ? And I took off this ring and put it on the side of the basin, and knowing George was waiting, I clean forgot it. Well, I said yes, she always wore it even on duty, and they said they were ever so sorry and would I like a cup of tea ? Their travelling van had just arrived and I was welcome. That made me laugh. I mean, it seemed so funny. Your friend's blown to bits, here's a ring we found lying about, how about a cup of tea instead ? I didn't take it, of course. I thought this was my chance. I went down to the country and I didn't come back to London till the bombing was over."

" I see," said Miss Pinnegar. " This, of course, was after Geoffrey had been posted as missing at Dunkirk ? "

" Well, we didn't get the bombs till then, did we ? Mind you, I never expected him to turn up again. I waited quite a while . . ."

" Did you make any particular inquiries, through any of the accredited agencies, I mean ? "

Violet stared. " How could I ? I was dead, wasn't I ? "

" But surely "—Miss Pinnegar knit her brows—" you were eligible for a widow's pension. . . ."

" Oh, I didn't bother about that. It wouldn't have kept me in cigarettes, anyhow. Besides, I'd made my own arrangements." She stared at Miss Pinnegar defiantly and the older woman saw the light.

" I understand. You'd married again."

" Well, what did anyone expect ? Nature never meant me to live alone. And, as I say, I thought I was a widow. When did Geoffrey turn up ? "

" In 1942."

" Oh, well, it 'ud have been too late in any case."

" Did you—er—marry your original cavalier ? "

" If you mean George Jenkins, I told you, he was married already. Besides, there was never much in that. No, I married a man called William Child. A widower, he was, a lot older than me, but with a nice house and a car—everything very comfortable—all except a daughter who hated me like poison. She was married herself and didn't see why she should have to share whatever her Daddy left with a step-mother. Some women *are* selfish, aren't they ? Still, I'm not put off so easy. William suited me, wasn't always picking on me, liked me to have nice things. And then when I told him about losing my husband at Dunkirk he was ever so kind. In the end, though, we got married by special licence. Had to sneak off like a couple of thieves. William 'ud never have dared take the plunge if he hadn't had me behind him. As for that woman, I don't know how anyone who calls herself a good wife and mother has the time on her hands to go round like something out of Sherlock Holmes, always spying. It's a wonder to me her last baby didn't have a face the shape of a keyhole."

" And—what happened to Mr. Child ? "

" Oh, he died about three years back. Mind you, it was all on the level. Pneumonia. He was one of these big men. When it came to the will, though, I was had proper. After all his big talk about his property and all the rest of it, it came out he'd been giving things away to that Mrs. Arbuthnot for years to save death duties, and all he had was an annuity. If it wasn't that he'd bought me some bits of jewellery and a fur coat—Russian ermine, it's not so common as mink— I'd have been left high and dry. But that's life all over. Men are all the same, liars and cheats, and Geoffrey was no better than the rest. What's this woman he's living with like ? "

Miss Pinnegar would not trust herself to reply.

" I see," said Violet in the same disparaging tone. " All to the harps and haloes, or kids you she is. Any family ? "

" Two little girls."

" And both of 'em baskets."

Miss Pinnegar looked as if she were about to repeat the slap and her companion withdrew sharply out of arm's reach.

" Say she's an angel it doesn't make any difference. I'm still Geoffrey's wife. Even if he did believe I was dead when he married her it doesn't make any difference in law."

" Always supposing," said Miss Pinnegar softly, " (a) that you can persuade a reputable authority you are the person you say you are, and (b) that you are in a position to dispute the issue."

Violet looked startled. " What do you mean by that ? "

" I mean firstly, you will have to prove your identity."

" That's easy. I'm Violet Pinnegar."

" Who says so ? "

" I do."

" And what proof have you to offer ? According to the official records Violet Pinnegar died ten years ago. Unless

16

you're going to claim you've been suffering from loss of memory you're going to find it a little difficult, aren't you, explaining why you didn't come forward before? And suppose no one recognises you?"

"You recognise me, you old bag."

Miss Pinnegar allowed the vulgarity to pass unchallenged. "Do I? But in court I might admit that in ten years it's easy to be mistaken."

"So that's your game? Well, Geoffrey will know me all right."

"Suppose he doesn't? What other witnesses can you produce—people who know you as Violet Pinnegar, I mean? No, really, you're in a very unenviable position. Unless, of course, you've been in the hands of the police. . . ."

"Here," shouted Violet, "you can keep that sort of suggestion to yourself. I've told you already the police haven't got anything on me."

"I'm afraid, Violet, you're not telling me the truth. I don't think you'd have come here simply because you've had a quarrel with one of your paramours. Well, if the police have no records there's another door closed. I'm afraid you aren't going to be popular. The civil servant's a remarkably orderly person, and dislikes nothing more than having to tamper with old records. However, perhaps you can suggest some other method of identification."

"I've got my marriage certificate," said Violet, with sullen triumph.

"Which one?"

"I've got them both. That proves it."

"It proves nothing beyond the fact that you're in possession of two marriage certificates. In what name is the second one made out? Did you marry Mr. Child as Mrs. Violet Pinnegar?"

Clearly she had caught her companion on the hop. Violet looked positively alarmed. "I hadn't been using that name for some time. I was Mrs. Jenkins, see?"

"Mr. Jenkins being—— ?"

"George. The one I told you about. His wife got so high and mighty he couldn't stand her any longer. . . ."

"And you accepted a situation as her stand-in?"

"Well, I couldn't marry him, could I?"

"And your identity card was made out in his name?"

" I told them I'd been bombed out and lost all my papers, and they gave me another card in the name of Jenkins."

" In the assumption that you had a legal right to it. Well, then, you married Mr. Child as Mrs. Jenkins. What happened to Mr. Jenkins ? "

" Oh, he had a bit of bad luck. I told you about this little place in the country where he used to go of a night. Well, would you believe it ? One evening a Jerry bomber unloaded one of its eggs just casually, trying to get away, see, from our boys, and poor George's place got a direct hit."

" And poor George was on the premises ? "

" That's right."

" And you ? "

" I happened to be away at the time. Bit of luck, wasn't it ? "

" For whom ? However, that is beside the point. You married Mr. Child as Mrs. Jenkins. I'm afraid, my dear Violet, you're not going to find it as easy as you think to establish an identity as someone who was buried in 1940."

" Geoffrey 'ull recognise me. He's got some moral sense, if you haven't. And it won't do him any good to have his name in all the Sunday papers."

" You think of everything, don't you ? Well, then, we must see that you don't have the opportunity of approaching Geoffrey. There aren't so many satisfactory marriages that we can afford to have even one broken up by a silly trollop." Miss Pinnegar had lived for years in a community where people spoke their minds and had neither the time nor the taste for verbal frills.

" You can't stop me."

" No ? You always underrated my capacities, my dear Violet."

" You think you hold all the winning cards, but you're wrong. Wait till I tell my story. All they have against me is that I laid low in the country in 1940 because I didn't want to come back to London. Well, that wasn't patriotic and brave, but I never set up to be a heroine. They can't send you to gaol for not calling for what was yours. I believed I was a widow—I did, too—and I married again. Then, when I found out the truth, through seeing Geoffrey's picture in the paper, and that's the first time I did know about this Marcia creature, I didn't come forward because I didn't want to bust things up for him. Why, people 'ud think it was rather decent. . . ."

Grim, who had been lying placidly on Miss Pinnegar's knee, suddenly rose and hissed. His owner put him on the floor, and he stalked out of the room.

" You make me sick," said the older woman simply. " At the same time I don't propose to ring up the police to-night. I've always found it a mistake to act on impulse."

" What are you going to do then ? "

" I am going to make myself a cup of tea. As you are my guest, even though entirely against my own wish, I will offer you a cup."

" Mind you don't put any poison in it," gibed Violet.

" Unfortunately I don't keep poison on the premises. If I did, and if I knew of any way of administering it that would not involve me in a trial for murder, I should not hesitate."

Even Violet was taken aback. " I say, you do hate me, don't you ? I believe you're more than half dotty."

" But only because any such development must inevitably harm Geoffrey," continued Miss Pinnegar as though Violet had not spoken, rising and plugging in an electric kettle. " I propose, therefore, to sleep on the problem, and will give you a bed for the night. When I've decided what to do I will let you know. But I should like this to be clearly understood. I should have no more compunction about putting you out of the way than I should in squashing a bluebottle. Sometimes," she added thoughtfully, opening a tin and producing some very plain biscuits, " I have allowed a bluebottle to live because I detested the thought of fouling my windows. But I have always got him in the end. I think it only fair—though doubtless misguided—to warn you of my attitude."

" Now I know you're crackers," cried Violet, really alarmed. " You talk of putting me out of the way as you might talk of washing your hands. You'd be a murderer."

" It may surprise you to know that murderers are quite ordinary people in extraordinary circumstances. The impulse is in us all. I consider you, for instance, to be a proven murderer. You deliberately destroyed your child—I don't for one instant believe it was your husband's—while, to be a little more subtle, you did everything in your power to take Geoffrey's life, though not by poison or a knife. You wouldn't hesitate to take it again in a similar way. So, stay here for the time being if you wish. But please never regard my house as a place of refuge. I shall not cease from mental strife, as William Blake says, until I have discovered some way of saving Geoffrey from you, and I shall stop at nothing. You understand that ? I shall stop at nothing."

Reluctantly she guided Violet into Florence's room. There were only two bedrooms in the flat so she had no choice, but what Florence would say if she knew this trollop was sleeping between her sheets Miss Pinnegar didn't like to think. Violet looked round at the photographs of chapel friends on chimney-piece and chest, the tear-off calendar of the Lord is my Shepherd by the bed, the biscuit box with the picture of King George V and Queen Mary on its painted tin sides.

"Whose room is this ? Florence's ? Oh, well, I suppose you have to pamper them these days to keep them at all." She flipped open the lid of the biscuit tin. "Not left much for the mice," she remarked.

Miss Pinnegar closed the tin quietly. "Florence is a great sweet-tooth," she said. "I will show you the bathroom." She swept Florence's few treasures into a corner drawer and turned the key, that she then removed. She provided a nightdress and slippers and a towel and said with her frostiest smile, "I am afraid I can be of no assistance where cosmetics are concerned."

"That's all right," said Violent carelessly. "I carry my own stuff about with me. Is there a key to this door ?"

"Neither Florence nor myself has ever required one," returned Miss Pinnegar. "However, I dare say I can find one."

"And you better see that cat stays away from me," added Violet.

Miss Pinnegar said good night in repressive tones and left her guest. Grim, contrary to his usual custom, came into her room and settled himself at the foot of her bed.

CHAPTER II

" MOST DAMES," said Arthur Crook, " have damn all respect for the law and, in a way, you can't blame 'em, seeing how little they've had to do with the making of it." And Frances Pinnegar had rather less respect than most. In the world where she had spent most of her life people obeyed what was roughly called Nature's law. If you wanted a thing badly enough you got it—fair means or foul. If you got sick of your old woman you didn't go through the tedious (and costly) business of airing your dirty linen in public, you simply made fresh private arrangements, leaving her free to do the same. If you thought the Government's planning silly and not suited to your particular case you just by-passed it and, as a rule, no one was any the worse. Live and let live was their motto, and philosophically they went to jail when they were caught and the country kept their wives and families. Some wives wished frankly that unsatisfactory husbands could get a life sentence, and so, said Miss Pinnegar, do a great many on the other side of Aldgate Pump; but they wouldn't say so for the world. So that the idea of somehow getting the odious and destructive Violet out of the way did not shock or appal her as it would have shocked or appalled any other tenant of Allenfield Mansions. She did not seek to justify her point of view ; it was against the law and to that degree immoral ; but Violet alive was a danger and an expense to society, and Miss Pinnegar was so old-fashioned that she thought all this psychiatric stuff pure bunk where such women were concerned. When she went to bed that night she was resolved by hook or crook to prevent Violet from telling Geoffrey the truth.

In a detective story she would put her out of the way without any scruple at all. It was done every day of the week. You noticed—as Miss Pinnegar had noticed this evening—that your enemy put saccharine in her tea, and you watched your opportunity and substituted pheno-barbitone. (See Gregory Gaunt in *Cups and Killers*.) But even if she were prepared to go to these lengths there was the insuperable objection that Violet would probably collapse in Allenfield Mansions and any number of uncomfortable questions would be asked. And even if she, Miss Pinnegar, could keep her mouth shut, and it was a trap that had closed on a good many secrets in its time, you could be certain that Geoffrey would get special leave from the B.A.O.R. authorities and come bustling home. Geoffrey was like Miss Pinnegar's own son.

His mother had died when he was an infant, his father had been engaged in work overseas and had left the baby to be looked after by his aunt. Miss Pinnegar had no intention of giving up her career as a nurse to look after the child, but she had engaged a children's nannie, and had contrived to be with him a good deal. Later, when her brother re-married and the new wife, who was very young, didn't want a noisy four-year-old in the home, she had virtually adopted the boy. Gerald, his father, had been killed in a motor accident a few years later, and his widow had re-married in her turn. The boy had a small income from his father which paid for his schooling and when most of this disappeared during the depressed thirties, Miss Pinnegar met all necessary expenses out of her own pocket. So, in one way and another, she had managed to keep him at a good preparatory school until he won a scholarship to one of the public schools and ceased to be much of an expense except in the holidays. She had insisted on his going abroad each summer to stay with a family, so that by the time Geoffrey was eighteen he spoke two languages besides his own. The war, of course, caught him young ; it was then that he had his desperate affair with Violet, which ended quite deplorably, in his aunt's view, in marriage. In June 1940 he was reported missing and a few months later Violet was presumed killed in an air raid. In 1942 Geoffrey turned up again to learn that he was a widower, and since he had hardly felt he was married to Violet in any case, it surprised no one when, at the end of the war, he married Marcia Edwardes and settled down to establish a family of his own. Of course, Miss Pinnegar was bound to admit to herself that, even if she could discover the perfect way of getting rid of Violet, it would not make Geoffrey's marriage legal or his children legitimate, but since no estate or family title was involved, it seemed to her natural feminine unscrupulousness that it would be ridiculous to let Geoffrey know the facts. Violet had ceased using his name years ago; she would be identified by the one on her ration book, Mrs. Violet Child, and as such she would be buried. Absurd to dig up an old story better forgotten by everyone. No, that part of it did not trouble Miss Pinnegar at all. The important thing was to keep out of the limelight herself.

And, anyway, she reminded herself, she hadn't got any pheno-barbitone and it might look odd if she bought some twenty-four hours before Violet died. Or, again, in films and crime stories, the killer lured his victim on to a platform and pushed him in front of the oncoming train. (See Killer Robinson in *Death Goes Underground*.) But this method, too, presented a good many difficulties. You had to get your victim on to the platform and then inveigle him (or her) to the edge, and the crime itself must be a miracle of timing. A shove a second too soon and the driver would contrive to draw up, a second too late and you'd fail. Then there was the problem of would-be Galahads, what they called Nosys in the docks and Crook called Buttinskis, only too eager to get a little limelight by saving someone from a horrid death —or others, equally anxious to give evidence that might involve a murder charge. And, anyway, you wouldn't get Violet to stand for five seconds on the same platform as Miss Pinnegar.

" Dear me," reflected the old warhorse, turning on to her right side, " I can't imagine how murderers ever get away with it. And yet they do. Victims have been strangled with nylon stockings (Miss Pinnegar had never owned a nylon in her life) suffocated with pillows, stabbed, drowned, pushed over cliffs or into quarries. . . . But I could never persuade Violet to come for a walk in the lonely countryside, and suffocation's easier on paper than in actual fact, and it's the exception rather than the rule for the victim to have two bottles of precisely similar medicine, similar in appearance, I mean, one lethal and the other a harmless digestive mixture. As for knives and firearms, they call for a great deal more skill than I know myself to possess, as well as being a very messy way of procuring death. And blood should be avoided at all costs." At this stage she realised with a shock that she was really weighing up the pros and cons of every kind of murder. " Before I know what is happening to me I really shall have committed a capital crime," she thought. She remembered a most interesting conversation she had once had with a detective in east London. " Murder," said he, " starts in the mind. It begins with a wish. If only So-and-So was out of the way I'd be a rich man." Or, " I could marry that little girl I've had my eye on for so long—or I could chuck this job I hate and start afresh. And pretty soon it becomes, When So-and-So is out of the way I shall be a rich man, etc. That's the moment when you see the red light and you want to apply the brakes." " Well," thought Miss Pinnegar, " this seems to be the time for me to apply the brakes, or I shall find I've got up and smothered Violet in my sleep."

She turned over on to the left side. There was always the hundred-to-one chance that Providence would intervene in the shape of a bus or a taxi, but Miss Pinnegar took a sensible woman's view of Providence. Heaven helps those who help themselves, and it was unfair to expect Heaven, whose hands must be full in any case, to relieve you of a burden you were too stupid or too cowardly to shoulder yourself. As she turned over, the night-light in her room began to waver oddly, throwing gaunt shadows across the ceiling. As a child Miss Pinnegar had had a wool-work motto over her bed—Thou God seest me—and she had never quite been able to overcome the feeling that it was divine cheating, since Providence, like cats, could presumably see in the dark. So she had asked for, and rather surprisingly obtained, a night-light and this habit she had never abandoned. At the Settlement it had been useful, and it was useful now. Because there was only one explanation for this sudden change in the small steady glow; the night-light was being affected by a draught. (It might, of course, have been burning out, but this was impossible, since Miss Pinnegar used a new light every evening, which was guaranteed to burn for six hours and invariably did.) So, then, someone was opening the door, and since clearly it couldn't be Grim, it must equally obviously be Violet.

Miss Pinnegar sat up in bed. " Yes, Violet ? What is it ? "

" I came to tell you," said Violet, " that I'm going."

" You'll have to wait till morning," said Miss Pinnegar sensibly, " because the front door's locked. We aren't accustomed to night-birds here, and it's always locked at eleven. If anyone wants to come in later they have to borrow a key from the porter before eight o'clock and sign for it. So you can take off that ridiculous hat and go back to bed."

" I'm not going to stay here to be murdered," said Violet.

" If you only had the sense to realise it," said Miss Pinnegar scornfully, " you're safer here than anywhere. I'm not likely to risk your body being found in my flat."

" I shall go in the morning," Violet assured her.

" Be sure to keep in touch," said Miss Pinnegar blithely.

" Not likely," said Violet.

" Ah, well, I dare say I can always get news of you through your landlady. It might help the police, too, to know where you've been living."

" That's all bunk. You're stringing me."

" My dear Violet, you are quite extraordinarily stupid. It shouldn't really be difficult to get rid of you. Have you forgotten that you are carrying your ration book in your bag ? "

" I . . . You . . . That's just bluff."

" Not at all. When you left me for a moment earlier in the evening you trustingly left your bag on the table, which gave me the opportunity I was seeking. I notice that you told the truth when you said you were registered as Mrs. Child, though, of course, you have no legal right to the title. However, I took the opportunity to memorise your address."

" You're a wicked old so-and-so," exploded Violet. " It would serve you right if I was to do the killing myself."

" I hardly see how that would help you. We are alone in the flat. Florence is at St. Mary Magdalene's Hospital. Even you are not stupid enough to suggest that Grim could be responsible. . . ."

" You're forgetting, aren't you, that nobody saw me come in, and you haven't talked to anybody on the telephone since I arrived, you haven't posted a letter to anybody and nobody's called. Nobody knows I'm here. I've only got to put you out of the way and get out first thing, and who's ever going to link me up with you, you silly old sausage."

" That's the first glimmering of intelligence I've seen in you," commented Miss Pinnegar, sitting erect in her long-sleeved crochet-edged nightgown and feeling for her spectacles. " All the same, you want to think twice before

25

committing deliberate murder. I've been thinking for three hours and haven't found any obvious solution."

Crook, of course, would have disagreed with her here. " If you're going to commit a murder," he'd say, " don't think about it at all, just whale in, do the job and leave the corpse weltering in its gore. Directly you try and build up a defence you start giving the police a platform on which to park their great flat feet." He could have quoted you scores of cases where this method has proved successful—the Silk Stockings Murder in northern England in the twenties, the Burning Car Mystery, the murder of Sarah Millson and Mrs. Noel, Mrs. Reville, the butcher's wife of Slough—for which no one ever went to gibbet or jail.

" You might, for instance," continued Miss Pinnegar, " be seen leaving the flat. Or—you say you have never been in prison ? Never mind—there are always fingerprints, or had you forgotten about them ? "

" Fingerprints ? "

" Yes. The police would certainly examine the flat for fingerprints and of course they would find yours. However careful you are you would be practically sure to forget something. Then, when you approached my nephew, they would instantly discover a motive, and—well, you doubtless think the police, like me, are silly sausages, but even they can do arithmetic with an accuracy that might surprise you. Well, as my friends at the docks would say, it is up to you." She leaned back on the pillow and pulled the blankets up to her chin.

Violet was clearly shaken. " You're no better than an old witch," she declared. " And that's what you are, black cat and all."

" Better and better," approved Miss Pinnegar. " I've frequently thought the same myself. And now, as I am extremely tired, will you kindly go back to bed and allow me to sleep ? If you have any other proposal to make in the morning I shall be prepared to listen to it. Kindly make no noise going back to your room. The tenant on the floor below is a poor sleeper and has to go to work each day."

Violet went out, flabbergasted. She clearly hadn't thought about fingerprints, reflected the old woman. But it was equally obvious that she hadn't been in the hands of the police or they would have had her record. Miss Pinnegar strained her ears to hear Violet's door close. But instead she heard faint sounds from the dining-room and grinned to herself. Violet was taking no chances. She was going the rounds polishing every surface that might retain fingerprints. " But she can't do it," reflected Miss Pinnegar confidently. " She's bound to overlook something." Then Violet's door closed at last and in the stillness her reluctant hostess heard the click of a key being turned in the lock.

" That settles it," she reflected. " She may remember to wipe off the door knob, but she's such a scatterbrain she won't think of the key. Anyway, she'll probably light a gas-fire—no, she'll have had one going all the time, she's the sort that leave everything burning when there's a fuel shortage just to embarrass the Government—and her fingerprints will be on the tap."

More sounds indicated that Violet was fixing a chair under the door handle. If only the gas-fire would go out of its own accord the situation could scarcely be bettered, Miss Pinnegar decided. Except, of course, that she'd still be in Allenfield Mansions. Still, the thought opened new possibilities.

As she turned over for the last time she remembered Arthur Crook. " I wonder what sort of advice he would give me," she reflected, " if I were to call upon him and ask his help in committing a murder." She remembered the big red face, the confident voice, the unexpected sense of support he gave. He had another quality, too, you wouldn't look for in such a man, sympathy. " Well," she decided, " perhaps it will come to that, but I shall do nothing in too much of a hurry." She had at that instant no notion of how much was going to happen during the next twenty-four hours.

CHAPTER III

THE NEXT MORNING the mystery of Violet's sudden reappearance in a state of terror was solved. Miss Pinnegar, reading the morning paper over her frugal breakfast of coffee and rolls, learned that the stolen car, reported in the B.B.C. news on the previous night, had been found seriously damaged at Grange Park cross-roads, where it had been in collision with a motor cycle. The driver of the motor cycle, a young man called Richard Carter, had been found unconscious a little distance from his wrecked vehicle; the occupants of the side-car, his wife and three-year-old child, had been killed outright. The driver of the stolen car was still unidentified; he was a man of about thirty who had been so seriously injured that he was not expected to live. The utmost the police could look for was a statement if he recovered consciousness before the end. All this would have been ruinously tragic but nothing more if it hadn't been for a police suspicion that the driver of the stolen car had had a woman companion who had disappeared from the scene without giving the alarm or calling a doctor or ambulance. The police theory was based on the fact that a green button, clearly from a woman's coat, had been found caught in the hinge of the door; the owner of the car had failed to identify the button which certainly had not come from any garment in his wife's or daughter's wardrobe. Moreover, his car had been washed and cleaned the previous day and no button had been found.

" Well," said Crook, glancing through the column with his usual lightning speed, " if it was caught in the hinge it can't have been there before the accident." The police had found a witness who remembered being asked by a woman in a dark coat, obviously in a state of alarm, the way to the station. This witness added that it was too dark to see the colour of the coat, but it looked black or a very dark shade of blue. Asked if it might have been a dark green, he had looked doubtful and said Yes, that was possible. The woman had seemed very much upset about something and he had asked her if she was all right; she had said Oh, yes, she simply

28

wanted to know the way to the station. He had said tentatively, " You didn't meet anyone who frightened you, I suppose ? " for there had been reports of a man jumping out at women after dark in that neighbourhood who was still unidentified by the authorities. She had said something incoherent about a man and hurried away from him. He had thought of accompanying her, but was on his way home and thought she might misinterpret his motive, so had gone back to his wife to whom he had said, " I bet that chap's at his tricks again. I met a woman to-night—quite distraught, she was. . . ." And they had agreed that someone ought to do something about it. The police made further inquiries at the station, but without result. Grange Park was a small station and not many people travelled late. It was quite probable that the woman would have a carriage to herself. At all events, at the time of going to press the police hadn't found anyone who had seen her at all clearly. Miss Pinnegar put down the paper, shocked in spite of her years of experience of the vagaries of human behaviour.

" What an appalling thing," she thought. There seemed no limit to the abominations of which mankind was guilty. Life was really very disillusioning. There had been some pretty shocking affairs in dockland, but she remembered nothing worse than this. She thought of the woman, presumably unhurt, extricating herself from her wreck and hurrying away into the dark to find some anonymous shelter. What sort of woman could do such a thing and leave four people dying or dead on a dark road ? she wondered aloud, and immediately the answer came back from nowhere. " That's just the sort of thing Violet might do."

An instant later she was sitting bolt upright, her hands clenching on the paper, horror filling her mind. " Oh, no," she said aloud, " that's impossible." And yet—and yet— Violet had arrived in a dishevelled and clearly terrified state shortly before eleven o'clock the night before. Miss Pinnegar knew the Grange Park district. The cross-roads were just outside the residential area ; a walk of about ten minutes would take you into the town. Allow twice that for Violet's shock and the ridiculous heels she wore. There were frequent trains to London, even at night, that brought passengers to Victoria Station. From Victoria it was only a few minutes by Underground to Allenfield Mansions. It all hung together horribly well. Violet looked as though she had been in some sort of rough-and-tumble; Miss Pinnegar recalled the place on the coat from which a button had been violently wrenched, the broken feather, the damp, muddy shoes. No woman would leave home in such a state. Add to this the general impression of having come through a hedge backwards, and Violet's obvious terror and the conclusion was almost irresistible. The newspaper reproduced a photograph of the scene of the tragedy with white crosses to show where the bodies had been lying. Sprawling right across the road, they were; the impact must have been terrific. The car was large and heavy, and the motor cycle was a twisted wreck. Without knowing a great deal about cars, it seemed obvious to Miss Pinnegar that it was the car that had run into the motor cycle rather than the other way round.

" Jumped the lights," she thought. " Now, why ? " The answer seemed to lie in the fact that the car was stolen and that the theft had already been discovered and reported to the police. There had been that urgent message on the nine o'clock news. Miss Pinnegar glanced at the paper again. There was no record that the car was equipped with wireless, but it might well have been; or a nitwit like Violet might carry a minute portable set about with her. She'd never been able to stand quiet, afraid to give the still, small voice a chance, the intolerant Miss Pinnegar used to think.

She was still brooding on this problem when the church bell near by began to ring for the eight o'clock service. Miss Pinnegar hurriedly pushed on the knob of the radio. She heard about the weather—uncertain—and then the police wanted information about a woman passenger believed to have travelled in the stolen car, etc., etc., She had no heart to hear of further trouble in Korea, Persia and Paris, and switched the set off. Then she lifted the telephone receiver and asked for Tolls. By good fortune the matron of the Grange Park Infirmary had been a friend and colleague for twenty years; she always spoke of retiring, but couldn't face the thought of inaction. " I must make Grace talk," thought Miss Pinnegar grimly, giving the number to the operator. She had to wait for the connection, but at last she heard the welcome words, " You're through."

" This is Miss Pinnegar," she announced in her clear

fastidious voice. " I should like to speak to Miss Medlicott, please. A private call."

She had another brief wait, then a voice said, " Is that you, Fanny ? . . . This is early in the day for a gossip."

" Not a gossip exactly, Grace," said Miss Pinnegar. " But I need your help. I'm going to ask you to forget your admirable discretion for once and give me a little information off the record. I'm referring to the accident at Grange Park cross-roads."

" My dear Fan, you're not going to tell me you know who Anonyma is ? "

Miss Pinnegar almost fell off the bed with surprise. " Anonyma ? Oh . . ." That moment gave her breathing space to collect her wits. " No, I didn't ring up about her. But this young man——"

" Carter ? He's going to be all right—we think. They did an X-ray and his trouble is mainly concussion. Not that he's going to find the world such a delightful place to come back to. The girl and the baby are both dead, though Dr. Mead thinks—but keep this under your hat, Fanny—that if help had been summoned at once they might have saved the child. It only died on the way to hospital."

" I see. And the driver of the car ? "

" Oh, I wouldn't care to risk my summer holiday on his chances. Mind you there's a possibility he'll come round sufficiently to make a statement before the end. The police are buzzing all around us like a covey of bluebottles. The hospital hasn't had so much excitement for months, not since the National Health authorities took over. They're inclined to give the Government the credit. In fact, it wouldn't surprise me to know that if we had an election next month quite half our patients would vote for them, whatever their own political creed."

" Where the body is there shall the vultures be gathered together."

" Oh, come, Fanny, don't be censorious. It's pretty dull lying in bed week after week with nothing but visiting day to look forward to and that isn't always successful. As a matter of fact, the patients in the ward are running a sweep as to whether this man, not Carter, the other, lives long enough to answer the police's questions. They've all seen the papers or had the news. You know, in a place like this rumours are like bugs in a tenement. You can't keep 'em out."

" You believe there's no likelihood of ultimate recovery ? " speculated Miss Pinnegar.

" Well, there are always miracles," acknowledged Miss Medlicott, sensibly ; " but the Wizard of Oz couldn't work one here. No, the point is, will he come round sufficiently to tell the police the name of his companion and/or any of his confederates ? They believe he's a member of a car-stealing gang. *Do* remember to keep all this to yourself, Fanny, won't you ? Don't tell even the inscrutable Florence."

" She's in another hospital," Miss Pinnegar reminded her. It was a relief to realise that there was no extension to this telephone, so Violet couldn't be listening in. " I see. How about visitors ? "

" Absolutely *tabu*. The police won't risk him coming round and passing any message on."

" How about a wife ? "

" No visitors unless the police are present. Anyway, to date no one's claimed the poor fool."

" I shouldn't mind wagering that there are quite a number of people praying (for the first time in years) that he doesn't recover consciousness. Men near death don't see things in a normal perspective. He might blurt out quite a lot that would be highly inconvenient to people who aren't expecting to die in the next twenty-four hours."

" Such as the names of other members of the gang ? Apparently it's a widespread affair, Fanny, from what I've coaxed out of the police. A lot of cars have been stolen recently and never traced."

" I understand that it's customary to change the number and frequently to repaint the car. This only involves it being out of commission for two or three days. Of course, it isn't offered in the ordinary market, but the gangs have a rota of people anxious to acquire cars in a hurry—jump the queue, as they say—and not too particular as to where they come from."

" What a lot you seem to know about it. Oh, well, I suppose in our profession we can't hope to retain our innocence long. I suppose you don't feel like telling me the real reason for this call ? "

" I can't say anything at the moment, Grace. I shall ring

again later in the day to know if there's any fresh development."

" That harpy who left 'em all to die may wish she'd joined the majority before she's through," opined Miss Medlicott. " I wouldn't give her long with a man like Carter on her trail."

" No doubt it would be summary justice," said Miss Pinnegar sternly, and rang off.

She was by this time practically convinced that Violet was the missing passenger, though Crook could have told her she hadn't enough evidence to hang a dog. Still, only something desperate would have brought her to Miss Pinnegar's door at such an hour and in such a state. She must have been panic-stricken indeed to seek shelter in such a quarter.

" But not altogether a fool," Miss Pinnegar told herself. " When the cockroach was set down in front of the tortoise as an appetising morsel, it made a bee-line for the tortoise's armpit, the one place where it could be safe. Violet may well have employed the same tactics. There can be no doubt about the wrenched button. Of course, it may not be the same, that is pure guesswork on my part, but there are other factors contributing to *my* theory. She had no umbrella, therefore she hadn't intended to walk, yet her shoes and clothes were wet, *so* some reason had compelled her to be out in bad weather. Her hat was a wreck, she had mud on her cheek. She daren't go home, wherever that may be. Now, why was that ? Because she and the doomed driver were keeping house together and she couldn't go back without him ? Possibly. Because it was known to others that she would be out with him that night, and they would be justifiably horrified at her callousness. Horrified, that is to say, to the point of violent action themselves ? She had no luggage, so clearly she intended to return to her lodgings, if not last night certainly to-day. There was no luggage found in the car, or there would have been some mention of it, and, in any case, that would constitute a clue. Of course, it may simply be a case of a pick-up, but I hardly think Violet would be wandering about in the rain on the chance of finding anyone foolish enough to desire her company. Well, if she is involved it must soon come out. Dear me, I could find it in my heart to wish I had allowed her to go in the middle of the night as she wished. Then I could say with my hand on my heart that I had no notion of her whereabouts."

She found it impossible to remain in bed any longer. Experience reminded her that acting on the spur of the moment is almost always a mistake, so she went along to the bathroom, for which, she noticed, there was no competition, and turned on the hot tap.

Twenty minutes later, neat as a new pin, her pallor undisguised by a dusting of powder, she left her room and went into the passage. Violet was standing in the entrance to the dining-room, fully dressed. " Don't you have a wireless ? " she demanded without preamble.

" It's in my room. Did you want to hear the news ? I have the papers here."

Violet took them and threw them down with an assumption of indifference, but she couldn't prevent her glance stealing towards the front page where the story of the tragedy was given a large headline.

" Why not read it in comfort ? " Miss Pinnegar suggested. " By the way, did you know you'd lost a button from your coat ? "

" Let her say ' Yes,' I noticed it when I put it on yesterday,' " she was praying in her heart. " Let me be proved a stupid malicious old woman." But this sort of prayer never seems to evoke much response from the Powers that Be.

" It's a nuisance, isn't it ? " said Violet. " Must have dropped it somewhere, I suppose. Wonder if that shop across the road could match it up. I might try."

Miss Pinnegar's voice was scarcely recognisable as she said, " Oh, I hardly think that would be wise, and, in any case, it's not necessary."

" Not necessary ? Oh, I see. You mean you've found it. Why couldn't you say so at first ? " She stuck out her hand carelessly.

" I don't mean I have it, but I think the police have."

" The police ? " Violet whirled round, her eyes glazed.

" The police found a button torn from a green coat in the door hinge of the crashed car, which had been identified as the one for which inquiries were being made last night. You were short of a button on arrival——"

"Anyone can shed a button," exclaimed Violet breathlessly.

"This button was not shed, but violently torn off. In any case it would be easy for the police to identify it as there must be a scrap of material attached to the shank."

"I—I don't know what you're talking about," protested Violet.

"Perhaps you'll be able to explain better to the police."

"Who's going to tell the police I've lost a button?" demanded Violet. "Oh, I can see you're dying to have a little kudos—Lady Fanny of Scotland Yard—but it won't help Geoffrey. . . ."

"This thing has gone beyond Geoffrey," said Miss Pinnegar in her sternest tone. "Two people are dead and a third is likely to die. . . ."

"What's that?" A look of terror shot across Violet's plump powdered face. "Who—which of them is alive?"

"Oh, I see," said Miss Pinnegar, "you thought they were all dead. That's why you left them without so much as stopping to see if there was anything you could do. All the same, people are going to take rather a serious view of your not even telephoning for a doctor. You must have been out of your mind to imagine you could get away with it."

Violet with a tremendous effort regained control. "I don't know what you're talking about," she said languidly. "This accident at Grange Park cross-roads is nothing to do with me."

Miss Pinnegar snatched the paper out of her reach. "If that's the case, how did you know where the accident took place?"

"Why—it's in the paper."

"But you hadn't read the paper."

"I saw the picture." Violet's breath came jerkily.

"And recognised the surroundings? But why? Or perhaps you're perpetually going down that road."

"It's in the paper," repeated the goaded Violet.

"The paper was folded back; you couldn't conceivably have seen the name. The caption merely says 'Scene of last night's collision between the two cars.'"

"It wasn't a car," exclaimed Violet unguardedly; "it was a motor cycle."

" So you were there ? That's what I thought. You must have been mad."

" Not so mad as you if you're thinking of laying information. It'll all come out then, and I don't expect your darling Geoffrey will feel as public-spirited about it as you."

" It's out of my hands now," Miss Pinnegar pointed out. " When the police catch up with you——"

" Why should they—unless you tell them."

" Your friend in the car——"

" Les ? I thought you said he was killed."

" He hasn't recovered consciousness and isn't expected to live——"

" How do you know all this ? "

" The matron of the hospital in question happens to be a friend of mine."

" Have you told her about me ? You couldn't be such a fool."

" I couldn't tell her something that was no more than speculation on my part."

" He's only got himself to thank, the motor-cyclist, I mean," Violet asserted breathlessly. " He came tearing through with the lights against him."

Miss Pinnegar picked up the newspaper. " Before you tell the police that story it might be worth studying this photograph. The car, you will see, has crossed the main road down which the motor cycle was travelling ; the cycle has been thrown right across the road on to the corner ; indeed, the driver was pinned beneath it. The woman passenger—represented by this white cross—must have been thrown out of the side-car and struck her head on that boulder. As for the child, she was flung a considerable distance. Presumably, the mother would make an instinctive effort to protect her, probably by taking her in her arms. But the violence with which the woman was thrown out of the car wrenched the child——"

" Stop it," shouted Violet, " stop it, can't you ? It's disgusting. You're like a cat gloating over a mouse. It wasn't my fault, I tell you. There was nothing I could do."

" You could at least have rung the police," said Miss Pinnegar in the same tone of revulsion.

" How could I ? Why, the car was hot. And they'd found out about it already. That's why——"

" Yes," agreed Miss Pinnegar slowly, " I thought it was that. You turned on the radio, I suppose, and heard about the missing car. But what I don't understand is how your friend thought he was going to improve the situation by running down a motor-cyclist."

" Well, he didn't do it on purpose. He didn't know he was there."

" What about the lights ? They must have been against you."

" He thought he could just make it. If the cyclist had had any sense——"

" Oh, come, Violet, that sort of thing is a waste of breath. No driver assumes that a man coming at right angles is going to ignore the traffic signals. Besides, why didn't your companion stop when he saw the cyclist ? I see that the car was a Minotaur. Their braking system is usually excellent."

Violet said nothing. " Perhaps he had had rather too much drink," Miss Pinnegar suggested. " Well, the medical evidence will tell us that in due course."

" Les is funny that way," Violet muttered. " He doesn't drink. No, he was sober enough, it's just he'd had a shock hearing about the car, I mean, and he said, ' They're on our tail, we've got to keep going.' "

" Where were you going ? "

" I'm not going to tell you," said Violet.

" You were on the Brightstone Road. Brightstone's a big town with a fluctuating population. There's a lot of money in Brightstone, likewise there are a lot of cars. A stolen Minotaur would be less conspicuous there than in some smaller place. Of course your friends would have their own garages where they undertook the—er—renovating processes. . . ."

Violet stared. " You seem to know a lot about this sort of thing."

" You forget that I've spent all my working life among people who had to get a living somehow, by fair means or foul. Oh, yes, I have a deal more knowledge about the crooked ways of life than you imagine. There's one thing that puzzles me a little—what precisely you were doing in the car. Just having a joy-ride ? However, you'll be able to explain that to the police."

Violet seemed suddenly to harden in her resolve. " Who's going to bring the police in here ? "

" I fancy they'll come of their own accord. For instance, your friend when he is able to answer questions. . . . I know the axiom about honour among thieves, but in my experience it's honoured at least as often in the breach as in the performance."

" He may never come round."

" How you wish that, don't you ? "

" If he doesn't you can stop worrying, can't you ? " suggested Violet. " The other boys won't make any move. And if the police knew about him it would be all over the papers by now."

" Do they know you were with him ? Your gangster friends, I mean ? "

Violet shrugged. " I dare say they could guess. Les and me had been going together for some time."

" And all that time he had been involved in what I believe is called the car racket ? "

" Easy to call names," flashed Violet ; " but what does the Government expect ? Why don't they let people have cars now the war's over ; save themselves a lot of trouble if they did. Les has had his name down for two years. . . ."

" How remarkably quixotic of him ! " was Miss Pinnegar's smooth comment. " Seeing that he had found a way of getting them without having to pay for them. Well, when they identify him——"

" Who's to say they will ? Oh, I can see what you're thinking. Frightened for your own skin like all the rest. ' Oh, Inspector, I took her in out of charity. To me, she was simply my nephew's wife. Of course if I'd known you wanted her I couldn't have got to the telephone fast enough.' "

Miss Pinnegar shrugged. " You can hardly blame me for that. Why should I suppose anyone wanted you ? "

" Do you know what this place feels like to me ? " demanded the younger woman violently. " The Snake House at the Zoo."

" Then you must feel perfectly at home," replied Miss Pinnegar with swift cordiality.

" I can see just what's in your mind," Violet blundered on. " Then you realise that I'm remembering there are more uses for a bread knife than simply cutting bread. By the way, what prevented your going to your own address last night?"

" I wanted breathing-time, see? And that Mrs. Gordon's a nosy bitch if ever there was one. Mind you, I thought they were all dead, but even if they weren't they didn't mean a thing to me. Only Les and he seemed deader than mutton. I knew some other car would come along any minute. . . ."

" On a wet night off the main road? As a matter of fact, the disaster wasn't discovered for almost an hour."

" I dare say it didn't make much difference. Anyway, I couldn't afford to take chances. You have to think of yourself when you're all you've got."

For some reason this matter-of-fact statement shook Miss Pinnegar's composure for the first time. She thought it was one of the most tragic remarks she had ever heard.

" This friend of yours——" she began.

" Les? " Violet's tone was openly contemptuous. " You don't know their kind. Oh, you think you've knocked about a lot, but you've always been protected in a way, always knowing you were on the right side and living a good life and a blessing to everyone—Geoffrey was the same. You were born safe, see? Only your sort never understand about that. Chaps like Les can't be counted on—ever. Irresponsible. That's what a magistrate said once about Bernie —he was another fellow, but he got caught. Since we're taking down our back hair, I may as well tell you I knew Les was planning to give me the air, and I meant to know the reason why. He said he couldn't stop and talk, not to-night, he'd got to go down to Brightstone on business. I said that was all right, I'd go with him. I'd enjoy the ride. For one thing, I needed money. I couldn't go back to my room without it."

" And you thought you'd get it from a shark? "

" I didn't think he could afford to refuse. I knew too much about—him and the others."

" And—were you successful? "

Violet looked sullen. " He said he hadn't got any. That's when I said I'd go with him. He said, ' My bank account's at Brightstone and, anyway, the bank won't be open at this hour of the night.' But he never told me it was a stolen car, How was I to know? "

" You've just told me he'd had his name down for one for

a considerable time. You must have known the car wasn't his."

" I wasn't to know it hadn't been lent him. I didn't know anything about his private life. Only he was one of those fellows who can't help boasting, always telling you what a genius he was. That's how I cottoned on to the rest of the gang."

" Perhaps in the circumstances you could apply to *them* for assistance," suggested Miss Pinnegar unhelpfully.

Violet gave a bitter laugh. " Not likely. They'd say what you've been thinking ever since you knew what's happened. Why on earth couldn't you have got yourself bumped off with the rest ? No tact, that's her trouble. Well, I wasn't bumped off, and I don't mean to be—see ? I'm not like you. I'm not a lady. I'm just a girl who didn't make good on the stage and had to take anything she could get. That's why I married Geoffrey. And you needn't think I made a good bargain there, because I didn't. He was a dead loss to me from the start."

" You married him as a speculation," Miss Pinnegar pointed out, in icy tones. " It's no use complaining now if you didn't get the immense profits you hoped for. Speculators have to take chances. You shouldn't go in for gambling if you're not prepared to risk making a loss." But against every inclination she felt a pang of sympathy for this wretched creature who had nothing—no integrity or security or friends. It was all very well to despise a hyena for being a scavenger, but there was no justice in blaming it for being true to its own nature. Blame, if you must, the power responsible for creating the hyena.

Violet was still urgently considering her own plight. " If Les dies," she said without a particle of feeling in her voice, " there's no reason why I should ever be dragged into it at all. Even if they do know there was a woman there, there's no reason they should pick on me. The others won't want to say a word, even if they guess, as most likely they will, because they won't want any limelight. So unless you go to the police . . ." She paused expectantly. " It'll be just malice if you do," she said. " It won't help anyone and it'll do Geoffrey and that woman of his a lot of harm. Whereas if you keep your mouth shut I could agree to do the same. Well, what do you say ? "

Miss Pinnegar observed mildly that it took two to keep a bargain, but as she went back to her room she thought, " Much as I detest Violet, I have more understanding of her in this crisis than anyone else would have, because in a sense I'm in the same position. She must have been panic-stricken and, since she's always considered her own interests first and anyone else's so far second they're almost invisible, her obvious course would be to put as large a distance between herself and the car as possible. And she came here because the other members of the gang will hear the news and realise the identity of the driver. They'll be round her lodgings like bees round a honey-pot. This is the only place in London where she can hope to be safe even for a few hours, particularly now she knows about the button." She was reminded of a rat hunt they had had once in the early days of the Settlement. The rat had terrorised a child and there hadn't been a rodent officer in those days. Miss Pinnegar and a helper had gone after the rat themselves. They had got it into a corner and Miss Pinnegar had gone in to dispatch it. The creature had turned with bared teeth and leaped, but his enemy's eye had been true and the blow she aimed with the old-fashioned poker had struck it fairly on the skull. All the same, she had felt a spasm of pity even for the rat which, when all was said and done, was only behaving after its nature, and had at all events put up a fight. But even if you felt sympathy for the rat you killed it just the same.

She turned to find that Violet had followed her. " I know you wish it was me in his place," she said. Since this was just what Miss Pinnegar did wish, and since her companion had the sense to recognise the fact, the old woman saw no sense in comment. The telephone rang and Miss Pinnegar went to answer it. It was someone at the Settlement wanting to know if she could do a friendly visit urgently that morning.

" We really haven't anyone to send right across London," explained Miss Ross, the new head, " and you know old Mrs. Scanlan . . ."

Miss Pinnegar said automatically that, of course, she would go.

" I don't believe it," said Violet flatly. " You're going to the hospital."

" Not till this afternoon," said Miss Pinnegar. " Wednesday is visiting day at St. Mary Magdalene's."

" But he's at—I mean, who's at St. Mary Magdalene's ? "

" Florence."

" Oh, her. I thought you meant you were going to the Grange Park Infirmary."

" There would be no sense in that. I have never set eyes on either of the young men, and if I want news I can telephone. Now, Violet, listen to me. You're a free agent as far as your own movements are concerned. If you wish to leave the flat nobody will try and stop you, but do remember that you're not an invisible person any longer."

" Invisible ? You're bats. I never was."

" Theoretically speaking, we are all invisible until we do something that brings us into the limelight. My neighbour across the passage, Miss Michael, is curiosity incarnate. It's an extraordinary piece of luck that she didn't see you come in last night, and I feel certain she didn't or she would have been over here before now. She's one of those unfortunate women who have no lives of their own and so must live in other people's. My telephone never rings (provided she's at home) but she is hovering on the landing, dying to know who has rung me up and why. If I have a visitor she always ' happens ' to be stepping out of the lift or opening her front door or anticipating a caller of her own ; she takes in every detail and is sure to try and pump me at the earliest opportunity."

" Poor old cow ! " said Violet. " I bet it's as easy pumping you as getting blood from a stone."

" So you will see the necessity for discretion," Miss Pinnegar wound up smoothly, as though she had not heard Violet's ill-bred interruption. " If you intend to go out and don't wish to be observed you'd better use the stairs. It's fatal to ring for the lift ; for one thing, it's quite improbable you would get it, with Hume in the state he is at present about his wife—she is quite gravely ill and he is seldom on duty. And for another, you would certainly be cornered by Miss Michael, and whether you believe me or not, I can assure you that she would have your whole story out of you as neatly as a surgeon removing an appendix. As it is——"
She stopped dead. The front-door bell had begun to ring.

" You see ! " said Miss Pinnegar.

" You don't know it's the old geezer."

" I have been listening to that particular peal for six years," Miss Pinnegar reminded her.

" Aren't you going to open the door ? "

" In a moment." The old woman put on her hideous brown hat, collected gloves, purse and umbrella and moved casually into the diminutive hall. She left the sitting-room door a few inches ajar. " Good morning, Miss Michael," Violet heard her say. " As you see, I was just going out."

" I was wondering if you had a postage stamp to spare," improvised Miss Michael hurriedly.

" I'm afraid not. But you can get them from the slot machine just outside."

" Such a nuisance," gabbled Miss Michael, with her tinny laugh. " I'm right out of coppers. Dear me, aren't you going to wait for the lift ? "

" I doubt whether Hume is on duty at this hour." Miss Pinnegar made for the stairs.

Miss Michael perforce fell into step with the indomitable old spinster and continued to chatter at a great rate as they descended the endless flights of stairs. " Really, I think one has a right to complain. This old-fashioned lift is most inconvenient, as well as being positively dangerous. Don't you agree ? "

" Dangerous," repeated Miss Pinnegar absently.

" Yes. Really, these old-fashioned contraptions should be swept away. Shoo ! Shoo ! " She made a humorous sweeping gesture and Miss Pinnegar's hat came off. " Dear me, how unfortunate. Still, it's lucky your hair's attached to your head, isn't it ? Just think how disastrous if you'd taken advantage of Mr. Bevan's generosity—I must say misplaced generosity——"

" I hope I'm not dragging you down against your will," suggested Miss Pinnegar, ramming the hat on again over her bony imperious forehead.

" Not at all. My stamps, you know. The little woman at the draper's can sometimes oblige. Of course if we had a reliable porter—but, really, with a lift operating on the pulley system that can be run up and down with all the doors and gates unlatched. Did I tell you I found the landing gate wide open on the third floor the other day ? "

" Yes," said Miss Pinnegar.

Miss Michael persisted. You had the impression she had been at odds with life for so long that it did not disconcert her in the least to find herself frustrated at every turn.

" Such an exhausting day I had yesterday," she observed. " A dear, dear friend most gravely ill. I was there from dawn till dark. She died soon after I left. Exhaustion, the doctor said. I'm just popping over again. I know what a death in the house means. Whole flights of relations who never bothered in the least while the poor dear was alive come simply sailing out of a clear sky to perch and peck. I feel it's my duty to dear Harriet to keep a weather eye open. If anyone knew her wishes I did. . . ."

Miss Pinnegar took advantage of a momentary break to slip in a few words. " Will it occupy you all day ? " She contrived a note of sympathy in her voice.

" Well, a good part of it, I'm afraid. I shall try to slip back for tea. I do think a cup of tea in one's own house is worth half a dozen in anyone else's."

Miss Pinnegar breathed a sigh of relief. It looked as though the coast would be clear for some hours. Until matters were smoothed out a little she had no desire for Miss Michael to know even of Violet's existence.

It was approaching the lunch-hour when Miss Pinnegar returned carrying a large rather untidy brown-paper parcel, that she dumped on the table, saying, " That, Violet, is for you. I am thankful you had the good sense to remain indoors until you had some alternative clothes."

Violet didn't offer to touch the parcel. " Is that something for me to wear ? "

Miss Pinnegar repressed a schoolgirl desire to ask if she'd supposed it was something to eat, and replied, " Certainly. You can hardly expect to go out in a coat that is being looked for by every policeman on the beat and escape detection."

" Coat, eh ? How did you know what size I took ? "

" I described your figure to the saleswoman and she recommended a medium stout."

" What bloody sauce ! I never heard of such a thing. I'd sooner go out in my birthday suit."

" I can think of no more certain way of being taken to the police station," agreed Miss Pinnegar, with a false cordiality that nearly took your skin off. " Now, Violet, stop behaving like a matinée idol and open that parcel. Be careful, it's not very well packed. It almost came to pieces in the bus."

" You would bring it back in a bus," sneered Violet. " Too mean, I suppose, to help a taxi-driver to pay his rent."

" The bus puts me down at the corner, and I'm not conceited enough to suppose that anyone will notice where I go when I leave it. A taxi would bring me to the door and, in the unfortunate event of questions being asked later, it would certainly be remembered that I had arrived in a cab."

" I believe you think you're royalty," exclaimed Violet.

" My income certainly doesn't allow me to indulge in taxi-cabs," said Miss Pinnegar in the same voice. " Can I not impress upon you the fact that the less attention you attract the better ? Now, open the parcel, please, and don't leave the brown paper on the floor."

Sulkily Violet opened the package to reveal a coat of drab cloth and universal cut, and a perfectly plain fawn-coloured beret.

" Do you really think I'm going to wear these ? " she demanded derisively.

" If you drive me much further you will require nothing but a shroud," Miss Pinnegar warned her. " Put it on at once, please."

" I don't wear ready-mades," grumbled Violet. But she put it on. " No style," she complained.

" It is what is called the classic style. Perhaps that doesn't appeal to you."

" When people tell you a coat or dress is cut on classic lines it means it's something that isn't smart now and won't be smart ten years hence."

" I can conceive of nothing more suitable. It's the greatest possible contrast to the green one you were wearing."

" And I've never worn a beret in my life."

" If you're to be believed, you've never had the police looking for you before. There has to be a first time for everything. Whatever happens you can't wear the green coat again. You must appreciate that. In fact, it might be as well to leave it here. I'll dispose of it."

" Not thinking of disposing of me at the same time, I suppose ? Where am I supposed to go ? "

" Somewhere where you are not likely to be recognised, I suggest," returned Miss Pinnegar crisply.

" And what do I use for money ? "

" Are you quite destitute ? "

" If I've got to cut myself off from everyone I shan't be able to draw much."

" I believe there is plenty of work to be obtained in seaside hotels and boarding-houses during the next few months. I commend the idea to your notice. In the meantime, here are twenty pounds in single notes. If you will later send me an address—I don't want one for the moment so that if questioned I can truthfully say I don't know your where-abouts—I will send you a small allowance (my own means are strictly limited) on condition that you remain in obscurity. And if it occurs to you," she went on, giving Violet no opportunity to make any comment, " that you could do better by applying to my nephew, let me tell you that with two children and a third arriving at any moment he is in an even less affluent position than myself."

" Oh, all right," said Violet sulkily. " I'm sure I don't want to stay here any longer than I have to. I don't feel safe here and that's a fact."

" Oh, you mustn't count on feeling safe anywhere," said Miss Pinnegar. " You can hardly expect that."

" I wish to heaven I'd never come," continued Violet passionately. " Then if Les does die without speaking, nobody would have known I was with him that night."

" You can scarcely imagine I shall reveal your secret."

" You wait. Suppose the police come asking nosy questions ? You won't risk your precious conscience. You'll be a danger to me."

" You should have thought of that before," said Miss Pinnegar indifferently. She knew that Violet's calculations had all gone astray; she who had supposed that she could shut the old woman's mouth by revealing her continued existence, hadn't anticipated defiance. Now she took the coat and the money, and sloped off without a word of thanks.

" If Les does die without saying anything I shall come back to London," was her final word. " Shan't have anything to fear then. It'll be your word against mine."

CHAPTER IV

MISS PINNEGAR was not the only person to take an interest in Violet's whereabouts. At about the time that the old woman returned to Allenfield Mansions a short dark man waited with considerable impatience in a room off Euston Square, eager for news. He didn't stand at the window— for who knew whether the house was being watched ?—but his ears were alert for the smallest sound, and when at length he heard steps on the stairs, he drew a sharp breath as he turned to face the newcomer. The door opened and a tall thin man with a face as sharp as a rat's came in.

" You've taken your time, Stan," observed the first. " How's it go ? "

" Couldn't be much worse," said Stan. " The place is alive with bluebottles."

The other sneered. " You always look for them round a corpse."

" Corpse might be the word."

The dark man's face changed, the apprehension deepening. " Bad as that ? Didn't get a word with Les, of course ? "

" Don't be a fool, Joe. I tell you, I didn't even dare go in. They're waiting for the first chap who inquires for Les, and then it'll be, ' And what's your business with him ? Name, address, identity card. You know this fellow ? Who is he ? ' "

" So they haven't got that yet ? "

" Not yet. Les always kept in the background, see. But they'll find it. Trust a flattie to nose out anything you want to keep quiet. I hung around, asking a question here and there. You know. He hasn't come round, the cops are waiting in case he gets a chance to say anything before he goes under."

" No chance for him, you mean ? "

" They don't seem to think so. In a way, it might be better, though we shall miss Les."

The dark man whose mother had never christened him Joseph, stubbed out a cigarette viciously. " What possessed the fool to take a skirt with him ? " he demanded. " That's

47

Les's trouble always. Can't do anything without a dame in tow. Frightened in the nursery when he was a kid, perhaps, and can't bear to sleep alone ever since. Any idea who the girl was ? "

" You never know with Les. He's like a quick-change artist. There's this woman, Vi, he's been going with her for some time, but lately it's been more her going with him."

" Trying to shake her, eh ? Seen a new love-light gleaming ? "

" Well, you know Les. And this one's been around a bit. On the other hand, if it was Vi she might have tried to get in touch."

" You've a hope," said Joe grimly. " Expecting her to come to Les's pals and say, ' I left him dying in the middle of the road and didn't even ring a doctor.' No, I wouldn't blame Vi if she does want to lie low."

" All the same," urged Stan, " a new one might not want to get mixed up with this car racket. Vi knew about it, but that's not to say Les told another dame they were travelling in a car he'd pinched a couple of hours earlier."

" What happened to the car ? "

" The bluebottles have got it. It was damaged, all right, but nothing too much. The motor-cycle's had it."

" To hell with the cycle. How about the rider ? "

" Concussion, that's all. They're hoping he can tell 'em something when he comes out of his long sleep."

Joe drew a deep breath, flipped open a packet of cigarettes and took one out. He didn't offer them to Stan, which showed just how deep his anxiety was. Joe was no good, but he wasn't mean as a rule. " The police never learn, do they ? How much do they expect a chap caught amidships to be able to tell them about the car that hit him ? "

Stan produced his own cigarettes and lighted up. " That's the trouble, Joe. We don't know if he was knocked out right away or if he saw anything of this dame."

" Couldn't ha' seen much in the kind of weather we had last night. Why, the chap who says he was stopped by this woman wouldn't recognise her, according to his own story."

Stan kicked at an empty match-box on the floor. " What the hell was Les thinking of to go through those lights ? "

" That way, was it ? "

" I'd say. I went down to take a look. Usual crowd all nattering—anything for a free show. It must have been practically a massacre. They haven't moved the car yet, traffic being diverted. Collision took place in the middle of the cross-roads and you know what the police 'ull say, that a chap with a wife and kid in a side-car doesn't take a chance of crossing against the lights with a car the size of a Minotaur coming at him. Les must have been out of his mind. Just heard the nine o'clock news, I suppose, and realised there'd be a cordon out to get the drugs—enough on board to poison a village, though Les didn't know that—and thought he'd take a chance. God, what a chance ! "

Joe looked sceptical. " Much more likely he was having a bull and cow with the girl. My bet is it was Vi—she's got a green coat, remember." (Stan didn't. He never noticed what women wore. As bad as a husband, the girls complained.) " And he was trying to shake her—I do know that. Why the hell he ever took up with her beats me. She's no chicken, and she's the sort that finds she's wanted on the phone when it's her turn to stand a round."

" Tried to get her ? On the blower, I mean ? "

Stan shook his head. " Better not. Never know how much the cops suspect. If they've an idea who the dame was they may be tapping the line. Or they'd question her landlady."

" All the same "—Joe sounded uneasy—" it 'ud be a good thing for us to have her where she couldn't talk. She's the sort that 'ud split wide open to save her own skin. No, I've got an idea. If she's there she's bound to go in or out during the day, so if we keep an eye on the house . . . Hallo ! " He stiffened as he turned towards the window.

" What is it ? "

" Police car."

" Coming here ? "

" Dunno. No, false alarm. Gone by."

They waited a few minutes to see if it came back in its tracks, but there was no further sign of it and in that long road there was no convenient corner where it could hide. Joe was jumpy. " Maybe we shouldn't try and contact Vi," he said.

" Maybe we shouldn't let the police have the first word. Hell, we've no idea *how* much has been given away. And there's plenty. If she knows about Collis I wouldn't give much chance for either of us. I tell you, that dame 'ud write our names down on a bit of paper without a thought." He clapped on a green fedora and buttoned his coat. " Come on ! "

" Think we should both go ? "

" I do. Sometimes a witness can be useful."

They came swiftly down the stairs, pausing a moment on the step to light fresh cigarettes, looking expertly this way and that to see if there was any sign that they were being watched. But there was nobody about—nobody, that is, in their sense of the word—and they got into the little black car Stan had left by the kerb.

Violet, meantime, with the twenty pounds in her purse and the new coat on her back, made her way to the Underground station. Catching sight of herself in a mirror in the lift, she scowled at the unbecoming and inexpensive brown beret Miss Pinnegar had thoughtfully provided. That should find its way into a garbage can at the first possible moment. With so much money burning a hole in her purse Violet could afford something more likely to attract the passing eye. She was through with Les and his friends, and would shortly have to start making fresh arrangements. Twenty pounds doesn't go far, and Violet realised that Miss Pinnegar's notions of what comprised an adequate allowance were not likely to accord with her own.

Mrs. Gordon heard the scrape of the latch key and came into the hall. " Bad penny," she suggested. " What happened to you last night ? "

" Went to see my auntie," returned Violet indifferently. " She made me stay."

" Brought the rent back with you ? "

" That's why I stayed. Bank doesn't open till ten." She snapped the catch of her bag and Mrs. Gordon saw a number of notes inside.

" Bought you a new coat too, did he ? Take my tip, dearie, and get what you can while you can. The ones that start mean get meaner."

" Mean ! " Violet looked affronted.

" Well, he didn't break himself over that coat. Buy 'em by the dozen at the Burlington shops. My niece got one last week, but then she has to pay for what she wears. Going to see Auntie again ? "

" She wants me to go to Bournemouth with her. I've only come for my things." She swaggered into her room and packed an imitation crocodile suitcase. Mrs. Gordon stood on the threshold.

" What are you afraid of ? " demanded Violet. " Think I shall pack the mantelpiece by mistake ? "

" Wouldn't be any mistake about it," retorted Mrs. Gordon grimly. " I've brought your bill."

" You'll never cheat yourself, will you ? " suggested Violet, looking through it. She threw down some notes.

" Shan't cheat anyone else neither," was Mrs. Gordon's reply. " I'll get you your receipt."

" And put a stamp on it while you're about it," called Violet.

" Aren't you going to leave anything for the girl ? " inquired Mrs. Gordon when, a little later, her lodger snapped the locks on the meretricious case and prepared to depart.

" What for ? " asked Violet coolly. " She's only done what she's paid for and if you don't think she gets enough you should put up her wages." She made for the front door.

" You're in a hurry," said Mrs. Gordon. " The Rolls isn't here yet."

Violet pushed past and, carrying the case, went down the steps. Mrs. Gordon watched her progress from a small gap in the carefully-parted lace curtains on the ground floor. She didn't believe a word of Violet's story about spending the night with her auntie—would probably have swooned to know that it was true. At least Miss Pinnegar was the aunt of the man she had married in 1940. And so she was not in the least surprised to see a man emerge from a small black car parked a short way up the road and politely relieve her late lodger of her suitcase—certainly not nearly so surprised as Violet herself.

" Here. What on earth——" she began.

" Come on," said Joe grimly. " Anyone 'ud think you'd been packing the Crown jewels, the time you've taken. We want a word with you. First of all "—he opened the car door and she got in—" about last night."

" It wasn't my fault," she said quickly. " I might have

been killed, too." Then she remembered. " What about Les ? Is he—— ? "

" Not yet. No thanks to you, though."

She said again angrily, " It wasn't my fault. I shouted at him but he didn't listen. Not that I'm sorry for him, the dirty, double-crossing——"

" Oh, let it ride." Stan sounded impatient. " We're not interested in your love-life. Come to that, I doubt if Les was. That seems to have been the trouble. Why the hell couldn't you leave him alone ? "

" What d'you expect a girl to live on ? Air ? Besides, I like to be the one to say when a thing's to break up."

" How was it ? " demanded Joe. " Who tipped you off he was making a trip to Brightstone last night ? "

" No one tipped me off. But I had to pay my rent, see ? And I rang his place and he said he was on to a job. I didn't believe him. I said I know your sort of job. I thought he was going off with this other girl, see ? So I went after him and said I might as well come too. I didn't know he was going to crash the lights—I didn't even know the car was hot——"

" And that's the yarn you're going to tell the cops ? Well, forget it, sweetheart. You're not going to tell the cops anything, see ? You're going for a nice holiday into the country till we see which way the cat's going to jump."

" Meaning Les ? But she said it was only a matter of hours ? "

" She ? "

Violet told them about Miss Pinnegar. Both men were aghast. " You mean, you told this old trollop—— ? "

Violet laughed uneasily. " She's not. She's a church worker or something."

" That makes it worse. She'll have a conscience to complicate matters, as if they weren't tangled enough already. Christ, Vi, this is a hell of a mess."

" What we want," put in Joe, " is a needle and thread to sew your mouth up. Why couldn't you keep it shut ? "

" I tell you, she knew. Don't ask me how. I believe she's a witch. Still, she won't say anything. Why, she's going to give me an allowance to keep out of the picture."

" Allowance hell ! She means to keep in touch. Can't you even register that far ? Who lives with her ? "

" The usual faithful servant, but luckily she's in hospital. There wasn't anyone else there last night. That's how I got a bed at all. I had dear Florence's room. She'd probably turn her face to the wall and die if she knew I'd been in her bed."

" Well, she'll tell her, won't she ? This Vinegar female ? "

" Not likely. She's going to see her this afternoon and she was hopping mad to get me off the premises first."

Stan looked across at Joe ; his eyes were as black as sloes and as hard as chips of glass. " I know these old family servants," he said disgustedly and, as it happened, inaccurately. " She'll spill all the beans with a drop of tomato sauce thrown in for luck. God, Vi, why couldn't you have got yourself killed with the rest of 'em. And for Pete's sake, stop bawling. You've made enough mess as it is. Now we've got to get you out of it."

" Les," began Violet uncertainly.

" You say your prayers and hope he doesn't come round. Though, mind you, if it hadn't been for you we'd never have lost that car."

" Can it, Joe," put in his companion. " This isn't getting us anywhere. What we've got to do is find some place where Vi can lie low for the time being. I'm glad you had the sense not to wear the coat. Where is it, by the way ? "

" *She's* got it."

" Who ? Vinegar ? Are you crazy ? "

" Better her than me. They'll never think of looking there."

" Honestly, Vi, you ought to be in the bughouse. Now she's got a hold over you you'll never shake off. *And that's the way she means it to be.* Nothing else you've forgotten to mention, while we're about it ? If you can make all this trouble without half trying what are you like when you really put your back into it ? "

They went into a huddle. Violet as always was voluble to a degree.

" Can't think why you ever wanted to take up with Les," said Stan wearily, after a time. " Cut out for a lady novelist, you are. And you wouldn't be able to complain you haven't any plots. You'd leave Ouida and that other dame "—he snapped his fingers—" Rita, was it ?—at the post and win in a canter."

CHAPTER V

WHEN SHE was sure that Violet had left the building Miss Pinnegar unshipped her telephone and put through a second call to Grange Park Infirmary, but Miss Medlicott had nothing new to report. There had been no callers, the police were still in attendance and there was very little change in the condition of either man.

" I suppose," she added, " you don't feel like telling me what your real interest is ? Oh, all right, Fanny. I know Clam is your middle name."

" Will you keep me posted ? " urged Miss Pinnegar.

" Yes. Better not ring again—the bell never stops as it is. I promise to let you know as soon as there's anything to tell—unless, of course, the police decide to put the telephone out of action. They appear to have all powers in heaven and earth—and the Press are almost as bad. When they hear he's going to defeat us in spite of everything . . . You do know who I'm talking about ? "

" I suppose you mean Les—I don't know his other name."

" Fanny ! Who told you his name was Les. No, don't answer. I'd rather not know. There's only one person who could have told you—and that's Anonyma. Nobody else knows. Unless, of course, you're in with the gang. Oh, Fan, do be careful. I've always said your luck was too good to last. And you do have the most extraordinary friends." She paused a moment, but Miss Pinnegar said nothing. " Oh, all right," said Grace Medlicott huffily ; " but I should have thought you could trust me after all these years."

" Surrounded by policemen as an island's surrounded by water ? Haven't you enough trouble as it is ? "

Miss Medlicott laughed reluctantly. " Oh, well. You never did take much care of yourself, and I suppose you can't teach an old dog new tricks. How's Florence ? "

" I shall be seeing her this afternoon. She would create like a maniac, to use her own expression, if I didn't turn up, but inwardly she's always hoping something will happen to me—not because she's malicious—she's absurdly devoted—

but because it would show how indispensable she is. She's always expecting me to get myself murdered——"

"And she's quite right," broke in Miss Medlicott warmly. "To be apprehensive, I mean. One of these days, Fan, you'll wake up to find you've been strangled and no one will be more surprised than you."

Miss Pinnegar said something that sounded like Tchah. But when she had replaced the receiver she sat for some time in thought.

Miss Medlicott's last remark made her think. There was unquestionably something in what Grace said. Like Agag it behoved her to walk warily. If Les did die without making any statement that meant, didn't it, that Violet would be safe? Miss Pinnegar had none of the guileless public's conviction about the abilities of the police to trace the woman, which meant that no one excepting Miss Pinnegar (apart from Les's cronies who must be expected to know the facts) realised the part Violet had played. And if the police didn't recognise Les then they'd be absolutely in the dark as to the names of Les's confederates. Miss Pinnegar wasn't afraid that Violet would tell them anything; she had too much to lose. "The boot will be on the other leg," she reflected. "I shall be a danger to her." And in that moment she realised that in Violet's world people who were dangerous were disposed of. If she were out of the way Violet had precious little to fear, whereas so long as she, Frances Pinnegar, was above ground, the gang must know she held their fate in her hands.

When she had worked this out the old warhorse crossed the room and routed out the card Crook had given her all those weeks ago. She dialled his number with a steady hand though her body shook as if she had an ague. Crook answered immediately; he might have been sitting on the other end of the line waiting for her call. Like a great ginger cat waiting for a mouse, she thought.

"This is Miss Pinnegar," she announced in her formal way. "Possibly you remember me."

"Could be," agreed Crook. "Coming out of the cage for a little run in the undergrowth?"

"I wish to consult you," said Miss Pinnegar in the same prim voice, "about a murder."

"My cup of tea," agreed Crook enthusiastically. "Whose body?"

" The murder I have in mind has not yet taken place."

Crook sounded frankly disappointed. " Can't expect me to act without a body," he pointed out.

Miss Pinnegar's voice assumed a tarter note. " Now you are talking like a policeman," she said with asperity.

" You win," chuckled Crook. " Did you want an accomplice ? Or any hints ? "

" I expect shortly to be in need of both," was his caller's grim reply. " At the moment I only want advice."

" Whose life's in danger ? Or was it just an experiment you had in mind ? "

" Mine," said Miss Pinnegar succinctly.

" H'm." It seemed impossible to take Crook aback. " How long have you got ? Before the villain strikes, I mean ? "

Miss Pinnegar considered. It all depended on Les. It could be that he was making a statement at this actual moment though that hardly seemed probable. Even if he said something stupendous the news would only be in the stop press column of the late night finals or possibly on the six o'clock broadcast news. Well, then, there was a little time to go. " Oh, I don't think I am in danger for the next few hours," she said. " It is quite literally a matter of life and death."

" Got anyone in the flat with you ? " asked Crook.

" No one. And I anticipate no visitors."

" You put up the chain," Crook warned her.

" I have to go to St. Mary Magdalene's this afternoon to see Florence. I should be back between three-thirty and four. I don't expect to be going out again."

" I'll be round about six o'clock," Crook promised. " Be good to yourself. I told you there was a pattern in these things," he added. And rang off.

No, reflected Miss Pinnegar wryly, hanging up the receiver, he was never likely to die from an excess of leisure.

There was nothing particular to be noted about Florence that afternoon. She was in her usual mood of brisk dissatisfaction with everyone, Miss Pinnegar included. She gave the impression, doubtless an authentic one, that she was convinced the flat was overrun with rats, food going stale, newspapers accumulating and the wireless battery requiring renewing. Miss Pinnegar was accustomed to all this and paid very little attention. She left the ward punctually at three twenty-five when the sister came in and began to clear the visitors out rather as the barmaid starts chanting " Time, gentlemen, please," just before the clock strikes.

" In a hurry, aren't you ? " grumbled Florence. It was an automatic reaction and equally automatically Miss Pinnegar replied :

" I have been a nurse myself. I know how important it is to get the ward cleared by three-thirty when the tea-trolley begins to go round, and someone must lead the way."

" It would have to be you, wouldn't it ? " said Florence, who believed in the democracy of the Kingdom of Heaven if she hadn't much use for the democracy of the House of Commons.

Miss Pinnegar said, " I shall be coming again on Sunday, Florence," and went out. Florence watched her back with affectionate eyes. Miss Pinnegar was her all, bracketed of course with the chapel. She had a sister in Scotland, but they did not correspond.

Miss Pinnegar had a word with the matron who told her it was a good thing Florence would be back soon, she looked quite washed out, and left the hospital just after three-thirty. It was only a short walk to Allenfield Mansions and she believed in regular exercise, so she accomplished the journey by Shank's mare, reaching South Kensington at ten minutes to four. This meant she would have the kettle boiling and her thin bread-and-butter cut by four o'clock. Hume was in the hall and brought her an unstamped letter on which he had paid fivepence. Miss Pinnegar recognised the hand-writing, and was about to say that it was dear at the price when she saw a second letter from dearest Geoffrey half-concealed by it. Hurriedly she gave Hume the fivepence and went upstairs in the lift. While the kettle boiled she read her letter, which was full of the most excellent news. Marcia's new baby was a boy who had excited interest even in the hard-boiled doctor and nurse by reason of his unexampled weight, colour, shape and beauty, mother and son were doing well, and Geoffrey only wished his aunt could disguise herself as a grenadier and come over in a service aircraft to see the latest addition to the family.

She turned the page. " And now," wrote Geoffrey exuberantly, " is my second piece of news, which I hope will stagger you. You remember old Colonel Godalming ? Marcia charmed him from the first and now we hear he died very suddenly last week from angina. He must have known about it, though he saw to it that no one else did. Luckily, he wasn't ill at all—it was as quick as that. But that's not the surprise. I heard of the death from the lawyer, who goes on to say : Colonel Godalming recently added a codicil to his will leaving the sum of £10,000 to ' the wife of his friend, Geoffrey Pinnegar.' Not to Marcia, you note, but to my wife. I like that touch."

Miss Pinnegar dropped the letter and sat staring at it in dismay. " The old fool ! " she exclaimed savagely. " Why couldn't he have said Marcia Pinnegar." Because in law Geoffrey's wife was Violet. Miss Pinnegar couldn't seriously believe that the law would award the legacy to *her*. Still, you could count on the thing arousing no end of a scandal. It was exactly the sort of thing the papers would leap on. Violet must inevitably see it. " And that will put up her price," reflected Miss Pinnegar grimly. " And sooner or later, probably sooner, Geoffrey will be bound to realise she's still alive. What on earth am I to do now ? How does one get rid of people who are not only superfluous, but dangerous ? "

She couldn't sit still. She threw down the letter for which she had reluctantly paid fivepence—you could be sure five farthings would be more than *that* was worth—and walked up and down the room. And behind her, like any Old Goody's sworn companion, pranced Grim, tail erect, whiskers bristling. The old body in the flat below endured this for a time, then she hunted out her broomstick and jabbed fiercely at the ceiling. This made no difference to Miss Pinnegar who did not even hear her. All her thought was— How to put Violet out of the picture ? This, she thought hazily, wondering if she really was getting a bit cracked, is where we came in. The clock in the flat below chimed the half-hour and her door bell rang. Miss Pinnegar thought, " That must be Mr. Crook come before his time," and she went eagerly to the door. " He will be able to advise me . . ." Though whether she meant about getting rid of the tiresome Violet or ensuring that Colonel Godalming's legacy went to the right wife, she didn't specify. Only as she came into the hall did it occur to her it was more likely to be Miss Michael.

However, it wasn't either of them, but Murder waiting on the doormat.

Shortly before five there was a development at Grange Park Infirmary. Les—the police hadn't yet learned his name, which was Les Strutt—moved, stared with unseeing eyes at the police and hospital authorities gathered round his bed, and made a sudden frantic move to rise.

" Easy ! " said the doctor, slipping an arm under the dying man's shoulder. " No hurry, son."

His patient was struggling violently. The police had their ears on sticks. This was what they'd been waiting for ever since the chap was brought in. Les moved an arm in a fruitless endeavour to hide his face. No, not hide—protect. He found voice at last.

" The lights ! " he croaked. He thought he was shouting. " My God, Vi ! Put on the brake. The light's against us."

Over his face passed a look of terror and apprehension. It was his last gesture, his final speech, as a living man. Though they watched beside him for nearly another hour he did not again recover consciousness.

" Pretty clear ! " said one official to the next. " No wonder this girl doesn't want to show up. *She* was driving : *she* crashed the motor cycle. Bad luck for her he came round for even those few seconds."

" You can't put that in as evidence, can you ? " suggested the doctor. " It's just a conclusion you've drawn from what he said when he didn't even know he was talking. Don't you need proof ? "

" We'll get proof all right," said the official grimly. He looked at the doctor with dislike. These chaps—laymen from his point of view—were a crowd of professional Buttinskis, always wanting the limelight. When the time came that the police had to rely on signed statements they could shut up shop and call it a day. Crook didn't often agree with the police, but he was at one with them there. The Israelites thinking themselves so hardly used because they had to make bricks without straw, didn't know what hard work was. Crook—or any rozzer—could have enlightened them.

When she heard the news Miss Medlicott shut herself up in her study and rang Miss Pinnegar's flat. She had an uneasy feeling that Miss Pinnegar knew a lot more than was healthy. She intended to advise her to make a clean breast of things to the police. Like Crook, Grace Medlicott had no use for amateurs. " And if Fanny thinks she can pull wool over the sergeant's eyes, she's got a nasty shock coming," she reflected. " She doesn't want to end her days in jail." And she thought bitterly that if Florence hadn't been incapacitated this situation would never have arisen. Which was perfectly true, though Fanny wouldn't be best pleased to be told as much. But all Miss Medlicott's good intentions were foiled because, though she could hear the telephone at Allenfield Mansions ringing away like mad, there was no answer. Clearly Miss Pinnegar had gone out.

" She'll have to wait now till my five o'clock visitor departs and I shall be lucky if that's less than an hour," thought Miss Medlicott. " Why can't Fanny be content to settle down quietly like any other ageing female ? "

But the answer to that was that in that case she would cease to be Miss Frances Pinnegar.

CHAPTER VI

CROOK, RELIABLE as the Bank of England used to be, drove the Scourge into the courtyard of the Mansions just as the B.B.C. announcer said " This is the weather forecast for to-night and to-morrow "—that is, at five minutes to six. Two small boys, who were amusing themselves taking down the numbers and makes of cars, looked at this intrepid (to their minds, barmy) driver as he hopped over the side as agilely as a flea, and goggled at each other.

" Can't count that one," said the elder. " Must ha' come out of a circus." The younger was more enterprising.

" Never can tell," he remarked stoutly. " More likely it came out of the Victoria and Albert. Relics of the Victorian Age. If so, the cops 'ull be round." And defiantly he added this cartoon of a car to his list.

Crook, paying no attention to these mannerless brats, pranced into the hall of the Mansions to find a disgruntled Hume hanging a notice—OUT OF ORDER—on the lift, whose gate stood open.

" Having a bit of trouble ? " suggested Crook breezily.

Hume turned his head. He was a sallow sulky little chap, carrying too much weight for his height.

" These mucking women ! " he said. " Nothing to do all day but gab, gab, gab, and can't even walk up a few stairs. If I didn't put the porter's bell out of order sometimes life wouldn't be worth living. Not that it's worth much, anyway," he added gloomily.

" Too bad you missed the Atom Bomb," suggested Crook, cosily. " What's happened to the lift ? "

" There's a notice up," continued Hume, not bothering to conceal his feelings. " No unauthorised person to work this lift, but you'd think nobody in the place could read for all the notice they take of it. And now one of 'em's brought it down so hard they've gone and put the perishing thing out of order. I've had No. 10 on at me already. I'm a porter and liftman, I told her, not a perishing mechanic. I'll get someone in in the morning and that's the best I can promise. ' I'm not accustomed to insolence,' she told me. The airs some of them put on. Not that I take any notice. Easier to get tenants than porters any day of the week, and the boss knows it. As if I hadn't got a pack of trouble anyway, with the wife the way she is."

" Soured," reflected Crook, bouncing cheerfully up the stairs. He was so used to mounting under his own steam, having no lifts either in Bloomsbury or Brandon Streets, his professional and private addresses, that a mere dozen flights were nothing to him. They were only short flights, anyway, and what are a hundred stairs to a chap of fifty-six who never takes any exercise and drinks beer as an old maid drinks tea ? Ask Arthur Crook. He wasn't even puffed when he stood outside No. 15 on the fifth floor and pressed the bell. He wondered how a sharp old body like Frances Pinnegar had got herself involved in murder, but he wasn't exactly surprised because he had sensed at their first meeting that, like himself, she never found it much fun to stand and shout —or boo—with the crowd. She wouldn't have been one of the elderly Roman virgins watching from a ring seat the lions have a good time with the martyrs. No, she'd have been down in the arena all among the blood and sand giving the lion something he wouldn't forget in a hurry.

" Game old girl ! " thought Crook indulgently, sparing a

pang of pity for whoever had set himself up against her. He leaned against the banisters and looked down on the stairs snaking away in a discreetly carpeted spiral to the black and white paved hall that seemed an unconscionable distance below. " Funny," he thought, " it didn't seem any way coming up. But it looks a hell of a long way down." The banisters gave a warning creak, and prudently he removed his weight from them. If they gave way Hume would have an unenviable job cleaning the place up. " Nobody in the flats 'ud need to buy jelly for a month to come," was his characteristic way of putting it. It occurred to him that Miss Pinnegar was being a remarkably long time opening the door. Of course, she might be in the bath or changing her dress or answering the telephone. He waited another moment, then rang again.

" If you want Miss Pinnegar," said a cracked voice behind him, " you're too late."

He whizzed round. The door of the opposite flat had opened a few inches and in the narrow aperture appeared what Crook supposed to be one of the original Goodies, a thin female figure with a crooked mouth, a pointed chin, and a wild tangle of hair like January twigs sprinkled with hoar frost ; the vision had mad green eyes, a twitching upper lip and hands to match her hair—that is, they looked as though they were made of something plucked from the hedgerow. Emett couldn't have bettered her for his Festival railway. Crook looked at her in fascination. " First cousin to the Witch of Endor and probably twice as dangerous," he thought.

" I don't know who you are," said Miss Michael ; " but if you're waiting for Miss Pinnegar you're too late."

There was something about the repetition that disturbed Crook. Too late had an ominous ring.

" Too late for what ? " he asked briskly.

" Too late to see her. She's gone."

" Gone where ? "

" I don't know. She wouldn't stop and tell me."

Crook felt he could hardly blame her for that. The old girl would probably turn you into a broomstick or a pillar of salt by one flash of those uncanny eyes."

" Maybe she was in a hurry," he suggested. But he didn't like it. It didn't add up.

"She was carrying a suitcase," amplified Miss Michael. "I thought that was queer."

"Maybe she was going for a holiday. Sometimes the air in these parts isn't too healthy."

"On the contrary." She poked her pointed chin into the air. "It's notorious for being a most salubrious neighbourhood."

"Well, perhaps she wants a change." What it meant, of course, was that something had happened since she dated him, and for some reason she hadn't had a chance of letting him know. It was the nature of the chance that bothered him. "How big a suitcase?" he added.

"Her big one, the one with all her labels on it. She's been quite a traveller in her time, so enterprising. Of course, not all of us get the chance—family ties. You know. Not that you can get her to talk about it much. It's funny how the people that see the most are often the least communicative."

"There's a proverb," murmured Crook, fascinated. "Something about an owl in an oak."

"For instance," continued Miss Michael who, like a juke-box, would go on playing till the machinery ran down, "she'd been to Krakov. The old label—Hotel Francusi, I think it was—was still on the side—a bit battered, of course, but think of it! Krakov."

Crook thought. Somehow it didn't inspire him in the least. "I guess if Providence had meant me to visit Krakov I'd have got myself born a Pole," he offered. "Tell me more about Miss Pinnegar. What time did you see her go?"

"Let me see. It would be about quarter past five. This is my day for the Fellowship Meeting. (Crook ribaldly supposed this was the modern version of the Witches' Sabbath.) It was over at five sharp and I came straight back. I came up in the lift——"

"With the porter?"

"The porter spends most of his time in his own flat. He says he's looking after his wife. That seems to take the greater part of his day."

"Lucky he ain't a Mohammedan, or whoever those chaps are who can have four," suggested Crook, who believed in looking on the bright side.

"As I say, I brought the lift up to this floor and opened

63

it just in time to see Miss Pinnegar disappearing round the corner, though I hadn't heard her door close. I thought for a minute perhaps she was taking Florence some clothes— Florence is her maid who has been in hospital for the past month—so I called out, ' Are you going to fetch Florence home ? ' but she didn't even turn her head. She seemed in a great hurry and there was something . . ." She paused, and Crook said encouragingly :

" Yes ? "

" It was almost as though she didn't want to speak to me. Can you understand it ? I mean, why should she want to avoid me ? I've always tried to be a good neighbour to her. There must be some reason . . ." Crook made sounds that were intended to be both soothing and encouraging. Miss Michael continued. " I called out ' Are you going away ? ' I thought perhaps she'd like me to look after her kitty, but she just hurried off. Mind you, she has moods—and she's not much of a mixer. That's one reason why I try to take her out of herself sometimes."

" Maybe," said Crook, feeling this was enough for one instalment, " she left a message with the porter. He didn't mention it, but then I didn't mention who I was coming to visit. Hallo, what's that ? "

A faint crying came from within the deserted flat.

" That'll be the kitty," said Miss Michael in distressed tones. " I expect it's hungry." She approached the front door of No. 15 and started in on some lovey-doveying through the keyhole. " I'm sure something's wrong. She'd never have left kitty."

" It could be she's coming back," suggested Crook.

" Then why did she take the big suitcase ? She's got a small one. I did wonder if she could be getting something back from the cleaners, but this is early closing day. Besides, they deliver."

" I'll pop down and have a word with the porter," said Crook. " I suppose he'll have a master key ? "

Miss Michael looked shocked. " But you can't break into her flat."

" You'd be surprised." Miss Michael (poor old Goody) was so surprised already Crook expected to hear her eyes fall out with a plop and bounce in the hall below.

Hume said he didn't know anything about Miss Pinnegar's

movements. She'd come in just before four. After that he'd gone to get Minnie's tea and have his own. He hadn't seen Miss Pinnegar again. The tenant on the top floor was holding a meeting—something political.

" Conservatives," suggested Crook intelligently.

" Or communists. It don't make much difference. Neither of them's going to do me any good. There's been people coming and going for hours. Probably one of them broke my lift," he added viciously. " What do they think the stairs are there for if it isn't to walk up ? "

Crook said they were sometimes handy to shove people down. He then suggested Hume might open the door of No. 15.

" What ? Miss Pinnegar's flat ? Nothing doing. I don't want to roast before my time. Besides, why should I ? "

" Well, the kitty wants its milk. If that ain't enough I've got a hunch. Miss Pinnegar had one, too."

" You ain't even told me who you are," objected Hume.

" Lawyer. Come by appointment."

" What for ? "

" It could be murder," said Crook casually. " No, that's not my idea. It's hers. Now we had a date for six o'clock but Glamour Puss across the way says she saw her going down the stairs at a quarter past five."

" Going to see you, p'r'aps," suggested Hume.

"With a suitcase ? Be your age. I'll go bail she won't prosecute you for unlawful entry, always supposing she's still in some place where she can take proceedings."

" Here, what are you getting at ? " demanded Hume, growing momentarily more disturbed.

" I don't like it," said Crook frankly, " and that's a fact. What's happened between her telephoning me at midday and her sneaking out without even a kind word for her buddy just after five ? Oh, well, if you won't open up for me I suppose you will for the police."

As he had anticipated, that did the trick. No more than any other sensible person did Hume want the police mucking about on his premises. Reluctantly he agreed to accompany Crook upstairs.

The door of No. 16 was still ajar and Miss Michael poked out her witch's head and greeted them eagerly.

" You don't think——" she began, and Crook gave her

his alligator smile, and said : Well, no, not yet ; not till he was paid to.

As Hume opened the door of No. 15 the little black kitten came tearing at them and ran up Crook's trouser leg. " Think's I'm some kind of a rat," said Crook cheerfully. " I like spunk." He bent down and stroked it between the ears. " Where's Ma, you little basket ? " he asked affectionately. The kitten opened its mouth as wide as it would go. " Hungry, I suppose," Crook suggested. " How about some milk ? " He turned into the kitchen. " Hallo ! " he said. " She had someone to tea." A tray stood on the table containing two clean cups, a plate of biscuits, a teapot, milk jug and sugar bowl.

" Went out in a hurry," suggested Crook. " Or she'd have stopped to put the biscuits away. I know what dames are." He removed the tea-cosy and lifted the teapot lid. " That's another funny thing," he said. " The cups are washed, but not the pot. Milk still in the jug, though she's got a refrigerator. Did she live alone ? "

" Except for Florence."

" And she's in hospital." He padded out of the kitchen, followed by the kitten, mewing indignantly. He opened another door. This was Miss Pinnegar's bedroom—it was neat as a new pin. The silver brushes on the dressing-table shone as though they had been polished that very morning, a severe jar of cold cream and a tube of colourless lip salve stood beside the mirror. Crook looked round as if he thought the room had something to tell him, noting the plain felt slippers under the bed, the grey ripple dressing-gown on the back of the door. He didn't touch anything, but after a moment he said, " Let's go." They went into the living-room. There was a lace-edged tablecloth on the trolley and a cigarette end in the hearth. Obviously she hadn't had time to leave everything absolutely spick and span. Crook picked up the cigarette—a familiar make and unstained by lipstick.

" Does she smoke ? " he asked. " Miss Pinnegar, I mean."

It was a dead heat between Hume and Miss Michael to assure him that she didn't.

" Then she had a visitor who did, either a man or another of these old-fashioned girls who don't use lipstick. Well, that 'ud explain the two tea-cups though it don't explain the teapot not bein' washed out."

" Perhaps she had a telephone call while she was washing the cups," suggested Miss Michael. " If it was very urgent she might drop everything and fly."

" She stopped to dry the cups," Crook pointed out. " Wouldn't she normally wash everything first before she started drying ? "

" Dear me ! " said Miss Michael brightly. " What a fusspot ! Is it important ? "

" Could be," said Crook, not in the least offended. " What's through that door ? "

It proved to be Florence's room. Crook stood on the threshold sniffing like a hound at scent. " How long has Abigail been in her penitentiary ? " he demanded.

" Let me see. I should say about a month."

" Someone slept here no more than forty-eight hours ago," Crook announced. " Someone with a good strong taste in face powder. Look at that mirror—you could write your name in it. That wasn't Florence."

" Florence doesn't use face powder," interpolated Miss Michael.

" You're wasted in S.W.7. You ought to be at the Yard," Crook told her frankly. " Well, did Miss Pinnegar know anyone who did use face powder and smoked (he had pounced on the lipsticked cigarette butts in the china vessel inscribed " A Present from Tenby "), and used lipstick and wasn't too keen on washing before going to bed ? " He indicated a red smear on the pillow.

" I thought that was blood," said Hume in disappointed tones.

" If you ever see any blood that colour I'll buy it," promised Crook rashly. " No, I'd say Miss Pinnegar had a visitor last night, who cleared out bag and baggage sometime during the day. And she had another visitor to tea this afternoon. You're sure there wasn't anyone else on the stairs, someone who went down in front of her, say."

" No. I'm quite sure there wasn't anyone."

" Well, there's no one in the flat now, so whoever it was left before she did. And I'll tell you something else. It was someone she didn't expect and whatever his news it knocked her off her rocker, or she wouldn't have gone out shortly before I was expected, not without leaving a message."

He was still letting this sink in when the telephone rang. Miss Michael beat him to it by a short head.

" Who is that ? " she demanded, snatching up the receiver.

" Is that you, Fanny ? . . . You don't sound at all like yourself."

" Miss Pinnegar is out," said Miss Michael in quavering tones.

" Then who are you ? "

Crook snatched the receiver in his turn. " Really ! " panted Miss Michael.

" Miss Pinnegar's legal representative here," he announced. " Could be I'll be her chief mourner unless someone gives me a line."

" I don't understand." Miss Medlicott sounded very tart.

" Then we're in the same boat, and it's not often I find myself in a boat with a lady. I don't think you mentioned who you were ? "

Miss Medlicott informed him in the same sharp tone.

" Hey," exclaimed Crook, his voice changing magically, " now we are going places. That's the place where the cross-roads victims are in jug. Now, then, lady, spill the beans."

" I'm afraid you're under some misapprehension. I want to speak to Miss Pinnegar."

" So do I. So does Glamour Puss. So do we all. Point is, we none of us know where she's vanished to. We were looking to you for a bit of help."

" Well . . ." Miss Medlicott hesitated. " This is a confidential matter. Perhaps I had better ring later."

" Yes, do that," agreed Crook cordially. " You won't get any answer, but——"

" Why are you so sure ? "

" Because she's made a bolt for it in a hurry, such a hurry she didn't even leave a message to say where she was going. When did you last speak to her ? "

" She telephoned me about lunchtime, but I had nothing to report. I rang up again at five, but there was no reply."

" Hold hard," exclaimed Crook. " Quite sure of your time ? Careful now. A few minutes either way may make all the difference."

" Perfectly sure," returned Miss Medlicott, without any hesitation. " I was expecting a caller at five, and I was anxious to get in touch with F—— Miss Pinnegar—before this person arrived. I knew I should be delayed some time. In fact, she has only just gone."

" And—I wouldn't press the point if it wasn't important —she came on time ? "

" I wish I knew what all this was about," exclaimed Miss Medlicott fretfully. " I don't like all this mystery—first Miss Pinnegar and then ̸you. Yes, she came as the clock was chiming the hour. When we were in the hospital together she was known as Punctuality Pete—Peters being her name. I am absolutely sure."

" So your call was made a minute or two before five. Well, thanks a million." But he didn't sound very grateful as he rang off. Miss Michael was standing in the doorway, looking like someone who has received not an angelic but a diabolical annunciation.

" What is it ? " she breathed.

" Look here ! " said Crook. " I take it you're prepared to go into court and swear your meeting wasn't over till five o'clock ? "

" Certainly. Ask anyone."

" Maybe I will presently. And Miss Pinnegar was waiting for an urgent call, but she don't answer the phone. Now there's only two reasons why she wouldn't do that. One is that she wasn't. there—no, hold your horses. The other is she was here, but didn't want anyone to know it. That 'ud fit in with your story of her slippin' down the stairs and pretendin' not to hear you when you called to her."

" Now I come to think of it, I didn't hear her door slam as I came up. And I'm quite convinced she heard me."

" But had a good reason, that we'll come to later, for not wanting to answer. Now, to my mind, this all ties up with her mysterious visitor. When we know who he was we'll have turned our first corner."

" And what do you expect to find round that ? " demanded Hume.

" Battle, murder and sudden death it could be," replied Crook in gloomy tones.

CHAPTER VII

At this point Miss Michael uttered a scream that made Hume jump about six inches from the ground. "It's all right," he said irritably, "the gentleman was only talking turkey. Things like that don't happen in our flats."

It appeared, however, that Miss Michael's distress was occasioned, not by any fear for Miss Pinnegar's safety, but by the behaviour of the kitten, Grim, who was pouncing and worrying at something at the end of the hall.

"It's a mouse," whispered the Goody. "Oh, please take it away. I can't bear it. Seeing them tormented, I mean. That's why I won't have a cat. . . ."

"Beats me," said Crook frankly, "how any mouse would dare come into Miss Pinnegar's flat."

"You don't know her," retorted Miss Michael in the same faint voice. "She'd import mice to please that kitten. Oh, please, please take it away."

She was making a lot more noise than the mouse, Crook reflected, and after all, the mouse was the one to suffer. But he strolled humanely over to where the enchanted kitten was tossing his plaything about in a demented fashion, bumping it with his nose and nibbling at it with his tiny sharp teeth. As Crook stooped the indignant Grim lay down like a minute lion curling his raspberry-pink pads round his treasure.

"Tackle something your own size," Crook suggested soothingly, stooping to rescue the victim. A moment later his expression had changed. It wasn't, after all, a mouse that had engaged Grim's attention, but a round button of a dark green shade, the size you'd expect to find on a lady's coat.

"Button, eh?" said Hume, leaning over to look. The next instant he had uttered a shocked exclamation and snatched the button out of Crook's hand. "Crikey! That's green."

"Superstitious?" asked Crook pleasantly. But Hume didn't answer. He uttered a wild cry of pain and straightened up, allowing the button to roll to the floor where it was

70

instantly pounced on by the enraged kitten. "The little blighter." For Hume and the police could think what they liked about this treasure; Grim knew it was his. Finding's keepings was stamped all over his fierce little lion's face.

"Hold everything," said Crook, who held that women and cats had a lot in common and were always distracted by something new. He was busily tying a knot in his enormous handkerchief, and now he began to enact the age-old routine of I've-come-to-confess-oh-Venerable-Bede. The waving corner of the handkerchief held the kitten spellbound. It stood staring, its tail waving rhythmically. Then, forgetting the button, it sprang and caught the handkerchief's pointed corner in its tiny resolute mouth. At a nod from Crook the porter snatched up the button and stood staring at it as it lay in the palm of his hand.

"Crikey," he said again in a low voice.

When the kitten suddenly tired of the handkerchief and curled up, falling into the sudden sleep of the very young, Crook came back to the job in hand.

"What's biting you?" he asked the porter.

"You can see for yourself, can't you?" The man shoved out his hand. "A green button."

"Well?"

"Well yourself. You know the police are looking for a green button, and here it is."

"Funny notion of law you've got. There are several million green buttons in the country and that's one of them. Any proof it's the one the police want?"

"We could ask them."

"Oh, we could, if you want to give them a good laugh. They'll ask you where you found it and when you tell them they'll say what proof have you got that the missing dame was in the flat. Well, what have you? Ever seen a lady visiting Miss Pinnegar wearing a green coat? Any reason to suppose Miss Pinnegar's the sort of lady who'd hide up an accessory to theft and manslaughter? Now, look," he added in more persuasive tones, "why don't you give Miss Pinnegar a chance to do her own explaining? I dare say I don't know her as well as you do"—this with Crook was diplomacy at its highest—"but I'd say she wouldn't be too keen to know you'd been rumbling her flat and getting in the force on what's most likely a fool's errand."

" In that case," said Miss Michael in stubborn tones, " why has she disappeared ? "

" A dame can break an appointment without breaking the law," Crook pointed out, silkily. " And if anyone's a right to be sore it 'ud be me. And I ain't. Do I look sore ? "

Miss Michael's private opinion was that he looked like something out of the Zoo.

" Perhaps not. But I think we should tell them she's gone away. And with a suitcase."

" If you're goin' away you generally take a suitcase," Crook said, summoning his meagre stock of patience to his aid. " And it could be there'll be a letter in to-morrow's mail explaining why she had to beetle off at such a rate. Lookee, what say we wait till the morning ? For one thing," he added, " you may increase her danger by going to the rozzers to-night."

" Danger ? "

" That's what I said. Y'see, she was expecting a bit of trouble, that's why she asked me to call. Could be it's arrived earlier than she expected, and she had to get out in a hurry. You know how it is. He who fights and runs away lives to fight another day. It wouldn't surprise me," he added mendaciously, " to know there's a letter in the box at this moment. As for the button—well, maybe it came off one of her own suits."

" They're hanging in the wardrobe," Miss Michael suggested.

Crook looked really shocked. " It's one thing to enter a flat to rescue a so-called dumb animal, though who thought up that description was dumber than all the rest put together, but directly we start going through her belongings we're for the big house ourselves. Why, even the police can't come in without a search warrant. Anyhow," he added, " I'd say the lady expected to be back to-night, and when she does return she won't be too pleased to find her place crawling with bluebottles."

" IF she returns," prophesied Miss Michael darkly.

" The gentleman's right," put in Hume, but she made short work of *him*.

" Oh, I don't deny it would suit your book very well to keep things quiet," she snapped. " They might start asking embarrassing questions about your not being on duty to see who comes and goes."

" I'm not the Gestapo," pointed out Hume in the same sort of voice. " And, anyway, it was my tea-time. And," he continued before Miss Michael could once more get under weigh, " with all the people coming and going on the top floor I couldn't be expected to notice any strange callers. Besides," he added triumphantly, " whoever it was come *last night*. I'm not expected to be on duty twenty-four hours out of the twenty-four."

Miss Michael had a lightning vision of Miss Pinnegar marching in to find her flat invaded, and she quailed before it. " Very well," she agreed reluctantly, " we will wait till the morning. But if she doesn't come back then I think we should go to the police."

" My guess 'ud be that a lady in her right mind don't count as missing just because she's away for a night and didn't confide in you. She may have written half a dozen letters of explanation ; she may have had a telephone call. Got any near relatives ? "

" She's got a nephew to whom she's quite devoted."

" P'r'aps he's in a train smash or something."

" He's stationed in Germany," Miss Michael pointed out.

" P'r'aps she's decided to go over for a long week-end. P'r'aps she's taking her last night's visitor home. Still," he added generously to show that he had an open mind on the subject, " you've got your rights as a citizen and no one can deprive you of 'em, though they've shrunk a bit in the past few years. You're as free as air to go to the police on your own account, but if afterwards you wish you hadn't, don't say I didn't warn you."

" You don't really think anything can have happened to her, do you ? " quavered Miss Michael. She spoke with a little pause between each word, which gave her speech an odd impressiveness.

" I'd say if she was in danger the fact that the police had been dragged in would increase it," he said frankly. " As for danger—well, she hasn't called me in at short notice just to make her will. I ain't that sort of a lawyer."

" You do believe she's mixed up in this cross-roads case," Miss Michael accused him. " There was that call from the matron of the hospital—and the button—and her suddenly disappearing."

" She went under her own steam, remember," Crook reminded her. " You didn't see her being bumped down the stairs in a trunk or anything. And I'd say she generally had a good reason for what she did." All the same, though he didn't say so, he was bothered about that five o'clock telephone call. It was easy to say that dear Grace had got the time wrong, but she'd alibi-ed herself very neatly, and she gave the impression of a woman who knew what she was talking about. Which was another reason why he didn't want the police pulled in till he had a little more information. He glanced sharply at Miss Michael, but she was lost in a reverie, gibbering to herself like a Barbary ape, thought the scornful Hume, who couldn't abide her anyway. He didn't want the police called in, but on the other hand, he didn't want a raspberry from them if it should turn out that the tenant of No.15 was in some way involved in a police case. Still, Crook was a lawyer, and with those shoulders he could take any amount of responsibility. Must have been an ox in a previous incarnation, he reflected. Crook turned suddenly.

" My card," he said, pulling it out of his pocket with the air of a conjuror producing a rabbit from a hat in the time of an acute meat shortage. " If there are any developments, ring me. Never mind the time. All this slavery to clocks makes me tired."

" Nice to know something does," retorted Hume sourly. But he took the card. It didn't mean a thing to him. He'd never heard of Crook. He'd no notion then how much he was going to learn about him during the next few days. They went down together, followed by Miss Michael's yearning gaze. Grim refused all offers of hospitality and they had to leave him in the flat after raiding the Frigidaire to find his supper.

" Never thought I'd come to this," Hume ejaculated as they turned a corner of the stair. " Keeper in a loony-bin, that's what I am. There's another of 'em," he added, as the tenant of No. 17 was discovered standing in the lift pulling furiously on the rope.

" There's a notice to say the lift's out of order," he announced with scant courtesy.

" We ought to have a reduction in rent," said the tenant

74

in fierce tones. " Lift service was particularly stipulated in the lease."

" Listen, lady," said Hume. " The best organised lift can go wrong sometimes."

" Like the best people," put in Crook helpfully, with Miss Pinnegar in mind. He hadn't much doubt that she'd got herself mixed up in something pretty squalid, and he only hoped she'd be able to straighten herself out again in an upright position. He'd taken a fancy to the old girl, he told himself, and he didn't want to see her lying out on a marble slab like a particularly aristocratic sort of fish, at their next meeting. But he wouldn't have liked to bet on it.

" I shall complain to the landlord," said the disgruntled tenant. " I suppose there are such people as engineers."

" There's such a thing as the forty-four-hour week, too," Hume reminded her. " Chap's coming in the morning. If people didn't use the lift that aren't entitled to," he added darkly, " accidents wouldn't happen."

" What does she expect me to do ? " he added to Crook as, in scornful silence, the tenant moved up the staircase. " Carry 'er ? " He watched Crook depart in the Scourge and went back to his wife, who had reached the tiresome stage of convalescence, when she could criticise without being able to help.

" Anyone 'ud think my job was a honey," he burst out when she paused for breath and broke at once into the 1445th instalment of How Much Better Life 'Ud Be if I'd Never Left the Navy. Mrs. Hume (they were like boxers, each watching like mad for a break in the other's defence) waited for her opportunity and said tartly that the navy had her sympathy and he could take that any way he liked. In a minute or so they were at it hammer and tongs. The porter's bell rang perpetually as each newcomer discovered the condition of the lift and resolved to give the porter a piece of his or her mind. But they didn't pay any attention. They were used to it and they knew they could outlast any tenant, no matter how persevering.

In the meantime Miss Michael had closed the door of her flat and picked up the *Radio Times* to see if there was anything worth listening to during the evening. But her mind wasn't on it ; she felt she was involved in something far more interesting than anything the B.B.C. had to offer. She was haunted by the tantalising suspicion that she'd missed something vital in the situation, something she couldn't identify. The knowledge of what it was dodged in and out of her consciousness like a wireworm through a three-pronged fork. " Something's wrong," she told the canary hanging in a cage in the window. " Something the others didn't notice or they'd have said something." The canary followed the example of the others in maintaining silence but that wasn't his fault; he had ceased taking any interest in his surroundings years ago. Miss Michael had had him stuffed, on the ground that a dead canary was more company than no canary at all, and she still threw a green cloth over his cage at night. When that was in place she could forget darling Gerry was dead; a sleeping canary makes as little noise as a defunct one. As she went about the job of getting her simple supper—and you'd have thought she was entertaining a couple of Roman grandees by the state of the kitchen when her tray was at length assembled—this sense of being blindfolded continued to tease her mind. She kept her door an inch or two ajar so that if she heard Miss Pinnegar return she could rush out and tell her what had happened. It was improbable that Hume would be on duty and most unfair if he were to defraud her of her innocent delight in being the first to give the news, but no one came up. A little after eleven she reluctantly closed the door and shot the bolt. Then she realised that the wireless had been playing all the evening and she hadn't heard a single item. She switched it off and got into bed where she lay awake a long time pursuing this elusive clue. But when she finally dropped off to sleep she was, in all senses, still in the dark.

She was brushing her hair in front of the glass next morning when it came to her in a flash what she had missed, what, she believed, Crook had missed too. Now she was all impatience to enlighten him. She made her tea before the kettle had really boiled, with the result that it was speckled and unappetising; she forget about the toast on the grill until it had burned, but she couldn't be bothered to make more, so she perfunctorily scraped away the top layer and nibbled it dry. For form's sake she rang Miss Pinnegar's number, but no one answered. Then she jammed on something she called a hat, and that looked as though it had been prised from the hedge at the same time as her hair, and joined the rush-hour queue for the tube. She had had the forethought to look over Hume's shoulder and note Crook's address, and all the way to Bloomsbury Street she rehearsed what she intended to say. She knew lawyers, or believed she did. When they heard she had no appointment they'd probably keep her waiting an hour. "This," she would say impressively, refusing to take No for an answer, " is a matter of *Life* and *Death*. I have proof—unassailable proof. . . ."

She caught the eye of a man sitting opposite who, she thought, was regarding her very oddly and blushed. But a minute later she'd forgotten about him, and was chattering away again like mad when the train arrived at her stop. And, after all, she needn't have worried. She'd thought Crook a very unconventional sort of lawyer at their first meeting and this opinion was strengthened when she was bidden to " Come right in," and found herself in a large shabby room whose furniture even in these days of scarcity wouldn't, she thought, fetch twenty pounds at an auction.

" I shouldn't think he ever gets any clients," she decided disdainfully. If she'd been privileged to see Crook's income-tax returns she'd have fainted dead away.

" Well, how's tricks ? " he greeted her briskly. " Come to tell me the lady's come home ? "

" No. Oh, no ! I waited up till quite late last night, but she didn't return. I telephoned her flat this morning, but though I could hear the bell ringing nobody answered. That's what convinces me there's something wrong and she never meant to be away for the night. You see, when we went into her flat her *brush and comb* were on the dressing-table. Now, the first things you put ready to pack are your brush and comb——"

" Your slippers and your dressing-gown. Yes, it seemed to me a bit rum they should all be there."

" So you *did* notice." Miss Michael was dreadfully mortified.

" Sure, I noticed. That's why I said wait till this morning, in case she came back last night."

" Then, what was in the suitcase ? "

" Even more pressin'—where *is* the suitcase ? Y'see, if it wasn't used to take Miss Pinnegar's gear, it was used to remove somethin' from the flat."

" You mean something incriminating ? "

" Looks like it. Now, if you wanted to get rid of a suit-case, where would you put it ? "

" A rubbish dump ? " suggested Miss Michael doubtfully.

" Wouldn't be safe there long. If you want a thing to be discovered double quick time, put it on a dump."

" I suppose you *could* leave it at a bank," hazarded Miss Michael.

" Not without advertisin' the fact that you'd left it there, and not at a quarter past five."

" A left luggage office," exclaimed Miss Michael inspired.

" That 'ud be my guess, too. Lucky there's something about this case that marks it out from the ruck."

" You mean—the Krakov label ? "

" You're comin' on," Crook congratulated her. " We'll have you in the Ladies' Force yet."

" But—we can't go round asking for it—we haven't got the receipt."

" We don't want it," said Crook. " Besides, why should we do the police's job for them ? "

" The police ? But surely Miss Pinnegar has a right to leave her case wherever she pleases ? And if you're thinking there might be a body in it," she added hurriedly, " I can assure you it was much too small, though it was the larger case of the two."

" Ever tried shifting a dead body ? " asked Crook grimly. " As you say, Miss Pinnegar has a right to dispose of her own property—always supposing it is Miss Pinnegar. Y'see, we haven't accounted for her gentleman visitor yet."

" I can only assure you she was quite alone when I saw her."

" I believe you," said Crook heartily. " All the same, there's something screwy. Miss Pinnegar was hopping mad to know how things were shaping in the cross-roads crash, yet when her girl-friend rings up at five o'clock she don't answer. Why ? "

" Because she didn't want anyone to know she was there ? But—what reason could she possibly have ? "

" That," Crook told her (afterwards she said his voice had a *sinister* ring), " is what we've got to find out."

At Allenfield Mansions Hume was explaining to the

engineer from Hunt & Workman that if it hadn't been for Mrs. Hume he'd still be in the navy, and give him Germans any day, he said, rather than the mob who lived in the Mansions. Worry, worry, worry, morning, noon and night.

"Wonder they aren't all in the cemetery the state this lift's in," returned the engineer unsympathetically. He had been working on it for two hours and he wanted his tea.

"They won't die," said Hume in despondent tones. "Why should they? They've got nothing to do but fuss about keeping themselves alive—that and make trouble for other people. Look at this one who's missing—absent without leave we shud ha' called it—and Daftie, up on the same floor, wanting to call the police." Grumbling was second nature to him. His wife would have told you he did it even in his sleep.

The engineer stamped experimentally on the lift floor.

"'Ere, don't do that," cried Hume, alarmed. "That's sooicide. That floor was never made for the wild men of Borneo, and if you go through odds are they'll never find you again. Don't know what they was thinking of when they sunk the shaft. Underground passage to Australia, if you ask me."

"One of these days your guv'nor 'ull be had up for manslaughter," observed his companion judicially. "The next old girl you miss will be found to have taken a single passage to—Australia, I think you said."

"If you ask me," said Hume in the same peevish voice, "they put this lift out of action just to make trouble for me. 'Allo! What the 'ell do you want?"

This last was to Grim, who came stepping delicately down the stairs and paused, mewing loudly.

"Drat that cat!" said Hume. "It's been like that ever since last night. It was howling like a banshee this morning till I let it out. You should ha' heard the string of complaints I had from the tenant below. Said it had been carrying on that way all night. It's not my blasted cat, I said. I don't know why they allow animals in these flats. If Miss Pinnegar ain't back by to-night I'll drown it and tell 'er it's run off."

"Don't do that, mate." The fitter sounded really alarmed. "Never 'eard it was unlucky to kill a black cat? Means a death—this old girl 'ull be found with 'er throat cut from ear to ear if you go 'arming that cat." A little later he said, " What's more it wouldn't surprise me if you was to have a murder here. This type of lift—it's obsolete, ought to be done away with. Still, there she is, as good as she'll ever be." He pulled on the rope and the lift rose slowly. It would be hard to say whether it or Hume complained more in the course of the day's work. He brought it down again. " Better try it yourself, mate," he said. " You're the customer we've got to satisfy. Besides "—he grinned—" I want to find out if it's really possible to see Australia at the end of your tunnel."

Hume took his place with reluctance. " Rope's stiff," he announced. 'Ave the skin off my 'ands this will."

" 'Ave to indent the Ministry of 'Ealth for a new pair," said the other unsympathetically.

Hume rose slowly out of sight. He had barely reached the first floor when a shout recalled him.

" My God ! " said the engineer. " Come on down, mate. No, no. Leave 'er where she is. Come down on your great flat feet. I told you it 'ud be murder." Hume came back to the hall floor.

" What's all this about ? " he demanded angrily. " The tenants 'ull think this is Bedlam. Luckily, they mostly seem to be out this afternoon."

" I can tell you one who isn't," said the engineer, who had turned as green as a pea-soup fog, " and that's the one you've bin looking for. She's been on the premises all the time." He jerked a thumb at the open gate of the lift. " Take a look for yourself."

Gingerly Hume peered over the side. " God a'mighty," he said after a minute. " Great 'eavens ! To think of 'er being there all the time. All night and us not knowing."

" That's nothing," said the fitter trying to sound matter-of-fact. " In 1940 there was the case of a woman—Bannerman I think her name was—fell down a shaft in Stansford Mansions the other side of the Park, wasn't found for four days. People were always bolting because of the bombing and she'd given out she'd be away for the week-end, and it wasn't till the Tuesday that the lady she'd been going to stay with rang up to know if anything was wrong because she'd never arrived. Then questions began to be asked and it turned out nobody had seen her leave, so they took a look round and—there she was."

Something small and light brushed against his leg, and he drew back with a muttered exclamation. It was the little black kitten from No. 15. It stood on the edge of the abyss, looking down with its bright green eyes.

" Gives me the creeps, that does," muttered Hume.

" Poor little blighter ! " said the engineer. " Misses 'er, I dare say."

The kitten, however, exemplified the proverbial heartlessness of cats by drawing back from the edge, putting its tail in the air and strolling into the hall.

" You'd better get a doctor, hadn't you, mate ? " suggested the engineer. He peered a second time into the dark hole. " Better tell 'em to send a crane and pulley while they're about it. Or a cable to Australia to get going their end," he added in a lamentable attempt to lighten the situation.

" We, we don't know she's dead," muttered Hume in uncertain tones.

" Be your age," the engineer counselled him rudely. " After falling from the top or nearly the top of the building and lying there—how long is it ? "

" Best part of twenty-four hours," acknowledged Hume.

" Well, I ask you—is she likely to be alive ? Besides, look at the way she's lying, all of a 'eap."

But Hume had seen enough. He went out through the back entrance down to his own flat. " And you," he told the younger man, " you bring the lift down to this floor, see ? We don't want the Shrieking Sisterhood on our hands before the doctor gets here. And don't let 'em use it. We don't want one of 'em looking down from one of the upper floors and seeing—that ! "

He disappeared. Grim sat anxiously on the front step and the wind that had sprung up during the last hour caused his whiskers to tremble deliciously.

It was typical of Miss Michael that she should be the first on this macabre scene. She came marching in in a hat of emerald green felt, shaped like an upturned flower-pot, set well on the back of her head, trimmed with an appliquéd scarlet flower and two small black marabout antennæ, to find the harassed fitter, whose name was Owen, standing by the lift's open door.

" All present and correct ? " she suggested. (She believed

in being matey with the working classes, as they were called in her far-distant youth.)

" Out of order," said Owen sullenly, adding to himself, " And not the only thing either, if appearances are anything to go by."

" Really ! That's very inconvenient. What's wrong ? Can't you manage it ? "

" My mate 'ull be along soon," promised Owen.

" Dear me ! The same old story. Forgotten an important tool, I suppose."

Owen preserved a grim silence.

" Well, I hope it will be all right and stay all right," commented Miss Michael, preparing to trot upstairs. " I've never really trusted it—never ! A death trap's my name for it."

She was almost at the top of the first flight and just going round the bend when Hume burst round the corner, saying, " Police are coming right over."

Owen made a furious shushing gesture. Miss Michael, who could be quick-witted enough on occasions, hurried up the stairs as though she had heard nothing. Owen jerked an expressive thumb in her direction. Miss Michael clattered a little on the next flight, then came creeping back as quiet as any mouse. Screened by the corner of the banister she leaned over.

" There'll be trouble over this, you mark my words," opined Hume, more gloomy than ever. " Coroners think they're God Almighty."

" If it makes 'em put in a safety lift it'll be all to the good. That old witch was right. Death-trap's the word."

" It is the missing one, I suppose ? "

" Who else should it be ? " Hume stared.

Miss Michael nipped upstairs and dropped her latch key in her excitement, which held her up another thirty seconds. When she found Crook's line was engaged she nearly went crazy, and stamped up and down the room talking to herself more madly than ever. She got through at last and broke the news. She would have enlarged on it, but Crook in the most unmannerly fashion hung up in the middle of a sentence.

" Hold everything, Bill," he said. " I'm off to the death-bed."

He didn't like the development at all. It didn't fit in with his own ideas and characteristically instead of altering his own ideas, he tried to adjust the facts to fit in with them. The police were keeping people out of the Mansions—the news had spread like wildfire—but Crook barged his way in.

"I understand the deceased is my client," he said. "I represent the family."

They let him through—they had no option—and he stood in the hall while what Hume called dredging operations went on. The stairs were crowded with tenants who could only be appealed to, not dismissed, but the police saw to it that they couldn't really see anything. Grim, materialising from the crowd, rubbed his head against Crook's boot.

"Another candidate for Dr. Barnardo's," said Crook sympathetically.

The authorities had their work cut out, but at length they managed to draw the body out of the hole. It came up, a sickening dead weight, swinging and bumping against the walls of the shaft. The gates on all the upper floors had been locked to prevent ghoulish onlookers overbalancing and crashing down on the body already in the cavity. The less hardened of the watchers on the stairs hid their eyes as the body came to the surface, but they opened them again pretty sharply when Hume's amazed voice rang out.

"But that—that's not her. That's not Miss Pinnegar. I never saw this woman in all my life before."

CHAPTER VIII

UPON HEARING Hume's amazed denial a number of the heads that had been turned away came round to peer once more over the barrier of police. Old Lady Follett, who was a little deaf, asked, "Whose wife?" and her neighbour bawled, "We don't know." Lady Follett subsided to a whisper of, "How shocking," and Crook elbowed his way into the group surrounding the body.

"If this isn't your client," suggested Sergeant Cream nastily, "you won't want to stay."

"My client's still missing, isn't she?" demanded Crook,

sounding almost as surprised as Hume. " If this ain't Miss
Pinnegar, who is she ? "

" She's none of the tenants," declared the porter. The
dead woman was wearing an obviously new mole brown
coat of classic cut and an austere beret to match.

" Then she must have been visiting." Cream was crisp.
" Someone here must know who she is."

Miss Michael clawed her way through the crowd and
clutched at Crook's arm. " I don't understand," she began.

" You're in good company," Crook assured her.

The doctor who had been summoned by the police said in
impatient tones, " If you'd kindly stand back and give us a
chance . . ."

Old Lady Follett's cracked voice rose again in a banshee
wail. " Is she dead ? "

" We don't know," yelled her neighbour.

" Of course she's dead," said Miss Michael. " That lift
went out of order last night. Do you suppose anyone could
live in that airless hole for twenty-four hours ? "

" I do hope she didn't suffer," murmured stout Mrs.
Benson.

They were all silent for a minute, thinking of that trapped
creature, conscious perhaps after her fall, calling out with a
voice growing ever fainter.

" I've always heard, my dear," said skinny Mr. Benson,
" that a fall from a height has some fatal action on the heart
which involves—er—instant death."

" That's if you fall from the Eiffel Tower," said someone
else. " This was only a few floors."

That gave them fresh meat for thought. Because—which
floor ? It suddenly became very important to all of them
to know whom she had been visiting.

" Didn't the porter take her up ? "

" I never set eyes on her," said Hume hastily. " My
wife——"

" Does anyone recognise her ? " inquired Cream.

" Can one—now ? " whispered Miss Lemon from No. 12,
in the high-pitched voice that presages hysteria.

The doctor, who had been on his knees by the body now
rose and whispered something in Cream's ear. Cream
nodded. A number of voices could be heard declaring they
hadn't had a visitor on the previous day, or if they had they

had certain knowledge that she had reached home safely. Only Mrs. Rossiter of No. 18 had had more than one visitor (she had had the Conservative Bring and Buy), and she declared that the lift had been out of order before most of her guests departed.

Cream was saying, " Well, surely she had a purse or a handbag. Ladies don't come calling without their bus fares home."

" Perhaps she didn't need a bus," said one of the officers. " Perhaps she lived so near——"

" In that case it shouldn't be difficult to find out who she is." He looked up. " Perhaps one of you ladies or gentlemen could identify her." But none of them could.

" Well, she came here to see someone," insisted Cream. " And it must have been some time yesterday while the lift was still running. If it had been out of order when she fell she'd be on top instead of underneath."

" The lift was in perfect order at five o'clock," declared Miss Michael. " I know because I used it to take me up to the fifth floor."

Miss Mearns from the top floor began to speak. " She didn't come near my flat."

" She didn't fall from the sixth floor," said Cream, concisely. " She couldn't. She must have fallen from some floor *lower* than that at which the lift was standing."

" Someone," said old Lady Follett, whose hearing had improved remarkably during the past few moments, " must have left the lift gates open and she looked down perhaps and lost her footing. Miss Michael, are you sure—— ? "

" I always shut the gates," said Miss Michael firmly. " I step out, then I pull on the rope to send the lift down, and I shut the gate immediately. What's more, all the gates were closed when I came up. I make a point of noticing and if anyone should have been careless enough to leave one open I stop the lift and close the door. I'm most particular."

" Does anyone remember when the lift was definitely out of action ? " inquired the sergeant. " We have this lady's testimony that it was all right just after five."

Several voices said it had been out of commission when they wanted it—at eight, at nine-thirty, at half-past seven.

" It wasn't working when I came at six," said Crook. Nobody present claimed to have used it between five-fifteen and six ; but of course it might have been someone hurrying away from the Bring and Buy. Miss Michael had returned it to the ground floor when she left it at approximately a quarter past five. So, said the police, the dead woman was either in the well before Miss Michael used the lift, or she had fallen there between five-fifteen and five fifty-five when Crook arrived. Because the lift had been out of order then. Hume said that a tenant had complained to him about five forty-five, and he had tested the lift and found it wasn't working ; he had gone back to his flat to write out a notice to this effect and Crook had found him affixing it on his arrival. The trouble was that most people who want a lift look upwards if it isn't at their floor. Of course if anyone had wanted to come down they'd have looked down, but the well was so deep and the shaft so dark it was possible to overlook the presence of a body in those ominous shadows.

It seemed that they wouldn't make much progress until they knew who the woman was. A fresh tenant and his wife arrived at this moment, but they didn't recognise the body either, and anyhow, they hadn't had any visitors the previous afternoon. Crook, who had his own ideas, kept them to himself. He hadn't much doubt himself that the dead woman was Miss Pinnegar's late visitor, but until he had some notion how she came to tumble down the lift-shaft, minus her handbag (an ominous detail, that) he intended to keep his trap shut. Feeling Miss Michael was going to explode in a moment, he dragged her away into the doorway of the Mansions.

" Do me a favour, Glamour Puss," he said. " Don't say a word till I give you the say-so. You'll have all the publicity you want before we're through, believe me."

" Where are you going now ? " she demanded breathlessly.

He looked at her with a glance bordering on affection. " My luck was in when I set eyes on you, honey-bee," he assured her. " Come on, we're going over the road to the station."

" But—but I've only just come in."

" And in about five minutes you'll be coming in again. If you don't come you'll be obstructin' the course of justice," he added in more threatening tones.

Miss Michael came like a bird.

At the station—" Left luggage office ? " he inquired.

When the odd couple found it, a young man in a grey suit was telling a companion how he'd handle the international situation.

" Very interesting," said Crook. " But right now I've got another situation for you to handle. Lady left a suitcase here last night to be picked up by a friend."

The young man put out a languid hand for the ticket. Crook shook his head. " If I had that there wouldn't be a situation. This lady can identify it. It's got a Krakov label on it."

" Can't give anything up without the ticket," said the young man.

" But you must remember it. Left by a lady wearing a greyish raincoat."

" With the most *extraordinary* sleeves—that's why it's unmistakable," chimed in Miss Michael.

The young man remained unimpressed. " If I had to remember all the ladies who left suitcases——"

" Well, just take a look and make sure it hasn't been picked up," ordered Crook.

" If it's been picked up it won't be here, will it ? "

" There, sugar," said Crook proudly, turning to Miss Michael. " Now you know what you pay your rates and taxes for. I didn't say it had been picked up. I was just asking."

" I can see it," said Miss Michael excitedly. " It's on the shelf there——"

" Good for you," said Crook. " Do me a favour, honeybee, nip back and ask that snooty sergeant to step this way. If you ask me, this is the first corpse he's had to deal with."

" What's that ? " The young man was suddenly galvanished into life. " Did you say a corpse ? "

" That's right. Wouldn't surprise me if you had your picture in the paper yet. Come to that—were you on duty yesterday ? "

" Yes, I was."

" Then maybe you're the chap the police are looking for."

" What do you mean ? I haven't murdered anyone."

" Murder ! " ejaculated Miss Michael. " There hasn't been a murder."

" No ? " said Crook. " Well, if anybody wants my opinion, I'd say that's just what it was."

" But when ? How ? I don't understand," panted Miss Michael, as he drew her away from the luggage office.

" When ? Well, obviously it was after five-fifteen, because the lift was still running then and before six, by which time the lift was out of commission. Somebody took the lift down from the sixth floor—yes, sugar, the sixth, the sergeant's explained all that—and left it in the hall."

Miss Michael shook her dishevelled head. " It's too difficult for me," she said. " I could never do sums, even as a girl. And—where does Miss Pinnegar come in ? "

" That," said Crook, looking disturbed for the first time, " is what's bothering me, too."

Meantime, an ambulance had arrived at the flats and into it was put the body of the nameless woman. The doctor, whose name was Preston, had said to Cream, " So far as I can tell without a more detailed examination she died from a head injury and subsequent shock. If she crashed from one of the upper floors, as seems probable, that could account for the damage."

Sergeant Cream said nothing much. He didn't like the situation. Because a lift gate shouldn't be open unless the lift is standing at the appropriate landing, in which case you couldn't fall farther than the floor of the lift. He knew even before he started asking questions, that no one was going to admit to leaving a gate open. And even if it was open it's not so easy in broad daylight to fall down a shaft, though, admittedly, it can be done. And then—well, the lift had to be at one of the upper floors when the disaster took place. He didn't like the look of things one little bit. Still, the job had to be done. He knew how it would be. He'd get opinions, advice, denunciations and pleas for personal security, but nothing helpful or apposite.

Crook bustled Miss Michael back to the flats and accompanied her to the fifth floor.

" Shall I really have to talk to the police ? " asked the breathless spinster.

" Oh, no," Crook assured her kindly, " you won't be expected to do that—only answer questions."

" But—I don't really know anything."

" Operative word bein' really. Now, buck up, sugar, and

pull yourself together. This may be the last chance you'll ever have of the limelight. Make the most of it."

By the time he reached the fifth floor, Cream felt like the Shakespearian character who, lost in a thorny wood, knew not how to find the open air, yet laboured desperately to find it out. As for renting the thorns and being rent with the thorns, he thought ruefully that Sebastian, pierced by innumerable arrows, had very little on a sergeant of police trying to get evidence in a case that might prove less straight-forward than most of them seemed to realise. It was a bit of a shock to find Crook proposed to be present during his interview with Miss Michael.

" Legal adviser," explained Crook cheerfully.

" Does she require one ? " asked Cream, who appeared remarkably unlike his name.

" Could be she can give you some vital evidence, Sherlock."

Miss Michael, keyed up by what had occurred and by the fact that once in her life what she said might matter to some-one else, didn't wait for questions, but burst into her story with the velocity of a Niagara Falls. Cream and Crook were both completely swept away by it. She had returned, she said, at five-fifteen to see Miss Pinnegar disappearing round the bend carrying a suitcase. Miss Pinnegar hadn't answered when she spoke to her.

" Perhaps," said Cream managing to get a word in edge-ways, " she was in a hurry. If she had a train to catch——"

" Oh, but she hadn't. That's the mysterious part of it. Because do you know where she put the suitcase ? At the station just across the road. And if she meant to be away for the night, she'd take the case with her, wouldn't she, and if she didn't mean to be away for the night she'd have come back, wouldn't she ? And she hasn't. Oh, yes, and she had an important appointment with Mr. Crook here, and she was —is, I mean—a model of order. I'm sure she could put her hand on anything in her flat in the dark. And I shouldn't think she's ever broken an appointment in her life before, anyway, not without letting the people know, and she didn't, because Mr. Crook checked up at his office. Didn't you, Mr. Crook ? And," she swept on, oblivious to the efforts of the unfortunate sergeant to make a point, " there's her kitty. If she'd been going off for the night she'd certainly have asked someone to look after him. I mean, he was hungry, he was crying, we heard him, didn't we, Mr. Crook ? And nothing to Hume about stopping the milk or the newspapers. And her brush and comb and her sponge-bag in the bathroom. I don't mean the brush and comb—they were on the dressing-table, of course—just the sponge-bag. As a matter of fact, you could find out from Florence—that's her maid—she's in St. Mary Magdalene's Hospital—Miss Pinnegar went to see her yesterday. I'm sure she wouldn't have any secrets from Florence."

Here Cream did contrive to make himself heard. " Have you any reason, madam, to suppose any connection between the lady and the deceased ? "

" That's for you to find out," declared Miss Michael, looking madder than ever. " You've got a disappearance *and* a body on your hands in the same building at the same time. I should have thought putting two and two together . . . And it's no good asking me what I think of it," she added hurriedly, " because I was never any good at arithmetic even at school. Did I say that before ? "

Crook, who could scarcely contain his laughter—it was like seeing a Newfoundland dog completely put out of countenance by a small spitting cat—said, " Lady's got something there, Sherlock. And if you don't feel like acting on her information how about this ? As a citizen I am exercising my rights in reporting a missing female, to wit, Miss Frances Pinnegar. And I suggest, to begin with, you could take a peep at that suitcase across the way. Chap 'ull give it you. Wonderful what a uniform will do. Why, if I'd been so minded I could have become a Mormon myself during the 1914-18 war."

Cream, however, was the product of his age. Everything in triplicate and permission to blow his own nose, as Crook remarked vulgarly to Miss Michael later. He insisted that Miss Pinnegar had a perfect right to absent herself from her own premises if she wished.

" Ah, but that's the point," Crook pointed out. " Did she so wish ? I don't believe it. And you tell me, if you can, why she should ring me up and ask me to hustle over in time to prevent a murder—her murder to be precise ? "

Cream looked startled. " Why didn't you mention this before ? "

Crook grinned affectionately at his companion. " Glamour Puss here didn't give me much chance. And, anyway, what the soldier said ain't evidence—but seeing my lady ain't shown up for twenty-four hours, I'll throw this in as a tip, seeing you're bound to find it out for yourself and time's money," he added dryly. " Miss Pinnegar had a mysterious visitor last night."

" You could find out about her from Florence," repeated the irrepressible Miss Michael, as it happened, inaccurately. " Miss Pinnegar went to see her yesterday afternoon."

" You're identifying the deceased with Miss Pinnegar's visitor ? "

" I'm not doing anything of the sort, Sherlock. It ain't my job. I'm just handing you the facts on a plate. If it was me I'd make them something fit for the Lord Mayor's banquet, but this is your kitchen, so go right ahead."

Because he had no other notion who the dead woman was or why she had come to Allenfield Mansions in the first place Cream paid more attention to Crook than he would otherwise have done. There had been a number of mysterious occurrences in the past few weeks, many of them criminal, and the police were kicking out the toes of their stout black shoes in blind alleys in several cases : he was an ambitious young man and he knew something of Crook's record. The police, of course, are hampered in that they can't play their hunches, as a civilian (say, Arthur Crook) can, but that's no reason why they shouldn't on occasions benefit from them. So he agreed to the lawyer's suggestion and they surged over to the station in a body. Cream told himself that if the missing woman had come to the flats by appointment and if the tenants whom he had interviewed were speaking the truth, there was only one person she could have come to see and that was the missing Miss Pinnegar. He'd have preferred to leave Crook behind, but Crook had no intention of being so left. He didn't know what his dotty client might say away from his restraining presence. The young man at the left luggage counter showed a spark of animation when he saw Cream's warrant card and fetched up the case, which was instantly identified by Miss Michael. Cream gave the youth a receipt and took the case away.

" If you're going to the station," suggested Crook, " we'll come along with you." Cream gave him a hard look that was intended to quell, but Crook wasn't quelled so easily. "We're your only reliable witnesses," he pointed out. "Come to that, we're the only witnesses you've got, so you'll have to make the best of us. You'll want Miss Michael's statement and you'll want mine."

"Since neither of you knew the dead woman——"

"My dear chap, I'm not talking about a dead woman—at least, I hope not. It's Miss Pinnegar we're interested in, and the sooner you get down on the old trail, the out trail, the higher her dividends are likely to rise."

"It's very light," said Cream, weighing the case thoughtfully.

"Well," Crook pointed out, "she wasn't going far, only just across the road. She wouldn't need much just for that."

But no one, not even Crook, was quite prepared for what the case contained. There was nothing in it but a dark green coat with buttons to match, of which two were missing, and a bit of nonsense topped with a broken feather that Miss Michael instantly recognised as a hat.

Cream stared, Crook frowned, Miss Michael almost choked.

The sergeant was the first to speak. "The Yard'll be interested to see that," he said. (It was Crook's first intimation that the Yard had been called in.) "I fancy they've got one of the missing buttons."

Even then Crook had the last word. "I fancy," said he, "that I have the other."

And thrusting his hand in his pocket, he produced his treasure trove and set it on the table.

Cream was up in arms at once. "How long have you had that?"

"Since yesterday."

"You ought to have turned it in."

"Why? I didn't know the police were making a salvage collection of buttons."

"You knew they were looking for a button from a green coat."

"I wasn't to know it was this one," retorted Crook undaunted. "The police don't confide in me—much. Besides, my job's to look after my client's interest and I'd hardly do that by delivering her into the jaws of the wolves."

Cream didn't argue any further. He could see he was

wasting his time. " This gives us a slant on Miss Pinnegar's disappearance," he observed.

" Just what I thought," agreed Crook. " And seeing the police and me don't often see eye to eye, you might look a bit more pleased about it."

Now the police got to work in real earnest. They had already discovered Les's other name was Strutt, and had produced a witness who remembered the dead man, then apparently domiciled in Brightstone, offering him a second-hand car some months previously. He hadn't closed with the offer because a brother-in-law had died suddenly in Scotland, and he had been given the opportunity of buying a Monitor Minor very reasonably. But though his information proved helpful to the police, it didn't enable them to locate the dead man's partners. Les had been the active member of the firm, the partner (or partners) presumably putting up the financial backing and, possibly, making arrangements about acquiring cars suitable for their purpose. Even if Les were pinched he wouldn't squeal. His partners would take care of any liabilities he might leave and have a sizable wad stored up for him when he returned to the outer world.

The only associate of whom they had any definite know-ledge was the woman called Vi, and they knew precious little about her. Still that was point one. Point two took the mysterious Vi to Miss Pinnegar's flat. The finding of the button on the premises and the discovery of the green coat in Miss Pinnegar's case, coupled with Miss Michael's evidence, was proof enough even for the cautious police. So—step three—Miss Pinnegar had known " Vi " sufficiently well to give her a night's lodging. Then it was impossible to ignore Miss Pinnegar's *cri de cœur* to Crook. Murder she had said, and there was evidence and to spare that she was not a person given to hysteria or easily panicked. The police as well as the ordinary public knew of her record. She had taken some pretty grave risks during her years at the Settlement and had pooh-poohed all suggestions that she should exercise a little caution. So if she said Murder, and nothing would move Crook (who wasn't given to hysteria or panic either), the odds were there was a definite threat against her. Miss Medlicott was another witness who helped the police to build up their case. She told them that Miss Pinnegar had (doubtless in an unguarded moment) referred to the dying man as Les. The only person who could have told them his name was Vi, so on all counts (since you can't have too much of a good thing and what can be better than proof ?) it seemed obvious that " Vi " spelt danger to Miss Pinnegar. That was, as it were, Act I, setting the scene. Act II opened with Miss Pinnegar's disappearance, followed by the discovery of a strange woman in the lift-shaft. It looked as though this corpse, whom nobody claimed, must be that of the missing Vi. The police announced that she wore a wedding ring and a second ring of turquoises and diamond chips of no particular value. Her coat was new and of a pattern and colour common to many large stores. The police asked any shop assistant who remembered selling such a coat during the past forty-eight hours—for it was reasonable to assume that the coat hadn't been bought till *after* the cross-roads tragedy—to get in touch with WHITE-HALL 1212. This appeal had swift success. An assistant at Melgrave & Co. said she had sold a coat to a customer who stated she was buying it for a relative going to the country after an accident who was unable to come shopping herself. She gave a description of this customer that tallied with that of Miss Pinnegar.

The police's headache at this point was that they had no evidence at all of the nature of the relationship between Vi and the missing woman. The information came trickling in. Mrs. Gordon appeared on the scene with her story of a lodger known to her as Mrs. Violet Child who normally wore a green coat, but had appeared on the morning after the crash (and after a night's absence, mark you) in one of precisely the cut and pattern of the coat found on the deceased. Even Miss Michael, admittedly poor at arithmetic, couldn't fail to do this simple sum. Invited by the police to visit the mortuary, Mrs. Gordon had no difficulty at all in recognising the deceased as Mrs. Violet Child. This from the police point of view was excellent, but unfortunately it went very little further. Mrs. Child had only been Mrs. Gordon's lodger for a few weeks, and she had provided no references, offering two weeks rent in advance. Mrs. Gordon knew nothing of Mr. Child, he might be dead or there might have been a divorce or they might have " split up " without bothering about legal action. Mrs. Child had never spoken of him or of children. For all she knew to the contrary, her lodger might never have actually been married. She had had no letters that Mrs. Gordon could recall. She was the sort, explained Mrs. Gordon, that didn't go in for women friends. No, Violet had never confided in her, but one could always tell. No, in reply to another question, her gentlemen friends didn't come to the house either. She (Mrs. Gordon) had always been respectable and had a good name (she was very anxious *that* should be understood), she didn't care about gentlemen visiting ladies that only had a combined room. There were some, of course, that didn't mind and thought her strait-laced, but letting rooms was her living and it was her boast she'd never owed a penny, and so on and so on, till the cows come home. In other words, the police said thank you very much, there's the door, the exterior is particularly admired. They searched the waste-paper basket in the room Violet had occupied—Mrs. Gordon hadn't emptied it yet, she must have suited her late lodger pretty well, thought Cream, an intolerant man who believed that cleanliness ran neck and neck with godliness and might even beat it at the post—but it didn't help them at all. There were no torn-up letters, no documents of any kind. Then they came back to Florence's room in Allenfield Mansions, but they hadn't much hope of finding what they wanted there.

" The fact is," the sergeant acknowledged, " there's every reason to suppose this wasn't an accident at all. If it were that bag would be somewhere. Of course, I know it is somewhere, but it would be in the last place where she was, and it's not. So whoever is responsible for putting her in the shaft is probably the one person who could tell us where that bag is now, and you can hardly expect him to come forward."

He reviewed the facts yet again. Violet, in difficulties, sought refuge in Allenfield Mansions. That was Tuesday night. Wednesday midday she collected her belongings from Mrs. Gordon's house ; she was wearing a new rig-out, and was met by a man in a black car when she left the house. Then, for some reason the police didn't as yet know, she came back to Number 15. They had no doubt that Miss Pinnegar was somehow connected with the affair ; it seemed probable she had actually bought the coat and the beret. And yet she wasn't simply an accomplice, because, if so, why drag Crook in ?

It was pointed out to him that in the event it was Violet who was found in the shaft, and Miss Pinnegar who had left the suitcase at the station. So what ?

" Ah," said Cream ; " but she's disappeared, don't forget."

" May have her own reasons for that."

" All the same, her toilet things were all in her flat and there was no sign of any other luggage being removed. Miss Michael said she was only carrying one case and that one we've identified."

" Are you expecting to find her body somewhere else ? "

" It's so odd that no one should have come forward with information. It's not so easy to lie low these days, when you need a ration book to live, to say nothing of an identity card and a cheque-book."

" We know she drew thirty pounds in one-pound notes from her bank on the morning following the crash. Thirty pounds would last her quite a long time."

" Not in 1951," said Cream grimly. " And she paid for the coat in cash of course. That was nearly ten pounds. I know she can exist on unrationed goods for a time, have her meals at restaurants, buy sandwiches—though she'll be stymied for tea. Still, perhaps she's partial to coffee. However, deserters have been doing without ration books for years. But she can't go to a hotel and, if she gets a room somewhere, the odds are she'll be asked for references. It's not so easy for elderly women to go missing in this country in 1951."

Miss Pinnegar could have told him that she'd never expected life to be easy and life had never betrayed her expectations. But she'd spent the greater part of a hard-working existence overcoming difficulties and apparently she was still on the same lay, because the morning and the evening made another day and still she wasn't found.

CHAPTER IX

By this time the greater part of the country was taking a burning interest in the case, an interest that increased to white heat when the doctor who had performed the post-mortem on Violet Child gave it as his opinion death was not due to a fall down the shaft. The head injury that was the primary cause of death had been inflicted before the fall. He stuck to this despite close questioning by the coroner. " The blow on the head was sufficient to smash the frontal bone of the skull," he said. " At a guess I should say it was our old friend, the blunt instrument. When the body was found the beret was pulled well down over the head in a manner that could not have occurred after the fall. If anything, the beret would have been pushed away from the hair. The blow, in my opinion, was delivered before the body was introduced into the shaft and the beret was deliberately pulled over the wound. Had it been in place at the time the blow was struck it must have been driven into the skull." He would not say that the wound had caused instantaneous death, but he doubted whether the victim ever recovered consciousness. Another point he made was that a person finding him or herself falling automatically scrabbles for some handhold ; the shaft of the lift was narrow, the lift itself could hold only three people at a time, and since the deceased was not wearing gloves he would have expected to find scratches or contusions on the fingers particularly at the tips, but no such marks were apparent. " Also," he said, " I understand from witnesses who saw the body lying in the shaft that the right side of the head was against the wall, whereas the wound is fairly high up on the left side. If the blow had been inflicted before the fall and the body pushed or flung into the shaft that position would be compatible with the facts, but if she fell accidentally I cannot see how she came to sustain such an injury. My own opinion is that after the blow was struck—and I do not altogether rule out the possibility of a fall that would cause such a wound—some article such as a handkerchief was applied to the place to prevent the flow of blood, and that the cap or beret as I understand it is called was then pulled over the head and the body thrust into the lift shaft. In addition, I find it hard to understand how a person in normal health could step accidentally into the shaft in broad daylight. Admitted that the passages of the building are narrow, it would be impossible for anyone who was not blind to be guilty of such an error of judgment."

" If the deceased suffered from vertigo such a fall would not be beyond possibility," suggested the coroner.

The doctor said dryly that there was no evidence to this effect, and the identity of the person who had left the gate of the lift open had not yet been established. The coroner, however, said testily that the witness was only being asked for medical evidence, and Dr. Preston shrugged his shoulders and stepped down from the stand. Within an hour the presses were humming with the word—Murder. Mystery Victim's Death Fall, they flashed. Do the Police Suspect Foul Play ? Other headlines appeared in rapid succession.

WHO WAS VIOLET CHILD ?

Although the identity of the lift-shaft victim has now been established she remains a woman of mystery. No witness has come forward to claim her acquaintance, no relative has made inquiries. Did she spend the last night of her life at No. 15, Allenfield Mansions ? The only person who could answer this question is missing in circumstances that must arouse considerable speculation.

And the men selling evening papers outside stations and at street corners wrote in a hasty charcoal script on their boards :

Lift Shaft Mystery

WHERE IS MISS FRANCES PINNEGAR ?

A few hours later a handbag in crocodile leather, bearing the gilt initials V.C. ("And there's glory for you," said Crook, when he heard. Cream, being better educated, substituted " irony " for glory.) was found on a piece of waste ground about a mile from the flats. Its contents were quite impersonal—a compact, lipstick, tiny box of cream rouge, and a purse and notecase, both of which were empty. There were no letters, no diary, nothing to identify it but the initials. These, however, were sufficient. Mrs. Gordon recognised the bag at once. This discovery crystallised the police suspicion that the dead woman was a victim not of accident but of foul play. The next inquiry concerned her other possessions. Mrs. Gordon told her story of the girl being met by a dark man who carried her case to a small waiting car. This case was easily traced to one of the large London termini, where it had been lodged for collection the following day. This told them nothing but that Violet had no place to go; she might, of course, have intended to leave London, but if so she hadn't bought a ticket, or rather, no ticket was found in her bag. Whoever took the contents of notecase and coin-purse might also have removed the ticket.

The inquest was deferred pending further investigations, after evidence of identification and the medical report had been taken. Miss Pinnegar's name was bandied freely from lip to lip. Her disappearance was the major mystery of the two, and the impulsive public linked them in their (to Crook) irresponsible minds. Meanwhile, the funeral was fixed for Saturday. No relations had come forward and interment would be at the public expense.

Crook was working in his office at about 9 p.m. on Friday when he heard rapid steps climbing the stairs. This aroused in him a sense of pleasurable anticipation. He was by no means unaccustomed to late callers, but as a rule these approached as unobtrusively as possible. The point of a late night call was to avoid recognition. " But this chap can be heard in Piccadilly Circus," reflected Crook. The door of the outer office was pushed open.

" Come right in," he sang out.

A tall man of about thirty appeared on the threshold. He wore the casual khaki battledress of the modern army, was dark, clean-shaven and seemed in a devil of a hurry about something.

" Are you Mr. Crook ? " he demanded.

Crook seemed a little hurt. " Do I look like a baby-sitter ? "

" My name's Pinnegar. I understand you're acting for my aunt."

ANTHONY GILBERT

"What's called ghosting," agreed Crook with a grimmer humour than he normally displayed. "If you've got any notion where she is I'll be grateful."

"I haven't, that's why I'm over here on special leave. The whole thing's preposterous. Aunt Fran mixed up in this sort of case. I don't blame the police because they didn't know her. But you—you're her lawyer . . ." He paused, obviously perplexed.

"All right," said Crook resignedly. "Say it. You can't imagine how she came to pick me. Well, I'll tell you. She didn't. It was providence. . . ." He explained briefly.

"Well "—Geoffrey Pinnegar picked up the thread of his broken speech—"you must realise that she'd never have connived at concealment of a crime. She'd have gone straight to the authorities."

"You'd be surprised," said Crook seriously. "Y'see, the fact is she did give this woman a bed for the night."

"But she couldn't have known who she was," urged Geoffrey. "It would be just like her to offer hospitality to someone she thought was down and out."

"Tain't as simple as that," Crook demurred. "This woman must have known your aunt. You don't appear by accident on the doorstep of a fifth-floor flat at 10 p.m. or thereabouts. Sure you've never heard the name ? "

"Mrs. Child ? " Geoffrey shook his head. "Doesn't rouse an echo."

"Well, she wasn't always Mrs. Child," said Crook, reasonably. "One time she must have been Violet Someone else. Never heard auntie say ' Drat that Violet,' or, ' Talk about modest violets ; they can't have met this one ? ' Or . . . Hallo ! " He had been watching his companion narrowly while he was talking, and he saw a flash of horrified apprehension pass across the other's face. It was suppressed instantly, but it had been there.

"Come on," he said encouragingly. "Not much use coming to me if you're going cagey on me in the first five minutes. Who was she ? "

"I told you, I don't know. . . ."

"I heard. Only you've remembered something since then. Who was this Violet who just came into your mind ? "

"Oh, it was absurd." Crook waited patiently. "As a matter of fact," said Geoffrey in slow tones, "my first wife's

100

name was Violet. But she's been dead for ten years. Killed in an air raid."

He waited hopefully for Crook to say, "Well, then, it can't have been her," but Crook sat up more erectly, exclaiming, " Hey, hey, now we are going places. An air raid, you say ? You were at the funeral ? "

" At the time I was on the run in France. But Aunt Fran went."

" Attend the lying-in-state ? "

" There wasn't much of that." Geoffrey's lips twisted grimly. " There was a direct hit on the F.A.P. and a mass funeral."

" Of anything they could find ? You know what a ground-sheet case is ? At least, that's what we called 'em in my war, and I dare say it was the same in yours. A shell burst and when it was quiet again you went out with your stretcher party and collected the wounded. Sometimes there was damn all to collect, but you put whatever there was in a ground-sheet and said the burial service over that. You counted up the survivors and then you reckoned whom you'd lost. I dare say your F.A.P. funeral was much the same. When the smoke cleared away they called the roster and anyone who was missing was put down as dead. Mostly that's pretty safe, but there's always a hundred-to-one chance you can be wrong. Say the lady had slipped out for a quick one or wanted to have a word with a boy-friend—well, a friend, say —at the corner, or got lost under some wreckage and didn't come round till some time later ? "

" I suppose that would be possible, but it wouldn't explain her staying quiet for ten years."

" You'd be surprised," said Crook again, " the queer things people 'ud do to avoid the man-power authorities. I dare say she wouldn't want to go back to the post wherever it was set up afterwards ; or maybe she had plans of her own. Mind you, I don't say that's the way it was, but it could be. Or she might have lost her memory. There were quite a lot of these cases during the bombing."

" That might be all right for a few days or even a few weeks," urged Geoffrey ; " but sooner or later someone would have recognised her. There were some survivors from the raid and they'd certainly have been asked to help. No, that can't be it. And, anyway, what about her allowances as the wife of a serving soldier ? They were never claimed after the raid."

" Well, if she was officially dead they couldn't be," Crook pointed out reasonably. " Mind you, I don't say this has anything to do with her, but I suppose there could be female Enoch Ardens as well as male ones. And if she thought you copped it out there—well, she might have thought she'd start all over again."

" Then why suddenly do a resurrection act on my aunt's doorstep ? "

" Because she was in a tight corner and wanted someone to pull her out of it. From what the police think, she was driving the stolen car, and though she may not have known it was stolen, and there'll be no way of proving now, with both witnesses underground, she must have known that to run over the lights and kill a woman and child is manslaughter for which in the circumstances she'd get the stiffest sentence allowed by the law—might be ten years. She'd only have two choices—she could go to dear Les's pals, and from what we know of them, I doubt if they'd have any hesitation in sending her to join her victims, or she could go to someone who, for private reasons, wouldn't immediately hand her over to the police. Mind you, I don't say the old lady knew anything about the accident at the time, but the police have made a mort of inquiries and nobody ever heard of a woman called Child, not this one anyhow, in connection with Miss Pinnegar. Her faithful Abigail, who's been with her a good many years, had never heard of her, and what's more, Miss Pinnegar didn't mention she'd got a visitor when she went to the hospital on Wednesday afternoon. So it was something, someone rather, that she wanted to keep dark. Then, there don't seem much doubt that she bought the coat and cap—Mrs. Gordon's evidence shows that they were worn by Violet Child on the one day only—and the news of the smash was in the papers by that time."

" Even so my aunt need not have associated her visitor with that."

" Then why buy her a new outfit ? Why leave the green coat and hat in a suitcase at the station ? Still, it's lucky your turning up to-night. To-morrow 'ud have been too late."

" Why do you mean ? "

" Funeral ain't till the morning. The body's still at the mortuary."

" You suggest that I should go down . . ."

" Well, what did you think ? Don't you want to be sure you are a widower ? Oh, I see. Got another wife, have you ? "

" And three children. I'd no reason to imagine——"

" Quite. Well, it's bad luck, but worse things happen at sea. No question of entailed estates, I take it ? "

Geoffrey's face changed again. " I—look here, you're a lawyer. An old chap we know died last month leaving ten thousand pounds to the wife of my good friend, Geoffrey Pinnegar."

" Just like that ? " said Crook. " No name mentioned ? "

" None"

" Chap who drew up that will ought to have to pay the damage. How did this old boy know you wouldn't have changed wives before he handed in his dinner-pail ? All right, all right, if that's the way it is. Did your aunt know about this ? "

" I'd told her. She should have had the letter."

" Since there don't seem to be an unopened one lying around the odds are she did. You know, this is going to make things very unpleasant for her, always supposing, of course, that the deceased is your wife. Best thing we can do is go down right away and clear that point up, because if she ain't we're wasting our time."

" Can we go this hour of the night ? Will they let us in ? "

" They'll let me in," promised Crook. " Only got to tell 'em who you are and say you thought you'd take a looksee at the body in case you could link it up with your auntie. . . ."

" No," protested Geoffrey ; " no, I can't do that. Don't you see, if it should prove to be Violet and this really isn't a case of accidental death, it ties Aunt Fran up with—with murder ? "

" So it does," said Crook unemotionally. " But then she's tied up with it already, unless and until she comes forward and tells her story."

" That's what defeats me. Why hasn't she come forward ?"

" Maybe she can't."

" You don't mean—you can't think she's dead, too."

" Now, look," said Crook firmly. " You're in the army,

you fought in the war. I dare say you've seen there ain't many lengths to which desperate men won't go. I saw some pretty ugly things in World War I. If I'd had any illusions to lose I'd have lost them then. If this gang, which operates on a pretty extensive scale and has one hell of a lot to lose, very likely including their lives and most certainly their liberty for a whale of a time to come, if they think she's in their way and they get the chance, they won't stop at what 'ud seem to them a feeble sort of scruple. Why, I wouldn't mind laying my last income-tax assessment they couldn't spell scruple if you offered 'em a thousand pounds a letter. On the other hand, no one's got any proof at present that they've had a chance to rub her out. It ain't so easy to get away with murder as amateurs suppose. Why, this looked safe enough, a fall down a lift-shaft, and it hasn't deceived anyone for more than about half an hour. Well, that could be one reason why she ain't turned up, one possibility rather. The other is that she feels it's healthier to stay put. And if that's the case then it's all Lombard Street to a china orange that she's got an accessory after the fact. The police have circularised all hotels and boarding-houses and service chambers and hospitals for news of a dame answering to her description arriving on the Wednesday night, and so far, they've drawn a complete blank. If Glamour Puss is right she didn't take any but the one case with her, and we know what happened to that. And I think G.P. *is* right, because she's left all her toilet articles in her flat. Of course she might have bought fresh supplies—we know she drew the money, a much larger sum than she'd ever drawn out in one fell swoop before—that morning. That alone shows there was something up. My guess 'ud be she got it out to finance Violet. Besides, she couldn't hope to stay hidden unless some pal was covering her up. And she don't seem to me the sort of dame who'd drag someone else into her mess."

" I'm quite sure she wouldn't." Geoffrey paused. " I suppose there is a third alternative."

" That she's put out her own light ? But in that case why bother about the lift shaft ? She must have known the body 'ud be found. Did she hope it would never be connected with her ? And even if she didn't want to die in bad company why not take her overdose in her own premises ? Anyway, no body's been found anywhere and there ain't many convenient quarries or nice deep ponds in this part of the world."

" Then—what do you think, Mr. Crook ? "

" I think we'd better go along to the mortuary and clear up Point Number One, and then we can decide where to go from there."

Geoffrey said with nervous vehemence, " I hadn't seen her for ten years, you know. People change."

" Not all that much," said Crook. " Besides, I dare say she had distinguishing marks."

" If—if you're right, do we have to inform the police ? " was his next question.

" Oh, come," said Crook. " You're of age, ain't you ? And an officer in the army ? Then you should know your duty as a citizen." He stretched out his hand and swung open a cupboard door near by. " One for the road," he suggested, expertly knocking the top off a bottle of brown ale. " Shocking stuff, but nations that win wars only get the fruits of victories." He poured out a couple of glasses. " One member of the family in the police's black books is enough," he continued, " and though I'm all against wet nursing the force, you do have to remember they're investigatin' a crime, and it's your job to help them all you can. They'll get round to it sooner or later anyhow," he added frankly.

Geoffrey picked up his glass. " If I didn't tell them, would you ? "

" No sense wasting time," said Crook a little testily. " You know you've no choice. Finish that muck and we'll get cracking." A moment later he switched off the light and the pair of them came clattering down the stairs. " How old would she be, this wife of yours ? " asked Crook, approaching the Scourge. Geoffrey didn't reply for an instant. Crook glanced up and found he was staring at the little car with the same kind of amazement as an entomologist might display at the sight of a insect whose existence he had never hitherto suspected. " All right," said Crook encouragingly, " she won't bite."

At the mortuary there was no trouble about seeing the body after Crook's brief explanation of their presence at this late hour. Geoffrey stood staring at it for what seemed an unconscionable time. At this stage she seemed to have no connection with the woman he had married, yet he hadn't a doubt after that first glance.

" Well, you may as well give the police the gen right away," Crook told him, not looking very pleased about it. " Y'know, this may have one good result. If your aunt should hear you've identified the woman and she's hiding of her own free will, this 'ull drag her above ground." But he didn't sound very optimistic. He thought it more than probable that Miss Pinnegar would never reappear walking on her own two feet.

Cream was on duty and listened intently to what Geoffrey had to say. " And you had heard nothing of your wife for ten years ? "

" No."

" I see." Geoffrey wondered how much he saw.

" Oh, they've all got second sight, these bobbies," said Crook scornfully. " See round corners and through stone walls, but some of 'em could do with some of these spectacles the government's been showering round the country during the last five years. Anyway, let them stew in their own juice. If they can find her—well, that'll be something to be grateful for." But his voice was unconvincing.

When they'd said good-bye to the police they came back in the Scourge to Crook's flat. Geoffrey said he'd booked a room at the station hotel, but Crook, knowing how little sleep there'd be for him to-night, said there was no hurry. Presently Geoffrey remarked, " If this Miss Whatsername hadn't seen her leaving with the case, and she couldn't allow for that, there'd be nothing to tie Aunt Fran up to the murder. I suppose we may as well call a spade a spade ; the police seem to have made up their minds."

" You're forgetting the button the kitten had. That of itself would be enough."

" Always supposing the police knew about it. Ah, no wonder Aunt Fran wanted to slip out without being seen. She must have cursed the old woman's sharp eyes. I suppose it wouldn't go through her mind that the case would be identified through a luggage label. She—why, what on earth's bitten you now ? "

" Why didn't I think of that ? " marvelled Crook. " If you want to hide something the police want you'd take every precaution. You're right when you say she couldn't have allowed for Miss Michael to come popping out of the lift like a jill-in-a-box—that's one of the fortunes of crime—but the label would be sheer damn carelessness. There can't be so many dames in the neighbourhood with that particular label on a suitcase. Besides, it was only a coat. Why didn't she use the small case she had ? Remember, Glamour Puss said—no, of course you don't, you weren't there—it was the bigger of her two cases. Oh, brother, you've said a mouthful. Now we start again from scratch." He glanced at the watch on his wrist.

"Are you going out somewhere again now ? " Geoffrey demanded in astonishment. " It's a bit late."

" Late ? It's not half-past ten. Here, I'll just call up Hume. They don't shut the front door till eleven o'clock, but I want to make sure he's around to open the flat for me. Well, well," he marvelled afresh, dialling the number, " fancy the police missing that too. But then they had their minds made up from the start. Hallo ! Crook here. . . . I'm coming over. I've got to leaf through Miss P.'s wardrobe. . . . What for ? The missing clue, of course. . . . Late ? Nonsense. The chap who invented clocks ought to be remembered as Public Enemy Number One. What are they for but to make things more difficult than they need be for chaps who want to work, and encourage idleness in the clock-watchers ? . . . I've told you that before. Now, listen. I've got Miss Pinnegar's nephew with me. You won't refuse to let him in, I suppose. . . . Miss P. 'ull give you socks when she comes back if you do. He's had an idea, and you can take it from me it's going to knock that pie-faced sergeant off his perch in a brace of shakes."

Hume, who had taken an instant dislike to Cream, wavered. " We close at eleven," he said.

" You're as bad as the pubs. Well, hold everything. California, here we come."

They piled back into the Scourge.

Geoffrey offered his cigarette case, but Crook shook his head. " Never smoke 'em," he said, pulling out some atrocious thin cigars. " Mind you, we keep some in the office, but they're strictly for clients. Bill — that's Bill Parsons, my A.D.C.—don't smoke at all, and if you chaps knew what you were putting in your mouths you wouldn't either. Old soldiers and chopped hay, that's all cigarettes

are nowadays, and a dash of floor sweepings for colouring."
Having delivered himself of this sweeping and slanderous
statement he proceeded to light up.

Hume met them in the hall of the Mansions. " You better
not take the lift," he said. " These old bundles of strife
complain it wakes 'em up after ten o'clock at night. Not that
half of 'em will use it anyway since what's happened. If you
ask me the local authority could change the name of this
place to the county asylum, and you wouldn't notice the
difference. A screwier lot I never set eyes on."

" The cat ought to have warned me," said Crook not
paying the least attention. " Glamour Puss called my
attention to it, too. ' Miss P. would never have left kitty,'
she said. And she had a chance to put in a word on Puss's
behalf "—he was climbing the stairs rapidly, Hume panting
at his heels—" when G.P. called out to her, and she didn't
even reply. That ought to have warned me."

" Warned you of what ? Mind you, I don't accept
responsibility for this," panted Hume. " Miss Pinnegar's not
one to like people messing about with her things."

" You might have thought of that a bit earlier," said Crook
in his briskest voice. " Don't expect me to bring you baccy
when you're in the workhouse. I never did have much use
for amateurs. If you'd been on duty I could have been
playing patience and listening to Edmundo Ros, instead of
chasing corpses."

" Are you telling me I neglect my duty ? " Hume sounded
threatening.

" Are you telling me I'm wrong ? Who called at the flats
the day Miss Pinnegar disappeared ? "

Hume looked at him angrily. " 'Ow the 'ell should I
know ? "

" My point exactly. Why, if I were the police, which
heaven forbid, I'd run you in as accessory. Now, now, keep
your shirt on. Remember it's late at night and much as I
esteem Glamour Puss I could do without her for a while."

They reached No. 15 and Hume, still faintly protesting,
unfastened the door. " What does 'e want now ? " he
demanded of Geoffrey, who remained outside. The young
man shook his head.

" Search me ! The missing clue, I suppose."

Crook was as good as his word. " Shan't be more than a

minute," he'd said and he wasn't. "Just wanted to glance through the lady's wardrobe. As I thought it's been returned." He didn't vouchsafe any further explanation. " I'll want a word with Glamour Puss," he went on. " But that can wait till morning. I know the answer already, but I like to check up as I go along."

" When may we expect the honour of another visit ? " inquired Hume sarcastically, as they picked their careful way downstairs.

" I'll be round first thing in the morning. Thank heaven, it's Saturday."

" Fancy you only working half a day," remarked Hume.

" Half a day, my foot. I'm thanking heaven on behalf of my essential witness who only does a five-day week. So long. Be seeing you."

And back he popped into the Scourge, as bright as a daisy and as fresh as paint.

" Are we any nearer a solution ? " inquired Geoffrey as the two drove away.

" Probably shall be this time to-morrow," said Crook a little evasively. " The fact is, I've established in my own mind, which means to my own satisfaction, that when Miss P. left the flat she'd no idea she wasn't coming back the same night. Well, I'd guessed that before, but now I'm beginning to understand what happened."

" And—do you think she's still alive ? "

Crook shook his head. " Can't answer that one yet. Y'see, we've one corpse on our hands already, and if Miss P. didn't dispatch the lady, then someone else did, and you can't hang twice. On the other hand, nobody's found a second body, but that don't mean a thing. I can remember a case where a body wasn't found for eighteen months, on one of these classy grouse moors. No suggestion of foul play, lady lost her way in a blizzard and, seeing she wasn't a good correspondent, nobody thought about her again till she was recognised by her rings and the suit she was wearing. And there's no getting away from it there must be a whole lot of hiding places the police haven't got round to as yet. Still, what we must hope for is that they're lying low till the stink dies down. Or they might try to fake a natural death."

" You have to register a death before you can fix up the

funeral," Geoffrey reminded him. He still looked a bit upset and Crook didn't blame him.

" Well, you don't have to register a lady in her own name. Mind you, it takes a bit of doing, but if I was to go round the corner and say, ' There's a dame passed out in my flat, name of Smith, and here's her ration book and identity card——"

" But they wouldn't be in the name of Smith," Geoffrey objected.

" They wouldn't, not if she was in my flat, but I ain't a gangster. And come to that, Bill's in the know ; Bill could fix me up with phonys if he put his mind to it. The trouble about that game is you have to play it with a partner, and a secret stops bein' a secret when you let a second person in on it. Of course the victim might count as a second person, but not in the eyes of the law, if you get me."

" You'd still need a doctor to certify cause of death," Geoffrey insisted.

" Well." Crook came to a dead stop. " Any time you want a job," he said, " you just come round to me. I'm always on the look out for fresh talent. That's the second pointer you've given me. A doctor. Of course." He slapped his big forehead with a huge hand. " Let there be light. Between you and me, brother, I believe it's grey dawn breaking."

He did nothing more that night. " Now don't get in a sweat," he told Geoffrey. " By the way, let me know where you're staying. We might do a little trip together to-morrow. Don't make any dates you can't break."

" Do we have to give these rogues another night ? " Geoffrey demanded.

" If she's above ground now she'll be above ground in the morning," Crook explained. " These chaps have no reason to suppose anything of importance is going to happen during the next twenty-four hours, and if they've held their hands, as the lawyers say, up till now they'll go on doin' it until they get a fresh suggestion that it's time to break it up. And even then they're not in the clear, because if it was difficult to put the old lady underground, at the time she vanished, it's goin' to be harder still with everybody on the *qui vive*. Y'know," he went on seriously, " I always find it a good rule to ask myself, ' Is there anything I can do in the next twelve hours ? ' and if the answer's No then put the thing out of mind. Get your beauty sleep, that's the most important thing. You don't know when you may have another chance."

Geoffrey didn't look as though he expected to shake hands with sleep for a week at least. He said something vague about the police.

" Yes, of course go to 'em if you've got any fresh ideas," said Crook cordially. " Only, if you haven't, keep out of their way. The police don't like Buttinskis any more than I do. If you take the advice of the expert, and don't forget my name's still in the Law List, though a lot of chaps who also figure there 'ud like to see it wiped out, you'll leave the police alone for the moment. You won't help your lady aunt by going to them again to-night, and things always look better in daylight."

And though Geoffrey couldn't pretend to be content with this cold comfort, he departed to the room he'd booked at the station hotel, promising to call Crook up first thing in the morning.

CHAPTER X

CROOK SAT UP for a long time doing arithmetic. He had spoken the truth when he told his companion he believed it was a case of grey dawn breaking. He was convinced that his reconstruction of the crime held at least the basis of fact. " Give me a foundation," he'd say, " and I'll build you any sort of house you like." And sometimes, though he wasn't a great reader, he would quote Artemus Ward. Get the evidence and then you can arrange it in any pattern you please. What mattered now was speed and accuracy, because if the real criminals got an inkling that he was on the track it would be curtains for Miss Pinnegar, and he was like the medico who tells you proudly he's never lost a father yet. He'd never lost a client and he didn't intend to start altering his ways at his time of life.

Next morning saw him bright and early at Allenfield Mansions.

" Lor, you again ! " grumbled Hume. " I wonder you don't take a room here."

Crook said, Thank you, and it was a nice idea, but he was very comfortable where he was. Then he asked, " Those kids who hang around this place—who are they ? "

" Kids ? "

" Yes. Takin' down car numbers. They were here the day I called."

" They're always around and a sight too many of 'em for my liking. The complaints I get from the tenants, as if it was my fault. You were all kids yourself once, I'd like to say to 'em, though to look at half of 'em now it's hard to believe. And where there's kids there's noise. Stands to reason."

" There was one taking down car numbers the other day when I called," Crook repeated. " Know who he was ? "

" Belongs to one of the housekeepers down the street. No, I don't know which one and I don't care. Charlie's his name. If you're afraid of missing him, don't worry. The only wonder to me is he don't bed down on the premises—like you."

Crook took himself off and established the Scourge at a convenient corner. About a quarter of an hour later he saw some boys emerge from various basements and soon identified the one he sought.

" Remember me ? " he demanded, popping out of the Scourge like a Jack out of its box.

The boy grinned. " I remember that." He pointed a derisive finger at the Scourge.

" One of these days you might be grateful to her," Crook warned him severely. " Now, how about giving me a hand ? "

" Pushing the biscuit tin into the nearest garage ? "

Crook clouted him dispassionately. " Got that list of cars you were mucking about with the other day ? "

The boy looked at him cheekily. " Expect to find a body in one of 'em ? "

" Could be," said Crook. " My guess is one of 'em took the body off the premises."

" Go on. Which one ? "

" You tell me. Where is it—the list, I mean ? "

The boy pulled a notebook out of the pocket of his shorts. Crook looked over his shoulder. " All a matter of timing," he explained. " When did you start listing 'em ? "

" Soon as I come out of school. We break at four. Gordon was with me."

" One of you's enough for me," Crook assured him. " Now then, first of all, are these cars that stopped by the Mansions or in the street or just any car ? "

" Well, if they stopped and we had a chance to look 'em over we could probably guess the year. Those that went by all we could do was put down the make and the number."

" Well, my car stopped some time between four-fifteen and, say, five o'clock. That is, I'd say it was away again by five. How many have you got there that might be the one I want ? "

He opened the door of the Scourge and the boy got in. " There were a few there when we arrived," he explained. " That 'ud be the first four. Some old geezer was having a party. Then there was a maroon Hillman Minx driven by a woman who'd brought her husband along." He looked sideways at Crook.

Crook shook his head. " Don't think that 'ud be my party."

" Well, there was a Morris and a Studebaker, smashing car, light grey chauffeur-driven." Crook shook his head once more. " Come again."

" There was a Monitor Beetle—doctor's car, that was."

" What's that ? Happen to notice the doctor ? "

" Not blooming likely. New car, though."

" How d'you know it belonged to a doctor."

" Had a label on the windscreen."

Crook frowned. " I thought they'd given that up by now."

" During the war," began the boy, who couldn't have been more than five when it was over, Crook reflected.

He broke in, " The number of doctors during the war operating in London must have given the B.M.A. heart failure. Haven't seen one for an age, though."

The boy pondered. " Come to think of it, nor have I. I suppose that's why we noticed this one. My dad says a lot of them don't like carrying a label because they don't want to be stopped on their day off to attend to some silly gink who's gone jay-walking."

" Your dad's a man of sense. Looks as though it runs in the family. Well, my guess 'ud be this chap wanted everyone to know he was a doctor. Notice if he came out of the Mansions alone ? "

But here the boy couldn't help him. There were plenty of people coming and going and a chap had caused a diversion by having a bull and cow with an old geezer with a Pekinese. Chap said the Pekinese had gone for his leg. Quite a lot of people had joined in. And by the time that was over the doctor's car had gone.

" Sure of that ? "

" Yes," said the boy, " quite sure. Because I said, ' Well, there's a doctor here,' but when we looked round the car had gone. I didn't see him go."

" Oh, well," said Crook philosophically, " nobody gets everything. We shall see you in the police force yet."

" Not till they start sending the police round in helicopters, you won't," said the boy scornfully, but he was grinning with pleasurable anticipation as he spoke.

Crook had his own way of getting information. It didn't take him long to discover that the car he sought belonged to a drive-yourself car company operated by a man called Mayhew. With Geoffrey as his companion, he drove round to the address, which was in north London.

" You might open up a bit," said Geoffrey.

" Plenty of time," Crook promised him. " We're going to ask as many questions as one of these government snoopers before the day's over."

Mr. Mayhew came to the door of his garage and gave the Scourge a look to which her owner was well accustomed.

" Cemetery's just up the road," he said.

" Must be convenient for you," Crook assured him. " I want to check up on a car you hired out on the sixteenth."

" Who are you ? "

" Acting for the innocent party."

" Innocent ? "

" I think so. Mind you, the police don't agree with me, but then the police don't often see eye to eye. Of course, I can't make you give me any information, but if it's not me it'll be them. Y'see, it looks like you've been had. This chap who hired XYA9910—he represented himself as a doctor, didn't he ? "

Mayhew checked up his books. " He was a doctor," he said.

" That's what you think ? "

" I verified it before I let him have the car. We have to be careful in this game."

" Did he tell you the name of his hospital ? He had a hospital appointment, hadn't he ? "

Mayhew said that transactions were confidential.

" My guess," continued Crook, as though the man hadn't spoken, " would be that he came from St. Mary Magdalene's, Felton Road."

" So you know him ? "

" Not yet, but I shall. And I'd be surprised to learn that St. Mary's knew him either."

" Then you'd be wrong," snapped Mayhew in disgruntled tones. " I checked up, and they said Dr. Weybridge was on their staff."

" If I came in and hired a car, and gave my name as Dr. Weybridge and you rang the hospital, and they said Yes, that was O.K. that wouldn't prove I was him. It was his day off, I suppose."

" That's right."

" Too easy," sighed Crook. " Fancy me not thinking of that before. By the way, you don't have a label stuck on the windscreen ? "

" Of course not. And there wasn't one when the car came back either."

" Well, no," agreed Crook, " there wouldn't be. But would it surprise you to know there was one there when the car stopped at its destination ? "

" That's nothing to do with me."

" It don't strike you as rum ? " suggested Crook persuasively.

" Lots of doctors used to have them, and I suppose some still do."

" What, put on a label when he was out for the afternoon ? You've just told me he was off duty."

Mayhew debated. " Well, I didn't know about the label. I never saw one."

" But I've got a witness who did. Now, any idea why a chap should want to make himself conspicuous ? None ? Then I'll tell you mine. Suppose you wanted to convince a passenger that you were what you claimed to be, a label might help ? "

Mayhew agreed sullenly that it might, but he added even more sullenly that it sounded bats to him. You didn't go round picking up strangers. . . .

" That's what you think. If it was all hunkydory why didn't the chap use his own car ? "

" It was in the garage—broken axle."

" So he says. Didn't seem to you queer, either "—he was as ruthless as a bulldozer—" that a chap who wants to hire a car for his day out should come the other side of London to get one ? Why, the district round Felton Road is stiff with garages, chauffeur-driven limousines, drive-yourself four-seaters and coupés—it wasn't likely they were all going to be out that particular day. And he had to come right across London to get you."

" It's not my job to think," snapped Mayhew. " I'm here to hire my cars to respectable clients."

" Well, if that's what you think you've fallen down this time," Crook assured him. " By the way, what time did the chap bring it back ? This may easily be a police matter, y'know. I'm the Good Samaritan, 1951 model, doing their job for them. If I'm in the red, though I don't believe it, you won't be bothered with them at all."

" A bit after ten that night," said Mayhew reluctantly.

" Mileage ? "

" A hundred and twenty-six."

" It all fits," said Crook. " You've read about this car-stealing gang, I suppose ? "

" The Cross-roads crowd ? Well, all I can say is this chap didn't steal my car."

" Maybe not. But unless I'm right off my track it was used to deposit stolen property."

Mayhew showed his first sign of distress. " They can't blame me. He said he was a doctor, gave me his name, paid on the nail, I rang the hospital and they confirmed it. What more could I do ? And, anyway, he didn't leave any of his precious stolen property in the car."

" What, nothing ? " said Crook, sounding disappointed.

" Not unless you count a long steel hairpin, the kind my auntie used to wear."

Crook looked as pleased as if he'd been offered a gold piece.

" Got it by you ? "

" What d'you suppose ? "

" Might be worth a packet if you had," Crook insinuated. It turned out that Mayhew's grandchild had taken it for some infantile purpose and had to be placated with silver before it could be persuaded to yield up its booty.

" That's just what I wanted," reflected Crook as he drove off. He'd seen similar murderous pins on Miss Pinnegar's dressing-table and nowadays when women mostly cut off their hair they weren't so common as you might suppose.

Geoffrey was waiting for him when he dropped in at Bloomsbury Street.

" I'm going to pay a visit to the hospital where dear Florence is staying," Crook announced, " and after that it's anybody's guess where we go."

Dr. Weybridge wasn't at the hospital, but Crook learned something from the matron—and it speaks volumes for his abilities that he was passed through to her in record time— that put another piece of the jigsaw in place. Miss Morrison said that Dr. Weybridge had nothing to do with Florence, who was under the house surgeon.

" You remember the last day Miss Pinnegar called to see Abigail ? " he asked.

" I remember that she did come, and she had a word with me afterwards, but she said nothing that might explain her sudden disappearance."

" Didn't notice anything special about her ? "

" I thought she was looking a little less—buoyant—than usual, and I advised her not to overdo it. She had no one to take Florence's place, and of course she's not as young as she used to be, and she's accustomed to everything being just so. I thought like too many women she was becoming a slave to her possessions. I told her to let the flat go a little, if she couldn't get a charwoman . . ."

" Florence has been here some time, hasn't she ? "

" Four weeks and three days."

" And you hadn't noticed Miss P. looking under the weather until the Thursday ? "

" I've a good deal on my mind," said Miss Morrison primly. " I can scarcely be expected to notice every change in every person I see."

" But you did notice it that day ? " Crook insisted. " No, really, this is important. If you'd been asked by the police would you have said she looked as if she had something on her mind ? "

Miss Morrison considered and said, well, now the idea had been mooted it was true that Miss Pinnegar hadn't been quite herself.

" That's what I thought," said Crook in satisfied tones. " Now, next point. Dr. Weybridge."

" What about him ? "

" He and Miss P. weren't acquainted, I take it ? "

" There's no reason why they should be. Of course she might have known him outside the hospital."

" But you never heard her mention his name."

" No."

" And he wasn't on duty that day ? "

" Dr. Weybridge was laid up with influenza last week. He wasn't on duty at all."

" So he wasn't likely to be hiring a car to go down to the coast ? "

" He wouldn't require to hire a car in any case. He's one of the lucky ones. He had a new model last year."

" And—one more question—does he generally carry a label announcin' his profession on his windscreen ? "

" I've never seen one. I cannot imagine why he should."

" Nor can I," said Crook, wringing her hand heartily. (She was so much surprised to find it engulfed in his that she didn't even try to pull it away.) " And what's more, I don't believe he ever did." He gave her his well-known alligator smile and hurried out. Miss Morrison followed him into the corridor.

" Mr. Crook ? "

Crook turned. " Yours to command."

" Have you any idea where Miss Pinnegar may be ? "

" Not yet. But if you asked me have I any idea what may have happened, the answer is, I have a hunch and my hunches are like Winston Churchill's, they generally come off."

" I suppose all this is part of a plan," acknowledged an exhausted Geoffrey as he and Crook stopped in front of a bar called the Live and Let Live ; " but I'm absolutely in the dark still."

" Give me a chance," said Crook. He found them a table, fetched beer and bread and cheese, and settled down with the air of a man who has just heard he's going to inherit a fortune. He spoke in a lower tone than usual, but the bar was so full and the voices about him so involved in personal concerns that he might have shouted at the top of his voice for all the attention he attracted.

" What puzzles me," said Geoffrey, " is why you're bothering about cars that arrived between four and five o'clock, when we've got a witness to the fact that Aunt Fran was alive and making her way down the stairs at five-fifteen. We know she reached the station and left the case. . . ."

" Pardon my left foot," said Crook, " we don't know anything of the kind. That's where we went wrong in the first place, taking the lady's word for gospel."

" You mean you think she went into a trance and saw visions ? "

" Well, of course I don't know what your standard for visions is," said Crook, " but that's not the way I'd have put it. And I think the lady spoke in perfectly good faith. More, I'd say she'd go into the witness-box and repeat her story and you wouldn't shake her in a single detail except the most important."

" And what's that ? "

" That she didn't see Miss Pinnegar at all. It's always a mistake to accept anything ready-made. You want to test your road step by step, and if I'd had the sense to remember that we wouldn't have wasted so much time going down a blind alley and I've you to thank that we didn't waste more. Y'see, what Glamour Puss saw was someone wearing a grey raincoat belonging to auntie and carrying auntie's suitcase, and she jumped to the conclusion that she'd seen auntie. But no." He shook his great bull head.

" Then who had she seen ? "

" Someone wearing auntie's raincoat and carrying auntie's suitcase," repeated Crook. " And the proof of the puddin' bein' in the eatin' you can take my word for it that auntie's raincoat is back in its proper place, inside auntie's flat. That's why I went back last night. And now you know the question I put to Glamour Puss on the phone this morning. No ? you surprise me. I asked her if the old lady had more than one grey raincoat. Mind you, she thought I was daft. ' Of course not,' she said, ' she couldn't wear more than one.' Then I asked her how she could be so sure it was auntie's she'd seen, and she said there couldn't be two like it in England. It was a kind of a cape with sleeves like the flukes of a whale. And I found that specimen hanging on the hooks in Miss Pinnegar's back hall. Now do you see where that gets you ? "

Geoffrey looked obstinate. " It simply proves that Aunt Fran came back to the flat after depositing the bag. Well, there's no evidence to show that she didn't."

" When you're up to your neck in a murder case," Crook told him, " negative evidence ain't much good. If you could show that Miss P. *had* come back—well, that might help us. All you can show is that somebody who had gone out wearing THE raincoat and carrying THE suitcase, came back, minus the second. Now my bet 'ud be that whoever came back was the one who went out, and I'd say she came straight back. It was five-fifteen when she left ; she had to put the case in and get the receipt—say it took her ten minutes. I was round at five fifty-five, so what matters now is what happened during the missing half-hour."

" And what do you imagine did happen ? "

" Oh, I think Mrs.—oh, hell, let's call her Violet—met her quietus. Now whoever administered that was a fast worker. He had to bump Vi off and you do realise the lift must have been at the top floor then. He had to go upstairs and take the lift down, hoping to hell he wouldn't see anyone en route, he had to get away and leave the coast clear for me. If he came in a car he didn't park it by the Mansions ; we've had our spies out and we've traced all the cars between four and the time I arrived and we know none of them—bar the one marked doctor—could be involved. Oh, yes, Bill's gone right through the list. Well, the odds are X came by tube, where nobody would notice him, walked into the Mansions and went upstairs."

" After five-fifteen ? "

Crook considered. " Well, no, he wouldn't have to. He might have come in with Vi. Look, I'll reconstruct the afternoon for you as well as I can, and you can pick holes in my story and then we can get down to patching it up. Miss P. came back from the hospital just before four. Hume gave her her letters and she went up to her flat. She had tea— say that 'ud be roughly four o'clock, and while she was having tea she had a visitor. Well, she wouldn't put out a second cup for the cat, would she ? And there were two cups on the tray. If she'd been expecting anyone she'd have told the porter when she came in and, anyhow, she wasn't, because she told me that once she got back from the hospital she'd be waiting for me. She knew I wouldn't be there till around six, and I told her to keep my visit dark, just to be on the safe side. Well, X comes in, and my guess 'ud be that he was calling himself Dr. Weybridge. We know a car jobbed in that name came to the flats. Nobody admits to seeing the fellow or expecting him, so it's pretty safe to assume he was your auntie's unwelcome visitor. And why should a doctor from that particular hospital be calling on Miss P. ? "

" To bring news about Florence, I suppose. You mean, it was a trick to get her out of the way ? "

" Don't it seem like that to you ? We don't know what story he told her, Flo's cut her throat, Flo's fallen out of bed and broken her neck, Flo's got bats and slugged the patient in the next bed—it don't matter. But it was something that made her put on her hat and go out. She didn't mean to be away long or she'd have left a message for me. She thought she had an hour and a half, so whatever she went for she didn't expect it 'ud keep her. Now the car we've traced to Mayhew didn't get back till ten o'clock that night, and when he was cleaning it down Mayhew found a long steel-grey hairpin dropped between the cushions of the driver's and the passenger's seat. When I was in auntie's room I took a look round and there were some identical hairpins in a box on the dressing-table. I suppose a few thousand people use that kind of pin—I wouldn't know—but only one of them was in a car with X that afternoon. X was alone when he jobbed the car and he was alone when he arrived at the Mansions. And he was alone when he turned the car in that night. The car had gone 126 miles, so it looks as though it deposited its passenger, say, fifty or sixty miles out of London, assuming the car went straight there and back. Well, that gives us a wide radius. It was out for six hours. Looks as though she was dumped." He frowned. " I don't like it," he confessed frankly. " A little less than sixty miles 'ud take you to the coast. Only, if they did put out her light, why ain't she been found yet ? "

" Tides," said Geoffrey in a choked voice.

" It's not so easy as you might suppose to lug a full-grown body to the top of a cliff. And then if she wasn't ' out ' why didn't she raise a hullabaloo ? She could have attracted attention somehow. No, it's more likely . . ." He stopped. " Hell," he said candidly, " I've lost my bearings. I don't know which is the more likely. As for what happened at this end, that's clear enough. Once the coast was clear back comes Violet to wash up the teacups—my first hunch was right, there *was* something in one of those cups that had to be washed—and don the waterproof cloak. She had to come back to destroy all signs of the tea bein' drugged, and to get hold of the raincoat. These criminals are a tidy bunch, like to leave everythin' shipshape. And that," he added grimly, " is likely to be their ruin. If they'd left the coat on the premises—well, I suppose they argued that 'ud tie 'em up to the old girl's disappearance."

" How did they get in ? " asked Geoffrey. " Aunt Fran was the most hospitable soul in creation, but she wasn't one for handing out latch keys right and left. Even I haven't got one. . . ."

" They didn't buy the porter because if so we should know. Besides, it's too risky. My guess 'ud be that X found some excuse to go back to the flat, pick up something—left his gloves, say, and only discovered it when they were back in the car. Then all he had to do was leave the door on the latch and Bob's your uncle. Let's work this out. Off goes the car and as soon as it's out of sight in comes Violet. How's that ? " For Geoffrey was looking as though his stomach was going back on him.

" I don't like to think she was in a plot to murder Aunt Fran," he muttered.

Crook reminded himself that she'd once been this chap's wife. He'd never been married himself, but he supposed it meant something, even after so many years and all the evidence on earth that she was a trollop all round the clock.

" I don't suppose by that she had any choice," he said. " She was in these chaps' hands and if she didn't play the game their way it was a date with the death-house for her. It was that anyhow as it happened, but she didn't know it. Well, up she comes, washes the cups but doesn't bother about the teapot or plates, collects the coat and hat, and shoves 'em into the first suitcase she finds and comes out, still leaving the door ajar. Yes, I think she did that because Miss Michael who's got ears as long as Jumbo's, makes a point of the fact that she hasn't heard the door slam. Into her flat goes Glamour Puss and starts an age-long conversation with her buddy. Out nips Vi and in, if I win my guess, nips Murder. Vi deposits the case and comes back to the flat. She must have done that or the waterproof wouldn't be hanging in the back hall. Besides, she must have had her handbag when she went out; she paid a deposit for the case and she must have had a receipt. Back in the flat she meets Murder and then either there's a row or he's got it all planned. Perhaps she sticks out for better terms, perhaps she wants something on the nail. She's got a lot of cards in her hand now, but it don't matter if you hold five aces if you don't know the rules of the game. And she didn't. Anyhow, whichever way it was, she came to grief. That's where Murder had to keep his head. My guess 'ud be that he took the lift up to the sixth floor and walked down one flight. Yes, that's what he'd do, anyway, it's what I'd do if I didn't want to advertise the fact that I'd just arrived opposite No. 15. Well, the job's done and Violet's out of the way. Miss P. likewise, and who is there now to blab to the police? Murder goes up, pops into the lift, takes it down and renders it unusable. It ain't difficult with a cranky old machine like that. Of course, it was chancy. He might have been seen going through the hall, but the porter 'ud be at tea and so would most of the tenants. Those who were out at parties wouldn't be back then, and there ain't much light in that hall, if he was seen leaving he might be any Tom, Dick or Harry from the top floor, no reason to suppose he's just pushed a girl down the shaft and is hurrying off to establish an alibi."

" You've got it all taped," said Geoffrey in the same dull voice. " All except the most important point of all—which is, Where is Aunt Fran ? "

" Give me time," Crook protested. " I've only just worked out this chapter."

Geoffrey straightened with determination. " I'm going to the police."

Crook caught him by the wrist. " Well, I'm jiggered. Fancy seeing you one of Murder Inc."

" What was that ? " Geoffrey's voice was threatening.

123

"Be your age," Crook pleaded. "Say you go to the police with this theory—because that's all it is. What happens? Either you're laughed out of court (and if that helps any of us you tell me), or they take it seriously, and to do the police justice, they're triers to a man, and they spread the net. And what happens? Bang goes Aunt Fran's last chance of survival. Once the gang knows the police are on the tracks they're going to obliterate every conceivable scrap of evidence. Mind you, I don't say we *shall* save the old lady, I don't know if it's possible, but I do know that if you start selling the story to the police and the Press you're signing the death warrant. You see," he went on a minute or two later, returning from the bar with reinforcements of beer and bread and cheese, " at the moment they're sitting pretty. Not a doubt about it they're involved in the head-on crash at the cross-roads. Three people could give evidence against them. Les was the first, and he's out. But before he passed out he implicated Vi. Well, Vi's out. But she couldn't let well alone, she dragged in your Aunt Fran. Well, she's off-stage for the moment and that's as much as we can say. But—before she disappeared she briefed me, and I'm still alive and kicking, and I expect to be when they put up the gallows, and may I be there to see. But suppose anything should go wrong—man is but mortal, and so forth—well, I falling, pass the torch, otherwise the buck, to you. It's all a bit like a folk dance," added Crook in a moment of expansive imagination, he never having participated in such a piece of frivolity in all his days. " Finished your beer? Well, go ahead, no heel-taps. There's no time to lose."

"If you're going to do a house-to-house inquiry in a sixty-mile radius, you'll have to hurry back to be in time to see the gallows erected," Geoffrey observed unenthusiastically.

But Crook only said comfortably, " You haven't met Bill yet."

" Not yet," Geoffrey agreed, and his companion realised he had set a literal interpretation on his words.

" You will," he promised. " He'll come into this any minute now. A nice chap, and especially useful to me because he knows both sides of the blanket. That bullet in his heel may have been the end of the career of the most promising cracksman in the country, but it was champion for Arthur Crook. What I'd do without Bill I don't know. Getting on for twenty years we've been dodging the police together and if they were to hear that we'd crashed a bus, and were laid out on twin slabs, I believe they'd be so damn pleased they'd pass the helmet round for a wreath. Well, here's to our next merry meeting." And on this optimistic note, they parted for the night.

CHAPTER XI

THE FOLLOWING MORNING at nine o'clock Geoffrey was called to the telephone.

" Captain Pinnegar ? " said a voice he didn't recognise. " My name's Parsons. I expect Crook's mentioned me to you."

" Yes, indeed," agreed Geoffrey cordially. " Any progress ? "

" We expect to clinch things to-day." The voice was as cool as though the speaker was announcing that after all he'd managed to get seats for a show that night. " All right if I come round for you in, say, half an hour ? " He wouldn't say any more on the telephone. Geoffrey ordered breakfast and found he didn't want it, drank coffee, crumbled toast, and was waiting on the step when a neat black car drew up, and a tall man who seemed approximately his own age got out. He walked with a pronounced limp.

" Captain Pinnegar ? My name's Parsons . . ." It was the telephone message all over again.

" Crook . . ." began Geoffrey.

" We'll catch up with him later in the day—I hope."

Geoffrey took his place in the car. The contrast between this man and Crook was almost as great as the gulf separating Dives from Lazarus, reflected Geoffrey. Here was none of the vitality, the infectious *bonhomie*, the crude human zest for the chase that animated the older man. There was a difference in their cars, too. Crook's Scourge would have won a prize in any exhibition for curiosities, but this was a modern car of comparatively recent vintage. Well looked after, too, thought Geoffrey. Crook took chances and his car had a battered if triumphant air. There was no need for its owner to proclaim he hadn't much interest in women; it would be a brave woman who would agree to travel in anything so conspicuous. And where Crook was loquacious this man was a model of silence.

Geoffrey set himself to break down that barrier. " Has Crook any further information ? " he asked doggedly. " He set himself a tough job."

" He lives on them," returned his companion. " One of these days he'll die of one of them, but what of it ? We've all got to die some time."

" I suppose so," Geoffrey agreed. He couldn't imagine Crook dead. It was easier to picture him driving the indomitable Scourge up the Milky Way; Elijah in his chariot of fire had nothing on Crook, decided Geoffrey irreverently. He sent an appraising glance at the locked face of the man beside him. One of these enigmatic chaps who treated words as though they were on the ration. Or perhaps, Geoffrey reflected, he doesn't think I'm capable of assimilating anything longer than one syllable. Yes. No. I see. I think not. He soon gave up all attempts at conversation and set himself to watching the streets through which they were passing.

Presently he exclaimed, " So Crook's hunch was right. This is the Brightstone Road, isn't it ? "

" Yes. Isn't that what you anticipated ? "

" I left all that to Crook." Geoffrey felt rather nettled. He could easily believe that this chap with the poker face had baffled the police for nearly twenty years, and proved an excellent lieutenant to Crook for almost as long again. He carried his years remarkably well, didn't look forty, though he must be nearer sixty. " Tell me this," he went on rather jerkily. " Does Crook think we shall find Miss Pinnegar at our journey's end ? "

" Not a doubt of it."

" And she'll be . . . in the land of the living ? "

His companion smiled suddenly. " No deader than yourself. Relax now. You're going to need everything you've got before the day's over."

" Rough house, eh ? "

The driver nodded. Geoffrey lay back. He found he was thinking of Violet, whose existence he had scarcely remembered for years. He had never been in love with her—as a very young man he had been infatuated for a very short time —he had made no promises of eternal fidelity—the marriage had been a legal agreement shorn of every trimming of romance. There had been no " Dearly beloved, we are gathered together in the sight of God and of this congregation to join this man and this woman." There had been no mention of God and the congregation had consisted of a couple of witnesses. He wondered, with a stab of compunction, if there had been any mourners at the graveside. It seemed highly improbable. To add to the general sense of melancholy a thin rain now began to fall, and a few minutes later the car seemed to hesitate.

" Damn that fool at the garage," said the driver, showing more feeling than he had done hitherto. " I told him to be sure to fill her up before he brought her round. Now we shall have to stop for juice at the first petrol pump we come to."

" Plenty in this part of the world, aren't there ? " murmured Geoffrey.

" Not open on a Sunday. Keep your eyes skinned and I'll tool her along. Luckily, she'll run downhill under her own steam."

Mechanically Geoffrey pulled out his cigarette case and handed it across. Equally mechanically his companion helped himself.

" There is a station round the next corner," he remarked. " Adjoining the Dragon Inn, if only it's open."

Geoffrey felt in his pocket for matches. " Light ? " said a drawling voice in his ear and he stooped his head to the flame of the smart little silver lighter. " You know Crook will have the laugh on me for life if I spoil his programme."

Geoffrey thought, " He's a pretty cool card." It wasn't Bill Parsons' life that interested him, but Miss Frances Pinnegar's. Already he knew enough about Crook to realise that he cut things finer than most chaps would dare, but the result was generally a pretty good fit. Still, five minutes on the wrong side might mean curtains for the old girl. However, this fellow didn't seem unduly perturbed. Probably taking other people's lives in his hands as well as his own, was child's play to him. It had been child's play to Geoffrey in a sense during the war, but—this was Aunt

Fran. He was shocked to find how difficult it was to keep his hands steady.

They turned the corner and there was the garage and, praise be, it was open.

" How about one for the road ? " Geoffrey murmured.

" As I reminded you a minute ago, you're in Merry England now. They don't open till twelve."

" Watch me," murmured Geoffrey.

The other swung out of the car and went down to the garage door. Geoffrey unfolding his considerable length, felt his foot strike some small object lying on the floor. He stooped and found it was the driver's cigarette lighter.

" Must have forgotten it was on his knee," he thought, picking it up. It was a charming affair, though a little too elaborate for Geoffrey's taste. Women might like these fancy numbers, but austerity should be good enough for men. There was even a monogram entwined in one corner. He looked at it idly. S.B. His brow contracted. What on earth was a chap called Bill Parsons doing with a lighter marked S.B. ? And on the heels of that question something exploded in his brain and he heard Crook's voice saying, " We keep a box of cigarettes on the office desk for clients, but I only smoke cigars, and Bill doesn't smoke at all." He repeated the words softly under his breath. " Bill doesn't smoke at all." He sat back, the lighter lying in the curve of his palm. He had no doubt whatsoever as to what this meant. He'd been caught by the oldest trick on the register, and one of the simplest. The gang weren't taking any chances they could avoid. His hopes for Aunt Fran dropped like Stock Exchange quotations after a speech by the Chancellor of the Exchequer. This chap, whoever he was—S.B., according to the initials on the lighter—had taken the precaution of ringing him up to find out if he'd met Bill Parsons, by observing that Crook was already on the warpath. That, of course, was to prevent him, Geoffrey, making a telephone call and spoiling the plot. But Geoffrey was not downcast for long. Indeed, within a few minutes he was seeing the hand of Providence in this unexpected development. He had wondered how on earth Crook expected to drop on the right building, that is, the one housing the gang and/or Aunt Fran out of, say, half a million. In his present perilous situation he found the answer. Now it was up to him.

" It all depends on me." The old wartime tag rang through his mind. He was a resourceful and by no means in-experienced adventurer; when he was lying up in France he had had a number of escapes quite as narrow as this one. He had the feeling now that Miss Pinnegar's fate might be tied with his, but in those days he had seldom been able to think of himself as a unit, in the horrible post-war jargon; always there had been one or more other men whose future might depend on his judgment. Now his problem was how to get the information through to Crook. He saw that the driver had given the necessary instruction about petrol and was looking at him in a rather curious manner. He slid the lighter unobtrusively into his pocket and got out of the car.

" Going to call Crook," announced the spurious Parsons. " If you think you can wheedle a pint out of the law-abiding landlord—well, good luck to you."

" I shall need it," thought Geoffrey, going round to the side door. From his place in the booth the impostor could see precisely what was happening. Probably trained in lip-reading. Geoffrey couldn't afford to take any unnecessary chances, so he simply exerted himself to put forward all the persuasive charm at his disposal. He had just won over the landlord when S.B. emerged from the box. " Be with you in a moment," he called, and made his way down to the Gents. The moment the door had swung behind him Geoffrey nipped into the booth. It wasn't a dial instrument, you had to get in touch with the operator.

" Number, please," said a voice, almost as he lifted the receiver.

" That number I had a second ago," he said quickly, making his voice sound as like the driver's as he could, " we got cut off. Can you put me through again ? "

" What was the number ? "

" Oh, bother. I'll have to look it up. I've forgotten."

" All right," said the operator. " I have it. Brightstone 1910."

" That's it." He waited in a panic of impatience. A sharp voice said, " Hallo," in cautious tones, and immediately he inquired in an assumed voice, as of some foreigner speaking English, " Ees that, please, Mrs. Chapman ? "

" Wrong number," said the voice sharply.

Geoffrey hung up and, turning, saw the driver walking up the path. With an easy air he pushed open the door.

" Trying to get a London connection," he said, emerging, " but they say there's no reply. I suppose this is a bit early for Sam to be up on a Sunday. I had a lunch date with him. I ought to have left a message with the hotel, but the fact is I clean forgot. Oh, well, may get a chance later." (Not if I know it, said that suspicious face looking into his own.) " If not, he can ring me for once."

" Why not send him a telegram ? " The voice was harsh and unsympathetic.

" I might, of course." He jiggled the instrument. " Can I send a telegram from this box ? . . . How much ? . . . Right ? " He fumbled for coins and pushed them through the slit. Then, with the other listening, he dictated a telegram to a non-existent friend, and hung up again.

" Got a pint apiece," he said confidingly. " On the house."

S.B. nodded. He'd pulled out his cigarette case again, and both men helped themselves.

Before the man could discover his lighter was missing Geoffrey had struck a match, and they went into the side door. Geoffrey chatted easily as they sat down. S.B. drank the beer as though it were medicine. Crook wouldn't have had a doubt about his character if he had been present. " A chap who'll murder a pint like that," he would have said, " wouldn't think twice about sticking an old girl like your Auntie Fran." In a few minutes it was Geoffrey's turn to produce a packet of Player's. This time he waited and allowed his companion to discover his loss.

" That's funny," said Stan (though Geoffrey didn't as yet know that was his name), " I had a lighter just now." He went through his pockets.

" P'r'aps you dropped it in the car. Shall I look ? " He half rose.

" No, no. If it's there it won't run away." Geoffrey saw that he'd got his instructions by heart. " Don't let the chap out of your sight," someone had told him. " Better make it snappy," he went on. " We've lost time enough as it is."

Geoffrey puffed for a few more seconds, then stubbed the cigarette out. " Maybe," he suggested as though the idea

had just occurred to him, " you dropped it down there."
He indicated the Gents.

" I doubt it. Still, I'll have a look. Have you settled with
this chap ? "

" I'll give it him while you look."

Stan vanished, and Geoffrey looked round. But the landlord was nowhere to be seen. He pulled an old envelope and
a pencil out of his pocket and scrawled a few words. Then
Stan was coming back, talking to the landlord. " Oh, it must
be in the car," he was saying. Geoffrey joined them, pushing
a folded note into the man's hand.

" Many thanks," he said. " Keep the change to drink our
good health." He hurried forward towards the car and Stan
hurried after him. " Left you a few cigarettes in there,"
Geoffrey shouted to the watching landlord, as they reached
the car.

Stan pulled the door open and looked round. " Don't see
it. Still . . ." " George " was still watching them.

" Look in the telephone booth," called Geoffrey. But
of course it wasn't there.

" Why should it be ? " inquired Stan sullenly. " I'd have
heard it fall and, anyway, you'd have seen it. Anyway, it'll
turn up. And so will our toes," he added, " if we're late for
that appointment."

" Sure it isn't in your pocket ? Or it could be on the
floor ? " Geoffrey stooped again. The landlord had gone
inside to clear away the guilty traces. He picked up the
cigarette carton. As Geoffrey had promised, there were half
a dozen cigarettes loosely wrapped in a bit of paper, part of
an old envelope. He unrolled it. He had a shock then, for
inside the paper was a pound note and on the back of the
envelope was scrawled in pencil : " Urgent. Ring Earl 2985.
Say the number is Brightstone 1910. Car number, AMB2803.
G.P." He turned the paper over. It had been addressed, in
a woman's writing, to Captain Geoffrey Pinnegar at a
German address.

" Pinnegar," he repeated. " Name seems familiar somehow." His glance fell on the Sunday paper he had been
reading when the travellers arrived.

No Trace Yet of Missing Spinster, ran the headline.
Where is Miss Frances Pinnegar ?

An instant later he was at the doorway. The car had

started, but he saw a face—not the driver's—looking over its shoulder. He waved the message reassuringly, and dived into the telephone booth.

It was about ten o'clock when Crook, lifting his receiver, asked for Glennan's Hotel. When he got through he inquired for Captain Pinnegar, to be told that he had gone out.

" What for ? " asked Crook impatiently. " Can't he get the stuff on your premises ? "

" I understand he won't be back before to-night," said the hotel porter.

" Must be suffering from loss of memory," snapped Crook. " He had a date."

" Yes, sir. The gentleman called for him some time ago."

" The . . . Put that one over the plate again," cried his correspondent.

" A gentleman in a black car. Captain Pinnegar was expecting him."

" The devil he was. He didn't happen to leave his name ? "

" I think the name was Parsons, sir. A tall gentleman with a limp."

" Lucky it was Sunday," reflected Crook ; " they'd never remember a casual visitor any other day of the week."

" You surprise me," Crook said in polite tones. " Be sure to watch the morning papers for the next instalment of our thrilling mystery." And he hung up. He saw at once what had happened, and he didn't blame Geoffrey, who could scarcely be expected to demand proof of his visitor's identity, but he supposed that between them he and Bill should have kept a close watch on the young man. According to the porter or whoever it was at the hotel the pair had left at about nine-thirty. Crook picked up the telephone again and dialled Bill's number. Bill, fortunately, was at home. As usual, he made no unnecessary comment, asked no teasing question, only when Crook had finished he murmured thoughtfully, " Where do we go from here ? "

Crook shrugged his broad brown shoulders. Bill could almost see him doing it. " It's up to the captain now," he said. " No sense us chasing off into the blue. After all, it's his auntie, and if he can't knock this chap over the head or dope his drink he don't deserve to get her back. But stay within reach, Bill, there's a good chap. I have a hunch this is the lást chapter but one." The last chapter, of course, would come when they'd corralled the criminals and found Miss Pinnegar. He only hoped she'd still be in one piece. He rang off and lighted another of his abominable cigars.

It was half an hour later that his telephone rang and the operator's voice inquired, " Are you Earl 2985 ? "

" Put him through," said Crook quickly, never doubting this would be the captain himself. But the voice at the other end of the line was one he'd never heard before. It took him a minute to get the hang of the message. " Hold on," he said. " Here, operator, don't cut us off unless you want to find yourself accessory to a murder. . . . Yes, that's what I said. . . . You can reverse the charges. . . . Now then, you, George, did you happen to notice what these chaps look like ? . . . Get the name, by any chance ? . . . Yes, of course, the torn envelope. Don't chuck *that* away as you value your immortal soul. You'll be needing it again and my guess is you'll be needing it p.d.q."

When he had rung off he sat for a minute, brooding. There wasn't a hope that either he or Bill could reach Brightstone in time to intercept Geoffrey and his driver ; they should be there in about half an hour, unless Geoffrey managed to put the chap out of action on the way. He was sorely tempted to trust his luck, but it was too big a risk even for him, so, reluctantly, he lifted the receiver once again and dialled Whitehall 1212.

CHAPTER XII

BRIGHTSTONE 1910 was the telephone number of 1 Yarmouth Road, a somewhat solitary house standing about a mile outside the popular seaside town of Brightstone. Before 1944 it had been the first of a row of houses running into Brightstone Minor, but a casually deposited German bomb had destroyed Nos. 2-5 and now it stood in mournful isolation, a small, not very convenient, not very pretty house with few modern amenities and no garden. For the previous owners had been an elderly brother and sister who spent all their time and money on the upkeep of a large, old-fashioned but practically indestructible car housed in a garage half the size of their own dwelling. After their death the car easily found a new owner, thanks to the dearth of motors in the country at the end of the forties, but it was 1950 before the house was again inhabited. Then it was bought at a very reasonable rate by a Mrs. Hilda Eberman, a widow with no children, who furnished it modestly and inserted an advertisement in the London Press:

Middle-aged lady, nursing experience, would take complete charge elderly person, male or female, moderate terms. Mild mental or senile not objected to.

From time to time some frantic relative, at his wits' end what to do with old Aunt May, old Uncle Ephraim, even old Nanny, who had become a positive witch as mental decrepitude overtook her, drove up and deposited some human wreck in the austere sitting-room. These patients never stayed very long, three months at most, and then Mrs. Eberman would write tactfully suggesting a change. She never had more than one at a time, she had no assistant and domestic help in such a neighbourhood was practically unobtainable. Brightstone was so full of hotels, boarding-houses and hospitals that the domestic help automatically migrated there to draw high wages and make their own terms.

" No," Mrs. Eberman would say, " one at a time is all I can manage. Besides, these mentals have to be watched. They get jealous like anyone else, and they don't see the necessity for controlling themselves or behaving like reasonable people. Because, you see, they're not." Reasonable, she meant.

" You'd hardly think it was worth her while," the neighbours said carelessly to each other when, more attractive topics of conversation being exhausted, they cast their line into the depths of inanity and fished up Mrs. Eberman. " All that work—she has her own little car, too, and we know what they cost these days—cooking and cleaning and shopping—I wonder how she makes two ends meet."

" I dare say she has a pension or something."

Stan and Joe could have told them it was " something." When he first set eyes on the house Joe was immensely impressed by its possibilities. He knew that once the police suspected that the stolen cars were coming to Brightstone they would examine the credentials of all the garage proprietors, particularly the new men. Private people who suddenly appear with cars of recent manufacture are likely to be watched; everybody wants a new car and if your neighbour gets it while you're still 144th on the list—well, the odds are there's something fishy. " So," said Joe who was nobody's fool, " what we want is a respectable set-up. And there's nothing more respectable than nursing—particularly people who take mild mental and senile cases."

" How about certificates from the local authority ? " enquired Stan, when the plan was under discussion. " Remember, we're living in the totalitarian age. Snoopers here and snoopers there—they've all got a right to come into your house."

" Hilda won't mind," said Stan serenely. " Anyway, she's not running a nursing home. She's simply taking in a paying guest, and she don't mind her being a bit crackers. She won't come under the Catering Wages Act either, since she isn't going to employ anyone. And that garage at the back is a gift. Take two big cars easy, and we never bring more than one down at a time. Then having only a bomb site next door is another gift. No neighbours to snoop, wonder why you spend so much time in your garage, think it a bit rum always changing the colour of your car——"

" Changing its shape and make, too," suggested Stan. " You've got something there, Joe."

Behind the garage the uncultivated undrained land stretched as far as eye could reach. During the war zealots had tried to make allotments there, but nothing flourished and presently it was abandoned to Home Guard exercises. Now a huge black and white notice-board announced " This Building Site for Sale," with a lot of blether about a fine situation and every amenity, but though Scotland Yard will tell you there's a mug born every minute, none of them had so far deteriorated to such a pitch that they made the poorest of offers. Well, there it was. What, asked Joe, could be better ? Mind you, most of the aged mentals were genuine. Mentals was Joe's idea, too. Mentals couldn't add two and two like you and me, and if they did no one would believe them. Mrs. Eberman had the reputation of being rather a silent woman, but civil enough on the rare occasions that she came into the town and would stop for a gossip.

" You must feel lonely cut off from everyone." That was a popular opening gambit.

Mrs. Eberman said, No, she had friends down to stay sometimes ; her brother came when business brought him to the neighbourhood, and the mentals were company of a kind. Those who weren't company were a responsibility. Either way they took up your time. " Of course," she would explain, " I never take dangerous ones. Mostly they suffer from delusions, like old Mr. Pocock, who thought he was the Prince Consort. He used to go round confiding, ' Everyone thinks I'm dead, but I'm not. Fact is, I couldn't stand the old girl any longer.' The bottle was his trouble rather than the brain."

It was known in the neighbourhood that she now had a new patient, an elderly lady suffering, as they all appeared to, from frustrated ambition. That was what delusions were called nowadays. Mrs. Eberman had dropped a hint, however, that this last comer was destined for a stay as brief as a butterfly's existence, " Though butterfly's hardly the word in connection with Miss Priestman," she said. " The fact is, families jib at the idea of insanity. You can't make them see, understand that a sick brain's no more of a disgrace than a sick body and sometimes more easily cured. No, they fancy people are saying, ' If the old girl's crackers perhaps it runs in the family.' " Life being what it is, a fairly humdrum affair for most people, it was mildly exciting to hear what Mrs. Eberman had to say.

" You mean the sort that comes for you with a bread-knife ? " suggested Mrs. Towle, the confidante of the moment.

" The sort that 'ud throw herself out of a window if there weren't bars to it," said Mrs. Eberman grimly. " I've had to put her on the top floor for that reason. The trouble is when people lose their own identity they just make up any other they hear of. I mean—Princess Margaret has a twenty-first birthday—well, she's Princess Margaret. Someone puts rat poison in her husband's tea, she's that person and why has someone taken away her wedding ring ? That kind of thing. I can't cope with it and I've told the family so."

" She might come for you next," said Mrs. Towle.

" Well, she might. No, I've asked them to take her away, and if they won't I'll have to get her certified. Still, they don't generally make trouble, the family, I mean. It was a nephew brought her down, she'd been living with him and his wife till it got too much for them. He's coming to take her off; I shall have a little rest before I look out for anyone else. My brother's hoping to come for a day or two —there's only the pair of us, you know—and it's nice not having anyone else there when he's about. What with the ones who think they're murderers and don't want to lose any chances, and the ones who realise how much publicity murderers get—well, it takes all your time."

So she had prepared the ground both for the unfortunate Miss Pinnegar's arrival and for her departure. Mental people are apt to go underground in every sense of the word, and it was in its most sinister sense that the expression could be used about Mr. Crook's latest client.

On the morning that Geoffrey Pinnegar set out with the man calling himself Bill Parsons, Mrs. Eberman found herself in an unusually restless and nervous condition. Like a good many other people who don't swim well but venture into the sea in spite of that fact, she found she was being rapidly carried out of her depths. The current was much stronger than she had anticipated, and when she decided she'd prefer to turn back and stay on the shore, it was too late. In a word, she was too deeply implicated. Joe, of course, wasn't her brother, but (though so far, only Stan was aware of the fact) her husband; she kept her first husband's name for professional purposes and the relationship was never anything but formal, a business proposal by Joe who knew that the law can't compel a wife to give evidence against her husband, and that that might prove useful if things ever went wrong.

The telephone call (from Stan, in the call-box by the Dragon Inn) came soon after ten o'clock and was simply to the effect that things were moving and she was to follow out Plan No. 2. There had been alternative plans, depending on which way the cat jumped, and like the contrary creatures that cats are, it was jumping in the one direction she had prayed it would avoid.

In the little comfortless room at the top of the house, with its barred windows and its desolate view, the woman referred to as Miss Priestman heard the bell ring far away, but didn't connect it particularly with herself. Although it was now some days since the outrage (as she thought of it) Miss Pinnegar still couldn't quite accept the fact that this was happening to her. " This "—i.e. battle, murder and sudden death—happens to other people, is reported in the Sunday Press and even referred to in police messages by the B.B.C., but elderly respectable women living on strictly limited incomes in obscure London flats are generally allowed to end their days in bed. It began to look to Miss Pinnegar as though she was going to be the exception that proved the rule. Because she had nothing to read and no visitors except Mrs. Eberman, who appeared at regular intervals with permission to go to the bathroom just across the passage, or instructions to " Eat this and no fuss, if you please," she relived the events of these last incredulous days over and over. It was like sitting in a cinema and seeing the same film come round and round. The appearance of Violet after ten years—and in what circumstances !—had been melodramatic enough, but what followed was pure Crime Club. It was so clear in her mind that she felt on her deathbed— and that, she told herself grimly, mightn't be far away—she would remember every detail. She saw herself returning to her flat from St. Mary Magdalene's Hospital, making the tea, reading Geoffrey's letter, scowling with impatience and exasperation for the old fool who couldn't make a will like anyone else, but had to involve them all in such problems, when the door bell rang and she had gone to answer it thinking, Mr. Crook before his time perhaps, but most likely Miss Michael come to snout round for any bits of gossip she can find. When she opened the door, though, it hadn't been either, but a tall dark man with a small black moustache, whom she had never seen before. She supposed, naturally, that he had mistaken the number and really wanted Flat 18, but before she could say anything he had murmured, " Miss Pinnegar ? " And then, " I am afraid I have some very bad news for you. Perhaps I may come in."

She hadn't guessed then that in inviting him over her threshold she was bringing Murder into the flat.

" I've come from the hospital," said the stranger at once. " Weybridge is my name. You may have heard your maid speak of me."

She shook her head. " I don't think so. Is something wrong ? "

" I'm afraid it is—desperately so. In fact, I scarcely know how to tell you. Matron would have telephoned, but I thought it might be best for me to come in person to—to cushion the shock, as it were."

Miss Pinnegar pulled herself together and invited him to sit down. " Has something happened to Florence ? It seems incredible. She appeared to be quite herself an hour or two ago."

He dropped his dark hat on a chair. " Miss Pinnegar, what I'm going to tell you is so melodramatic you may not be able to believe it. Unhappily, it's true. And it's not going to do the hospital any good either," he added abruptly.

Miss Pinnegar now realised that the worst had happened. " I take it there's been an accident," she suggested.

" It's worse than that. There's been a murder."

" Oh, no." The words burst from her. These things happened in films and in thrillers, a form of literature that had never appealed to her, but not to oneself. Then she remembered Violet and the cross-roads tragedy. Two or three days earlier she would have said that her present situation was incredible. The events of the past twenty-four hours should have cured her of such optimism. " But why Florence ? " she heard herself say.

" That's one of the things I wanted to know. Has she an enemy ? "

" Only the devil." Miss Pinnegar's voice was grim. Florence lived in perpetual juxtaposition with Beelzebub. He was always hovering round the door of the kitchen tempting her to lose her immortal soul, and when he wasn't there, according to Florence, he was in the living-room performing the same office for Miss Pinnegar.

The visitor's next words surprised her. " Has she an acquaintance called Beck, Mary Beck ? "

" Yes, of course. But she's in Edinburgh at the moment, or so I understood."

" Oh, I don't doubt she is. But naturally no one at the hospital realised that."

" Do you mean someone purporting to be Mary Beck has visited the hospital and—and done Florence mortal harm ?

But—she was in a public ward and, in any case, visiting hours were over."

" Precisely. You may be sure the woman calling herself Miss Beck was aware of that. Unfortunately, no one saw her except the porter, and he didn't pay any particular attention to her. She left a box of chocolates with him, saying that she knew Florence was a great sweet-tooth and these had been specially made for her. She was to eat them all, with her old friend Mary's love. Well, you can't blame the porter or the nurse who handed them on. You don't expect to find cyanide in a box of chocolates."

" Cyanide ! "

" Of course, there'll have to be a post-mortem, but the symptoms indicate that that was the poison employed. We've got the rest of the chocolates—she only ate two, and then she collapsed—but it's clear they've been tampered with. At first nobody suspected the sweets, they were at a loss to understand what had happened. Then the woman in the next bed suggested they might be the cause of the collapse. In any case—well, you know the rapid action of cyanide."

" And Florence is dead ? " She couldn't take it in. She had realised her enemies might strike, but that they might strike through Florence had never occurred to her.

" I don't know if you've a picture of Miss Beck on the premises," the man went on.

" Yes. There's one on the mantelpiece in her room." Miss Pinnegar, trained to keep her head in any circumstance, was already putting the pieces of the puzzle together. Violet would have seen the picture—With love from Mary Beck, was scrawled across the foot—any other name would have done just as well so long as it was one Florence would recognise—they must have imagined she would confide in her. Miss Pinnegar almost laughed. She confide in Florence about Violet ! She wouldn't have confided in her guardian angel. But the gang were taking no chances. " And it'll be my turn next," reflected Miss Pinnegar, not realising how very near her turn was. She recovered sufficiently to offer her visitor a cup of tea, and went to fetch the cup and the photograph. He asked her if she could come back to the hospital at once. They wanted a formal identification ; he had his car outside.

" I take it I shan't be detained at the hospital," murmured Miss Pinnegar, remembering her appointment for six o'clock.

Her companion shook his head. " A mere formality," he assured her. " We'll send you back in a car, of course. The inquest will probably be held to-morrow, but you will get due warning as to time."

All this while Miss Pinnegar was too much dazed to think of anything but that Florence, loyal, crude, clumsy Florence, was dead, and that she in some way was to blame. For she couldn't baulk *that* conclusion. If she'd handed Violet over to the authorities at once, instead of becoming an accessory after the fact, Florence would still be alive. She couldn't imagine existence without her. She could be maddening, stubborn and the reverse of flattering, but she was a part of Miss Pinnegar's life. And that she should die in this hideous fashion was intolerable. Miss Pinnegar added a little hot tea to the half-cold mixture in her cup (" That's right," said the doctor, " tea's the best medicine in the world for shock."), put on her hat and went down in the lift that the doctor had left at the fifth floor. In the car she found that her wits had wandered so much she had left the photograph of Mary Beck on the table. Her companion offered to fetch it, and she handed him her keys and lay back against the upholstery of the car. She felt suddenly so tired she scarcely knew how she would get through all that lay before her. She even wished she had not rung up Crook and made the appointment. The police would be in charge of the case now. She supposed they would hold her responsible but that was justice, since the responsibility was indubitably hers. She scarcely imagined she could be sent to prison, but the flat would be prison enough. She didn't believe she could live there any longer. But at the back of her mind the voice of reason said, " This is nonsense. This will pass as everything passes. When you heard that Geoffrey was missing believed killed, you thought your life had come to an end, but it put out fresh shoots and long before you heard he was still alive you were deeply rooted again. And so it will be this time."

She heard swift steps behind her, the car door clashed, her keys were dropped into her lap. " Feeling all in ? " asked a sympathetic voice. " I'm not surprised. Well, this shouldn't take us long." The car swung into the busy line of traffic that surged along Felton Road at this time of day.

They had been travelling some time when she looked at her watch and saw with perplexity that it was almost half-past five. It had not been much after half-past four when they left the flat. She looked through the car window but could discern no familiar streets. "Where are you taking me?" she asked drowsily. "Isn't Florence at the mortuary?" There was no reply and she flashed a look at her companion's face. "Where is Florence?" she asked in a louder tone.

"Florence?" said the driver in absent tones. "Oh, all right, I expect. Who's she, anyway?"

"She—she——" Realising in a flash the appalling danger into which she had walked, Miss Pinnegar struggled with the sense of exhaustion that threatened to overwhelm her. "What does this mean?" she demanded. "You said you were a doctor."

"So I am. Now, Miss Priestman, I beg of you keep calm. . . ."

"Priestman? That's not my name." She struggled erect and looked through the window. It was spotting with rain and umbrellas were going up everywhere. "Where is this place? Stop the car at once. Did you hear me? Stop the car." She knew that time was the essence of the situation. This overpowering drowsiness would soon make her incapable of any action at all. "I feel drugged," she thought, and at once knew that was the truth. But when? Ah, when she went to fetch the cup and the picture. No wonder the driver had been so insistent on her finishing her tea. She put out her hand and tugged at his sleeve.

"Look here," he said furiously, "you'll have us both in the ditch if you're not careful."

She said in foolish tones, "Another car crash." That seemed to her immensely witty. She chuckled.

"Oh, shut up," said her companion in violent tones. He braked violently as a lunatic jay-walker stepped unconcernedly off the pavement.

"Why did you do that?" asked Miss Pinnegar, feeling drunk as well as dazed.

"I didn't want to run that scarecrow down," said the man ungallantly.

"Oh, but why not? I thought death-dealing was your profession." She laughed again. "Was that funny?" she demanded hearing the laughter and supposing him to be the author of it.

" It won't be funny when we're both in the mortuary," he said. " Do you want me to knock you out ? You'll have the whole crowd . . ." He stopped abruptly ; he'd said too much, put an idea into her crack-pot brain.

" Of course. Why didn't I think of it." She made a last tremendous effort, pulling herself upright. Just ahead of her she saw buildings and people. This might be her last chance. As the car was stopped by traffic lights she began to pound on the window. " Help, police," she shouted.

In an instant the man had caught her hands and dragged them down on to her lap. " You old besom," he muttered. People were beginning to look at them ; she hadn't shouted as loudly as she supposed, but her wild expression, her hat that had been knocked crooked when the man caught her wrists, her open mouth and staring eyes, would have warned anyone something was wrong. Like a miracle a policeman emerged from the crowd. She tried to scream. At the same moment the lights changed. The driver looked as if he were about to go on, but wisdom prevailed. He leaned across and wound down the window.

" Want me for something, officer ? "

Miss Pinnegar began to speak, but the drug was doing its deadly work. The words ran into one another, became indistinguishable ; only a few nonsensical phrases dribbled from her panting mouth.

" Lady seems in trouble," said the officer.

" Florence," gasped Miss Pinnegar. " Poison. Mortuary."

" Yes," said the officer, and behind them an exasperated driver sounded his horn. The policeman straightened up and signalled to him to draw out ; he got over the lights just before they changed again.

" Florence," repeated Miss Pinnegar in stronger tones.

" Who's Florence ? "

" Ask me another," said the driver frankly. " She keeps muttering about Florence and poison, and it doesn't add up at all. Poor old lady, she's not quite—you know—and I'm taking her down to Langley." (Langley was the big county mental asylum.) " It's bad luck the nurse who should be accompanying us came to grief just before we started, sprained an ankle, but there'll be plenty of help the other

143

end." (They never thought of doubting him. Hadn't he got " DOCTOR " on the windscreen ?)

" Abduction." Miss Pinnegar brought out the word in triumph and stared hopefully at the constable's face. But she couldn't help laughing a little because it kept swelling and receding and broadening, just like a face seen in a mirror at a fun fair.

" Now, Miss Priestman," said the driver.

" Priestman . . ." she said idiotically. " I'm—I'm . . ." But it was too late—she couldn't remember. " P—P——"

" Oh, come," he interrupted. " Look at the identity card in your bag." Her fingers fumbled helplessly with the catch ; he snapped it open for her and there lay the card in full view ; she clutched at it. " Priestman, Bertha M.," she read, " 4 Singleton Crescent, N.W.4."

She waved it away feebly. " Not mine, impostor." That was a good word. She repeated it in a louder tone. A few people began to gather round the car. " Drunk, dear," said a voice clearly. " Dunno how they do it this hour of the day," said a second voice. " Keep it in the sideboard, dear," chimed in the first. " My Aunt Emma was like that. Sip, sip, sip, all day."

With a great effort Miss Pinnegar turned her head. " Smell my breath," she said dramatically.

" Of course she's not intoxicated," said the man in impatient tones. " I say, officer, can't you clear these people off ? This isn't a raree show. I knew we ought to have an ambulance, but there's such a call on 'em these days and we gave her a sedative . . ."

" Drugged," said Miss Pinnegar, her head falling forward. " Poisoned."

The constable shrugged. " Stand by, please," he said irritably to the crowd. " Don't obstruct the road. Never seen anyone ill before, I suppose." He waved the car on. The driver wound up the window, and they sped away, away, from the lights and the people and all hope of rescue into the perilous and the unknown.

CHAPTER XIII

" AND THAT," said Miss Pinnegar to herself, getting out of bed and walking on bare feet to the window, where she stared through the bars like an agonised and captive lioness, " is the last I remember. I haven't the faintest recollection of arriving here, I suppose somebody carried me up the stairs —that woman has hands like a butcher, I noticed them the first time she came in—they're not taking any chances."

For there was no sign of her clothes or her handbag, she hadn't even a pair of bedroom slippers, the night-gown she was wearing was not hers, or the type she would be likely to buy, the door was kept locked, the windows, narrow and forbidding, stared over a desolate countryside. Once she had seen someone moving there and had rapped imperiously on the window, but though she had attracted attention, it had done her more harm than good. The man had looked up, laughed and shaken his head. Even at that distance she realised what his expression meant. Another of the loonies. " But they can't get me certified," she thought in horror, " you need two doctors, and, anyway, it would be risky. They wouldn't take the chance." Well then, what alternatives were there ? They could keep her here, but that would be risky too, if her stay was likely to be of long duration. They could let her go, but clearly they wouldn't do that. She would beetle off to the nearest police station and lay information against them. So that left one other solution. The more she thought of it the less she liked it. " And nothing can we call our own but death," she murmured, marching up and down the room on her long bare feet. (On the floor below Mrs. Eberman heard her. " Thinks she's a sentry, I suppose," she muttered.) No wonder they tried to impress upon her that her name was Priestman. Doubtless they'd already destroyed her true ration and identity cards. If she died here, and it looked uncommonly as though she was going to and at no distant date, she'd be buried as Priestman. No doubt the word had gone round that she was crazy. It seemed fantastic that such an event could happen, but probably violent death was all part of the

ANTHONY GILBERT

day's work to the gang. What puzzled her was why they'd
kept her alive for so long. It couldn't be because they
thought she could be any use to them. But, of course, they'll
want the neighbours to know they've got a sick maniac here
—perhaps a manic-depressive, they'd call her—then no one
will be surprised to see a hearse draw up at the gate. She
stared down into the courtyard, but nobody moved there.
The garage doors were locked. " Is that where they hide
the stolen cars ? " she thought. " Most likely. They'd argue
the police wouldn't look here. Wouldn't look here for a body
either. Nobody will look for me," she thought. And then
in a flash she remembered Crook. Bulldog Crook—Crook
who always gets his man. You could be sure he came to
Allenfield Mansions as arranged—unless they'd contrived to
put him off, sent him a message in her name :
" Don't come after all. I'll ring you." Would he smell a
rat if they had ? Or wouldn't he come along just to make
certain. " Better be sure than sorry," he might say. Or
suppose he rang up the next morning, there wouldn't be any
answer. Perhaps he'd been told she was going out of town,
had changed her plans, was staying with a friend. It wasn't
likely the gang would chance Crook spoiling their plot. But
further reflection assured her that they didn't know Crook
was implicated. " Unless I said something in the car," she
wondered aloud in agony. " Did I mention his name ? "
But if anything had happened to him wouldn't it be in the
papers ? She hadn't seen a newspaper since she arrived.
" There's nothing you'll want to read," Mrs. Eberman had
said. " It's all very depressing. I'll fetch a book if you like."
The book had been a weekly woman's paper. " Waste
matter clogs the pores, look after your skin, your hair, your
nails. Fashionable women are wearing the hoop sleeves that
made such a stir when Lady Blank Blank appeared in them
at Somebody or Other's ball . . ." Only one phrase was
applicable there and that not in the sense intended by the
writer. " Look after your skin."
" There's no sense my getting into a panic or giving up
hope," Miss Pinnegar reminded herself severely. " All is
not lost. Why, at this very moment Mr. Crook may be half-
way here from London. Perhaps that telephone call—but,
no, he wouldn't do anything so silly as that. ' Surprise is
the best form of attack,' he used to say." She strained her

eyes as if she expected to see the Scourge come bounding and bumbling down the cart track visible from the window.

The key turned in the lock and Mrs. Eberman came in. " Now, dear," she said, " you've done enough exercise for one morning. We shall have you getting thin. I've brought you your elevenses." Miss Pinnegar shrugged them aside.

" I don't want anything, thank you." Queer how courtesy prevailed even in such circumstances as these. You said thank you when you were refusing a cup of cold pizen, as very likely this stuff was. " I never drink milk," she added. Milk, being an opaque substance, was excellent for disguising mysterious doses, powders, say.

" Now, dear," said the woman again, " don't start playing up. You're in safe hands."

" I don't doubt it," said Miss Pinnegar grimly " But safe for whom ? Hardly myself, I think."

" If you don't quiet down I'll have to tell the doctor."

" Doctor ? " Miss Pinnegar quite admired the effect of the sneer she contrived to produce. " You really expect me to believe he was a doctor ? If you can believe that you can believe anything. You might even believe my real name is Pinnegar."

" You should be grateful it isn't," retorted Mrs. Eberman. " Seeing the trouble that's piling up for her."

" Trouble ? " Miss Pinnegar in a rare gesture beat her hands together. " I feel like someone standing in the dark, not even able to feel her way because the floor may open under her feet. And the maddening thing is that you're standing by me with a lamp in your hands, and you won't light it, you won't light it."

" Now, take it easy," said Mrs. Eberman in a sharp voice. " If you're going to take on like this I'll show you the paper. Then perhaps you'll see sense."

She vanished, relocking the door behind her. Miss Pinnegar stood just where she was. She didn't give a thought to appearances and it was strange that even in that nonsensical nightdress with its pattern of rosebuds on a sickly pink ground, with a silly little shawl about her shoulders, she still looked noble rather than grotesque. She heard steps hurrying on the stairs, and Mrs. Eberman came in with the Sunday paper in her hand. " Look at that," she declared dramatically, delivering it to her captive.

147

Miss Pinnegar looked. She saw her own photograph and beneath it the caption :

Miss Frances Pinnegar, who is still missing from her flat in S.W.7. Police are anxious to question her in connection with the death of Mrs. Violet Child. . . .

Miss Pinnegar let the paper fall. " Violet dead ? " she whispered. " No, that I can't believe. Not dead."

Mrs. Eberman was impressed in spite of herself. " She was found in the lift-shaft," she contributed. " The lift-shaft of Miss Pinnegar's flats, probably fallen from the fifth floor. Now are you so anxious to say you're her ? "

Miss Pinnegar became instantly the brisk settlement warden. " This is something I hadn't anticipated," she said. " I must go to the police at once. Or, if you refuse to let me leave the house, telephone them and bring them here. You'll find they'll come the moment you mention my name."

" I don't doubt they'll come," agreed Mrs. Eberman in grim tones; " but I've my living to think of. If it gets about that I've had the police calling here I shall be ruined."

" Then let me go to them. Telephone for a cab or a car, I have ample funds—and that reminds me. I shall be glad to have my handbag returned with my own identity card in it."

" Whose else would you expect ? " the woman snapped.

" The last time I saw it it had been substituted for one in the name of Priestman," was Miss Pinnegar's somewhat confused reply. " Not that it's of prime importance. I can collect a dozen, two dozen witnesses to prove who I am. Now will you kindly bring me my clothes, I don't know whether there are facilities for a bath, but, in any case, a basin of hot water will do for the moment, and I will get in touch with the authorities at once."

Mrs. Eberman was staring at her as if hypnotised. " I could almost believe you are her," she said. " But in that case, where's Miss Priestman ? "

" At the bottom of another lift-shaft, I dare say," was Miss Pinnegar's crisp retort.

Mrs. Eberman took a step backwards. " I can't do it, not till after the doctor's been."

" Afterwards I doubt whether you will be able to. Doesn't murder mean a thing to you ? "

" I don't know anything about a murder. You read a case in the papers and then tell me you're the woman they're after."

" Pardon me, I told you that before I had seen a news-paper. I should know my own name, having borne it for over sixty years."

" I'll get your clothes," said Mrs. Eberman. " Then if he hasn't arrived—the doctor, that is, and don't go on saying he isn't a doctor, because how was I to know?—then perhaps I could work it for you. Only—don't waste time."

" I'm not in the habit of wasting time," returned the battleaxe, whose character hadn't been changed at all by several days' incarceration in circumstances of the utmost terror. " I shall be with you in a quarter of an hour." She washed in a cupful of hot water, dressed, sat on the edge of the bed to do her hair. She was folding her nightgown, unable to shed in a few days the habits of a lifetime, when Mrs. Eberman came in.

" All right ? You'd best hurry if you want to get off. Never mind about the bed, I'll see to that."

She hurried out of the room, Miss Pinnegar at her heels.

" I'll take you in myself," she said, but her guest negatived that at once.

" A most unwise suggestion. If this spurious Dr. Wey-bridge arrives and finds we are both gone he is bound to put two and two together. Besides, that method would court the very publicity you are so anxious to avoid. No, no, I should prefer a car."

The woman hesitated. Doesn't want a car here ? Doesn't want anyone to see me go ? Is playing some trick ? The alternative notions chased themselves through Miss Pinne-gar's brain. And, anyway, it was too late, for as the women hesitated in the hall they heard the sound of a car drive up and someone emerged.

" That'll be him." Mrs. Eberman seemed quite nerveless ; Miss Pinnegar took her by the shoulders and shook her.

" Where can I go ? " she demanded. " Where can I go ? " It was part and parcel of this grotesque affair that she should contemplate hiding in a cupboard or under a floor-board, in a cellar, anywhere.

Mrs. Eberman moved quickly. " I'll tell you. Hurry." A bell pealed through the house. " Come on, it's your only chance." She hustled the old maid to the back door and unlocked the garage.

" Quick," she implored. " Inside here." She swung open the door of the little car that stood in one corner. " That's right; down in the back, pull the rug over you, then if he should look in he won't see you. Know anything about cars ? "

" No," admitted Miss Pinnegar in a voice muffled by folds of dusty rug. " Geoffrey, my nephew, tells me I haven't a mechanical mind. I can't even distinguish between the accumulator—or do I mean the accelerator ?—and the brake."

" Well, it doesn't matter," returned Mrs. Eberman consolingly. " I'll have to take away the electric light bulb in case he gets nosey, but you're not afraid of the dark, are you ? "

She removed the bulb, returned to the car and fiddled about, there was a roaring noise that made Miss Pinnegar exclaim, " He'll hear that, surely ? " And then Mrs. Eberman was gone with a word of reassurance on her Judas mouth. The door closed, the key turned in the lock. " Must do this," whispered Mrs. Eberman. " In case he notices anything. Anyhow, I'll tell him I've lost the key."

Her footsteps moved rapidly away. Left to herself, Miss Pinnegar began to wonder if this dilemma was any improvement on her previous one. Here she was locked in a black shed, half suffocated in a car that didn't accommodate itself to her angular height, with enemies on every side, like the psalmist, a prisoner with no means of escape. She began to wonder how long she could remain in this airless den before she began to suffocate. Already the air seemed mephitic, she felt as though she were " going under " as they said in the theatre at St. Margaret's. The noise bothered her, too. Why on earth had Mrs. Eberman left the engine running ? Did she mean to seize an opportunity, leap into the car, drive them both away ? She was puzzled, wished she knew more about cars. The darkness seemed to be increasing; now it came not merely from without, but inside her head, her brain. The world was receding.

" I can't be going to faint," she thought scornfully. " But of course the air—the air . . ."

And then, though the atmosphere didn't clear, her mind for a moment did, and she knew why the woman had switched on the engine and why she had locked the door. Because, of course, she wasn't coming back, not till the carbon monoxide fumes had done their deadly worst.

" Really, I deserve to die," Miss Pinnegar told herself in disgust. " I hope when Mr. Crook discovers what has happened he won't blame himself." Commonsense whispered she might still stand a chance if she knew how to switch off the engine. She disembarrassed herself of the rug, and climbed into the driving-seat. But in the pitch blackness she was afraid. Suppose she touched the wrong thing and the car plunged forward into the opposite wall or backed into the door ? Did cars burst into flames as planes did ? It was fantastic to belong to the Atom Age and know so little. She wrenched furiously at the door ; let her at all events get out of the car. But this door was locked. She had just sufficient strength left to unfasten the other door and fall out before the blackness overwhelmed her. Her last thought was that when they'd achieved their aim the conspirators would doubtless drive the car away, with her still under the rug, and find some better place than a lift-shaft to pitch the body. Rubbish must not be tipped here, said the notices on waste ground. Well, she'd be rubbish.

" Oh, her nephew came to fetch her away," they'd tell inquirers, if there were any.

Who shall we send to fetch her away, fetch her away, fetch her away ?

inquired the old song.

It would be death who fetched her away. You'll be the death of me, people said, wiping the tears of laughter from their eyes. And Mrs. Eberman and her confederates would be the death of Frances Pinnegar, as already the self-styled Dr. Weybridge had presumably been the death of Violet, and Violet had been the death of Les.

" It's like the House That Jack Built," thought Miss Pinnegar, believing she spoke aloud. But the dark tide had carried her far, far from the shore, out of sight and hearing alike. Violet herself had fallen into no darker pit.

Mrs. Eberman returned to the house to find Joe in the hall.

" Oke ? " he asked laconically.

Mrs. Eberman nodded. " I don't like it," she confessed, her face chalk-white. " This is going too far."

" What d'you expect us to do ? " demanded Joe roughly. " We can't afford to take chances at this stage."

The woman laughed abruptly. " Not take chances ? What else are we doing ? "

" Keep your head," he warned her. " Stan 'ull be along soon, when . . ."

" When he's done *his* murder, I suppose. God, Joe, where's it all going to stop ? "

" She shouldn't have butted in in the first place. Once she knew about Vi and us she wasn't safe. We've too much to lose. Now, keep your head, Hilda, it'll be all right. The police half-think she pitched Vi down the shaft, and all the evidence points to it. She had every reason for wanting the girl out of the way and this must have seemed safe."

But the woman, who was his wife, refused to be reassured. " I don't like it, Joe. If she thought she was safe why should she do a bolt ? Why not stay and say she's never heard of Violet ? "

He made an impatient gesture. " Use your loaf. Presently they're going to find Miss Pinnegar's body in such a state that no one will be able to say just how she died, but it won't be inconsistent with a verdict of suicide. Stan will see to that. Stan's got his head screwed on all right."

" When's he coming ? "

" Any minute now. Fact is, I expected him before this. As soon as he's here we'll take care of that old besom. . . . Hallo, that'll be him." For a car had driven up and stopped outside the door. An instant later feet came up the path.

" Let him in," said Joe impatiently. " The sooner we're through the better. She ought to be out by now, and so long as she can't claw or scream that'll do for us."

Hilda Eberman moved slowly down the hall. She hated this traffic, feared and detested Stanley Browne, but whenever she thought of cutting loose and leaving Joe her heart turned over. The fact was she was utterly infatuated with this man, fifteen years her junior, who had gone through a ceremony of marriage in the same spirit as he'd have signed any other business agreement. He wouldn't let it prevent him from any more favourable coup or alliance that came his way, any more than he'd have let a contract interfere with his freedom. For herself, she knew she was crazy; he wasn't particularly handsome, intelligent or rich; he wasn't so much unscrupulous as quite without conscience; it seemed to have been omitted from his make-up. As some unfortunates are colour-blind and cannot distinguish between red and blue, so Joe was blind morally. Though, as Crook could have assured him in his grimmest tone, that wasn't going to help him much when he found himself en route for the little covered shed. As she took the few necessary steps down the hall Hilda wondered at the spell that engulfed her. She got nothing out of it at all, nothing but danger, work and blame if things went wrong. And in spite of it all . . .

" Did he get tired of waiting ? " called her husband's acid voice. " You could hardly blame him."

She fitted a false smile on her lips and threw open the door. " Come in, Stan," she started, and then gave a low cry and flung one of those enormous hands over her mouth. Because it wasn't Stan at all, but a nondescript-looking man in a grey suit who waited on the step.

" Mrs. Eberman ? " he asked. " I am Detective-Inspector Merriman of the Brightstone Police." He offered her proof of identity. " I should like to ask you some questions about Miss Frances Pinnegar, and I should warn you that anything you say may be taken down and used in evidence."

Over the woman's face passed a look of such terror he thought she would faint. Instead she turned her head over her shoulder, calling, " Joe ! Mr. Taylor."

Joe came forward. " What is it ? " He saw the visitor and stared. The inspector, a man of more intelligence than Joe generally allowed the police to possess, could see the thoughts moving through his mind like goldfish swimming in a bowl. " Can I beat it ? What's the odds ? "

Merriman said coolly, " That your car outside ? Then you don't live here ? "

He looked at Hilda again. She said jerkily, " He's my husband. I keep to my first husband's name for professional purposes—I'm a nurse." The words were torn out of her. She clasped her hands in front of her as though they could stem that reluctant torrent.

" I see. Then you're really Mrs. Taylor. I shouldn't worry about your car, if that's what's bothering you, Mr. Taylor. I've got my chaps back and front. No one can break

153

in if that's what you're afraid of. And," said the pitiless grey glance, " no one can break out either, which is more to the point."

He put down a soft hat on the little table in the hall. " Miss Pinnegar ? " he said again, and Hilda burst out :

" I don't know anything about her. I don't know who you mean."

" Oh, come. Don't you ever see a paper ? "

" That one ? " said Joe coolly. " Why the heck should we know anything about her ? "

" Information received," said Merriman in the same dispassionate tone. (He didn't add, possibly because he didn't know, that the name of the informant in this case was Arthur Crook. Joe knew of his reputation if Merriman didn't.) " I understand an elderly lady came here as a patient last week."

" That's right," said Mrs. Eberman more steadily. " Miss Priestman. She was brought down by a doctor, a relation. He said she had delusions and just needed care, but it was more than that. I had to ask him to remove her, and she's gone."

" When did she go ? "

" Quite early this morning." She started. " There now, I forgot about her ration book and identity card. They're still in the kitchen." She looked defiantly at Merriman. " What do you make of that ? " her glanced challenged him. But inwardly she was petrified with terror. Oh, this was something of which she'd never dreamed when she became Mrs. Taylor. Anyone might fiddle the income tax or play it a bit rough on the Black Market, but shutting an old woman up in a shed with a car's exhaust going full blast, that was murder and the day of judgment wouldn't make it any different.

" I see. All the same, I think we'll take a look round." He turned towards the door.

" Got a warrant ? " snapped Joe.

" What do you think ? " The officer produced it. " I should warn you," he said, " that Miss Pinnegar is wanted by the police to give information in connection with a murder. If you're concealing her you lay yourselves open to court proceedings."

" Oh, you can be sure we wouldn't like that, Inspector," said Joe in a rapid mincing voice. " Hilda, show the gentleman round. Don't forget the dustbins. I should think hunting through garbage was second nature to him."

Hilda threw the inspector an imploring look. "He's just joking," she said nervously, beginning to open and close doors with great rapidity.

"Not so fast," said Merriman, who had paused to give instructions to the men who had accompanied him.

"Expecting a siege, it appears," said Joe, standing sullenly in the hall.

The policemen did their job thoroughly; they opened cupboard doors and shook out curtains. Mrs. Eberman gave a half-hysterical laugh. "Sure you wouldn't like to look in the copper to make certain we're not boiling her to pieces?"

"It might be a good idea."

There was no getting past this chap's guard, and they both knew it. Hilda went upstairs slowly, trying to prepare herself for the inevitable questions. She wondered what plan Joe was evolving. She had no illusions about him. If he could dissociate himself from the whole affair he wouldn't hesitate. She could swing to-morrow for all the effort he'd make to save her, would probably cut out her tongue and paralyse her fingers to stop her making any statement that might get him on the rebound, if he knew how. Still, this fellow must know the law. You can't make a wife answer questions that may implicate her husband, though she's allowed to make a statement of her own free will, and that goes for the husband, too. If—oh, horrors!—if they found Miss Pinnegar in the garage, would Joe swear he knew nothing about it? With a dreadful sinking of the heart she knew this was quite probable. And Miss Pinnegar had never set eyes on him. Still, if they did find Miss Pinnegar it would be too late to expect her to give evidence of any kind. Methodically but wasting no time, Merriman and his assistant toured the house. There would be no sign of Miss Pinnegar in any place but the attic bedroom, since she had never entered any other room. When he reached this apartment the inspector looked round.

"What time did you say Miss Priestman left?"

"Only this morning. I haven't had time to put the place to rights yet."

"Left her nightdress behind, I see?"

" She must have forgotten."

" Not exactly an old lady, not if she wore that sort, was she ? " he asked. " What did she look like ? "

Madly Hilda Eberman plunged. " Fat, rather a raddled face, dyed hair, sort of henna. . . ."

" That's queer."

" What's queer ? "

The inspector stooped and picked something from a crease in the bed. He held it out on the palm of his hand. It was a long, grey, bristling, steel pin. " Funny a lady with red hair should use that sort of pin, I mean." He strode across the room and looked out of the window. " That your garage ? "

" Yes."

He turned and went quickly down the stairs. In the hall he stopped, muttered something to his assistant and made for the back door. Hilda had hoped against hope that somehow Joe would have thought of a plan to get the old girl out of the car before the police came in, but she saw at once that he would have no chance. There was a constable at the back ; as Merriman opened the back door this man came forward.

" Sir, I've been listening at the door. There's a car in there with the engine running." Merriman bent, the humming, hissing, call it what you like, came faintly through the barrier. He whirled round.

" Where's the key ? "

She shook her stricken head. " I—I haven't got it."

" Did you hear what I said ? Give me the key."

She shrank back, trembling and grey. Joe stamped down the passage. " Didn't you hear what she said ? She hasn't got it. Here you are."

He threw a key-ring across ; the constable ran a practised eye over it. " We'll need the key of the padlock," he said sharply. Joe had retreated, with Hilda in his wake. Merriman came charging back.

" Where's the key of the padlock ? Go on, give it me, unless you want the place broken down."

" We're in your hands, Inspector," said Joe suavely. " We can't prevent you. And we can't help you, because we haven't got the key. My wife lost it a day or two ago. That's why you see my car standing in the street. We were going to get a fellow to come and pick the lock for us in the morning—but p'r'aps one of your boys is an expert."

Merriman had no time to waste. He came up to Joe and said, " I don't believe you, and I'm going to search you."

Joe obligingly held up his arms.

" Frisk is the word," he said. " I dare say you know."

Joe turned round so that his back was to the policeman. This was the instant for which Merriman waited. There was a mirror on the wall nearby, and in this mirror it was possible to see Hilda standing distraught against the opposite wall. Joe had sent her a signal, one that she understood, for now she edged near a huge flower-bowl, thick with spreading leaves, and her hand was stealing into her pocket. Merriman was on her like a flash, ruthlessly twisting the wrist to make the great predatory hand open, snatching the ring with its two keys—one large, that would be the lock; one small, that would be the padlock—and leaping for the door where he almost collided with one of his own men.

" None of these opens it, sir," the fellow panted.

" These will. Go on. We may be too late as it is. You, Birch, ring up for an ambulance. And I shall want both of you "—he turned to the oddly-married pair—" to accompany me to the station."

" It's news to me," hissed Joe, " that it's a crime to lock your own garage."

" If there's a woman in there, as I believe, and she dies, you'll both swing," he told them rashly.

There was a cry from the yard as the big doors swung open ; two men dashed into the fumes, torches flashed when it was found that the electricity supply was useless.

" The car," said one man, but another shouted :

" No, she's here, on the floor. Give me a hand."

They stooped over that piece of human wreckage, limp, discoloured, beyond speech or sight. They scooped her up and brought her into the life-giving air. For a moment or two all was confusion, one man was on the telephone, another was standing at Hilda's side, a third fetched water.

" Is there any brandy in the house ?" Merriman demanded, and went himself to make sure. Joe took advantage of the momentary break to make a frantic dash for freedom. He was through the door and down the path, dragged himself away from a detaining constable ; the car was a few steps, a few breaths away. But as he came pelting out of the gate his path was blocked by a square solid brown figure, so compact that he bounced off the hard chest and the comfortable paunch; an instant later this apparition put out hands the size of legs of mutton and caught him like a vice.

" Where's the hurry, pal ? " said a voice. " Let's all sit down and be sociable. And, in case you didn't know it, this round's on me."

Gasping, red in the face, with black fear gnawing at his indomitable heart, " decks awash, barnacled and scarcely seaworthy " he'd have told you, but with flags flying for all that, the old Superb had arrived.

For Crook it had been one of those days, the kind of day, he confided later, that would warm his old bones when he sat in his alloted corner in the Eventide Homes a paternal government were going to erect for the aged, and bad luck if you had such poor taste you preferred an attic outside government control, because you could count on being hounded out, like the scapegrace daughter of Victorian fiction, to perish in the snow. As soon as he had got his connection to Whitehall and caused a flutter in the dovecotes that attracted the attention even of the eagles, he waited only to telephone his instructions to Bill, and then went downstairs hell-for-leather and jumped into the Scourge. " Make it snappy," he urged her. She obligingly jumped two lots of lights, carried away a bit of somebody's mudguard, turned a ladylike deaf ear to the language of a taxi-driver, ruined for the rest of her life the nerves of a refined party taking dear little Fido for a walk, and made Victoria Station in record time. True, she left a trail of summonses and shattered nerves in her wake, but as Mrs. Beaton, Boulestin, Philip Harben and Elizabeth Craig would all assure you with one voice, you can't make an omelette without breaking eggs.

As Crook leaped out again a policeman said sharply, " You can't park there, sir," but he pushed an official card into the man's hands. " Meet you in court, your choice of weapons," he panted, and was lost in the crowd taking advantage of a fine Sunday morning to take the excursion to Brightstone at cut-price rates.

" Can't come through here without a ticket," said the

collector at the barrier. Crook pushed him out of the way, one leg-of-mutton hand on his chest.

" Stand away there," roared the guard, as the Brightstone express began to move out of the station. " Can't get on. . . ."

" Can't I ? " said Crook. He made a wild leap and landed on a foot-board.

The carriage said " Ladies Only "; three of the six occupants screamed. " You can't come in here. Don't you see the label ? " they screeched, as he hauled open the door and fell over their long dusty feet.

" I'll be such a lady," promised Crook. " I'll make a duchess look like a housemaid." He sank into an empty place, where he wheezed and gasped like a bulldog.

Two of the ladies eyed each other belligerently; they talked without using words. One of them half-rose. " If anyone touches that communicating cord," said Crook in a mild voice, " there'll be another murder done, and we've got enough on our hands as it is. Two women to date. . . ."

They were terrified. By sheer bad luck this wasn't a corridor coach, they were mewed up with this lunatic— they hadn't any doubt he was a lunatic—until they reached Brightstone. Crook waited for the panic to subside, then he said, " Sorry to inconvenience you, but it's life or death— not for you or me, but for Miss Pinnegar."

" Miss Pinnegar ! " six voices echoed.

" That's what I said." He produced a sheaf of visiting-cards. " Heard of me ? Well, no, of course not. Easy to see none of you ladies has ever been in trouble." He gave them his alligator smile.

" But—but she killed this girl, didn't she ? " said the bravest of the six.

" That's what you're meant to think, and if she's dead and can't talk that's what people will go on thinkin'. This is her last chance and a pretty slender one." He grinned again. " Not referrin' to myself," he pointed out, looking down complacently at his plump form attired in its inevitable brown atrocities. " Even I can't help her much when she's dead."

" You can establish the truth," suggested one of his companions.

He stared at her in frank amazement; he really did think she was a bit dotty. " How'll that help her ? I'm not out to establish truth, I'm out to save my client. Still, I can see it takes all sorts to make a world and there's two sides to everything. Twenty-two more likely, come to that. Now, suppose my luck don't hold, just you remember what I'm telling you."

" You mean we might be witnesses ? "

" Not unless I win the Cemetery Stakes, and an also ran's good enough for me, but here's the way I see it."

He kept them absorbed until they reached Brightstone. Then, before the train had really stopped, he was on the platform and plunging into the stationmaster's office.

" Got a message for me. Name of Crook," he said. His quick eye sighted the orange envelope with his name on the outside. He snatched it up and disregarding the official's protests—" He wants me to sign a receipt in triplicate, I suppose," Crook reflected—he was out on the tarmac and flashing into a taxi. " 1 Yarmouth Road," he called, and pushed a pound note through the driver's window. " Step on it."

The driver stepped.

" In at the death," said the driver in a cheerful voice, as Crook tightened his hold on the frantic Joe.

Crook threw him a lopsided glance. " Just what I'm wondering," he said. " Is she ? Dead, I mean ? "

" The ambulance is on its way," said Merriman briefly.

Crook looked at him inimicably. He'd never had much use for grass himself, people said. Anyway, he never gave it a chance to grow under his feet, but, in his opinion, Nebuchadnezzar wasn't in it with the inspector. When the ambulance arrived he insisted on accompanying the sick woman to the hospital.

" Stand *in loco parentis*," he mumbled. " Owe it to her only relative." He twisted his great head nearly off looking round. " Where is he ? "

" Where's who ? "

" The chap who pressed the button, the chap who gave you your chance, who has saved the old lady here—because you ain't under the impression it's you, are you ? If it hadn't been for Captain Pinnegar you'd still be on your knees asking for light instead of bustling about and making a few matches for yourself."

Geoffrey hadn't arrived, nor was there any news of him, when Crook returned from the hospital with the comforting reassurance that the doctor thought well of Miss Pinnegar's chances.

" She's got great powers of resistance," said Merriman soberly.

" Oh, these old girls are like chickens," said Crook exuberantly. " The older they are the tougher they come. All the same, you'd better be able to produce the gallant captain before Miss P. comes round or she'll have a relapse and, as her legal representative, I shall press for a charge of culpable homicide."

CHAPTER XIV

WHEN HE HAD seen George of the Dragon move into the telephone booth Geoffrey gave himself up to consideration of his own future. If he wasn't careful, he thought, it was likely to be of short duration. Pretty soon the driver would have to show his hand, but he wouldn't do that until he was sure that there wouldn't be a survivor to tell the tale. It did not escape Geoffrey's notice that after leaving the inn his companion was steering clear of all main roads, and his hope that they might soon be pulled in by a police car searching for AMB2803 began to fade. He was under no illusions; he knew it was no part of the gang's plan that he should arrive in Brightstone in one piece. In fact, the odds were he wouldn't reach Brightstone at all.

" This isn't the main road," he said presently, hoping to draw his companion out.

" Seeing that we may be followed by chaps who won't stop at anything the less in evidence we are the better," was the curt reply.

" Come to that," drawled Geoffrey, " I think we are being followed. That green car seems to be trailing us pretty persistently."

" We'll soon see." Stan slackened speed and drew into the side of the road. He pulled out his cigarette case and handed it across. The green car drew alongside and stopped. The driver leaned out.

161

" Are we right for P—— ? " he inquired.

" You ought to have taken the right fork at the Harvest-Mouse," said Stan. The green car obligingly reversed and drove off. There was an old lady and a girl in the back seat. No, it didn't look as though they had any connection with the authorities. Stan twirled the wheel and they were off again. He began to lay himself out to be more civil. " Known Crook long ? " he inquired.

" He's been a buddy of my Aunt Fran for a long time," Geoffrey explained. " By the way, aren't we supposed to be meeting him some time ? "

." You'll meet him soon enough. If you want to know, our job is to draw the enemy's fire. Keep 'em guessing. That's the reason for all these by-ways." They twisted and turned till Geoffrey was completely lost ; if he had been asked which road they had travelled he couldn't have answered. That was probably his companion's intention.

" Whereabouts are we ? " he asked presently.

" Making for Amberley."

" Amberley ? I thought Brightstone was our objective."

" Is that what Crook said ? "

" I supposed the police were tying up the murder with the cross-roads crash, and that car was making for Brightstone."

" Plenty of time," said the other. " We want to give Crook plenty of rope."

Geoffrey shook himself like a dog emerging from the water. He didn't like the expression. You only gave a man plenty of rope when you meant him to hang himself. Crook's luck was a by-word, but even that couldn't last for ever. And now Geoffrey began to wonder if George had really got through. Or suppose Crook had been out ? Suppose there'd been no answer ? That thought shook him. He had consoled himself with the vision of Crook and the police all making a beeline for Brightstone 1910. But that was what the medical high-ups called wishful thinking. He looked again at the profile of the man beside him. No pity there, no weakening, no repulsion even at the thought of what he had in mind. Geoffrey knew the type, had met it in more than one army. The sanctity of human life has been greatly exaggerated— some well-known writer had said it, though the name escaped him for the moment, but a man like his companion would never consider any human life sacred. He was the flesh and blood prototype of the tank, that merciless juggernaut of battle that would crush any obstacle in its path.

Stan suddenly twisted the wheel and the car shot into the mouth of a narrow lane. " Short cut," he said. " We shall save about three miles. Besides, no one's likely to follow us on this path."

" We've had it if they do," suggested Geoffrey grimly. " You couldn't reverse, and if you met another vehicle you'd simply have a head-on crash." He felt himself tingle with apprehension. " This is it," he thought as he'd thought so often in the war when the crisis was at hand. " What's his plan ? The fellow couldn't have chosen a more remote place." Geoffrey didn't for an instant believe that it led anywhere or was even used as often as once a week. The country all about them was clear and bright, and quite deserted. " Landscape without figures," thought Geoffrey. " If a chap came to grief here the odds are he wouldn't be found for a month of Sundays." Was the same thought in Stan's mind ? Quite likely. Another consideration occupied him. What precise shape was his end to take ? You could shoot a man here without attracting attention, shove the body into one of the overgrown ditches, and it would be bones and rags before anyone discovered it ; the willow herb and the lady's parsley grew exuberant ; it would be autumn before the plants shrivelled and the rough herbage died, before the foliage on the thorn bushes were rags and some chance passer-by was curious because the birds were clustering—or some stray dog gave the alarm.

" I suppose you're sure of your road ? " he murmured. " It looks to me like arrow pointing nowhere."

" I know what I'm doing," Stan assured him.

Geoffrey didn't doubt it.

" Sooner your car than mine," he observed. " You'll have the springs out of her if you're not careful." His one chance would be to initiate the attack ; he'd learned some ugly tricks in the commandos. The lane was a series of turnings, and after each was negotiated it had narrowed perceptibly.

" What'll you bet this is a cul-de-sac ? " asked Geoffrey suddenly. " At best it only leads to a farm." He looked about with growing eagerness for some sign of life. The hedges on either side were closing in, the road became increasingly unnegotiable.

Relief came in a most unexpected form. A bull grazing at the top of a field on the left of the car became suddenly aware of intruders in the lane and came galloping down to investigate, making sounds indicative of extreme animosity.

" What the hell's that ? " demanded Stan, shaken for the first time.

" A bull," said Geoffrey firmly. " You know, I hate saying I told you so, but I did have a hunch this wasn't the right road. Bulls," he continued, " are particularly dangerous at this time of the year. It's the mating season." He knew that his companion being, as he inelegantly phrased it, a slum rat, would know as much about bulls as elderly ladies about the differential calculus. " One thing," he went on, " he can hardly jump the hedge, though it looks to me as though it were shortly coming to an end—the hedge, I mean. Still," he added encouragingly, " there's barbed wire between us, and that's something." His tone suggested it wasn't much.

The bull came level with the car and tore along beside it, bellowing and blowing smoke and making great play with his wicked little horns. " Oh, what a beautiful morning," carolled Geoffrey, whose spirits seemed to have risen miraculously. The bull seemed to be of the same mind.

" I thought farmers had to keep those brutes on the chain," exclaimed Stan, whose nerve wasn't proof against this sort of thing.

" Have a heart. How'd you like to live on a chain ? "

" Bulls are dangerous."

" Oh, well, so are some men." He tossed the remark off casually, but Stan threw him a sharp glance. Then he had to give his attention to the road again. It was just about wide enough for the car now, but a bicycle couldn't have passed it.

" I believe you're right," he said at last in chagrined tones. " I believe we are on the wrong road. Damn it. Now what ? "

" There was a gate a little way back," offered Geoffrey. " Just about where the hedge stopped. You could reverse the car that far, couldn't you, and back her into the gate. I'd open it for you."

" With that brute about ? "

" Oh, he's probably much more frightened of the car than

you are of him. He's young, you know," he added helpfully.
" All this show is just *joie-de-vivre*." All this while the bull
was cavorting beside them, looking about as full of *joie-de-vivre* as an inquisitor surrounded by heating irons and thumb-screws. He put his head over the (to Stan) infamously
insecure barbed-wire barrier and blew hot air at the car.

" Look here," suggested Stan, " get out and see what's
round the next corner, will you ? And be as quick as you
can. We might be able to turn there."

Geoffrey got out and walked round the bend ; as he had
suspected, the going became progressively worse ; soon it
deteriorated into a mud track. The choice lay between
trying to back the car the whole way to the original road or
turning it at the gate and chancing the bull. " Fun to see
which he chooses," he thought, looking round at the clear
sky, the waving trees and handsome figure of the bull,
silhouetted against the distance. And then he heard it, the
roar of the motor, the crash of the car as it rounded the
corner at full speed and saw what his enemy meant to do.
The road was so narrow he couldn't press back into the
ditch to escape that car, he couldn't hope to outrun it, in
another moment it would bowl him over, deliberately run
him down. It was for this, then, that the driver had
negotiated this impossible and unfruitful lane ; which, as
Geoffrey had just discovered ended only in a barrier of
ragged bushes. Once there must have been an exit, but it
had been closed long ago by the woody undergrowth. A chap
could lie hidden there for weeks, months perhaps ; you had
to hand it to these fellows, they didn't leave much to chance.
These thoughts flitted in an instant, swift and dazzling as
light, through his mind, that had been trained through years
of warfare to act on the inspiration of the moment. No time,
no time, that had been the tune of those desperate years
when any corner might conceal an enemy, any ruined house
a sniper or machine gun. As the car roared up to him, its
wheels looking as huge as those of the Juggernaut car, he
knew his only chance. He had once narrowly escaped being
run down by a tank in France ; there were times when it was
a choice of two evils and some risk had to be run. The
choice lay between Stan in the car and the bull in the field,
and for humanity and good sense his money was on the bull.
He leaped backwards and the car's mudguard grazed his

knee; the barbed wire caught his clothes, he heard the material rip, a button snapped off with the noise of a pop-gun. He could feel the bull's hot breath as he fought his way through the wire and found himself prone with the creature blowing into his face. His hoof at close quarters looked enormous. " So long as he doesn't start pawing," reflected Geoffrey. " One blow from that powerful hoof would reduce a man's face to bloody pulp."

A voice rose from the other side of the wire. " Trample him to death, you great brute," it shouted. " Worry him, tear him, leave him so that his own mother wouldn't know him."

" This is jam for Murder Inc.," flashed through Geoffrey's mind. " He can cook up any yarn he pleases, and even Crook won't be able to press a murder charge."

Stan was continuing to scream like a maniac. The bull, startled by the human voice at this pitch, changed his position and shoved his great head over the wire to observe the phenomenon in the lane. Cars came this way so seldom he didn't know what to make of them. Geoffrey took full advantage of this instant's respite. Rolling over, he was on his feet in a single movement and was racing down the field for dear life. He thought of the headlines—Bull Saves Man. " They ought to give him the medal of the Royal Humane Society," he decided. Then he heard the hoofs thundering behind him, as the bull came cantering down the field, full of frolicsome anticipation. He couldn't ever remember such a good day before. Geoffrey reached the gate with a couple of seconds to spare. He had it open and himself behind it as the bull shot past. The bull turned in his tracks, saw an opening in the hedge, tossed his head once more, this time with mischievous delight, and trotted into the lane. Geoffrey slammed the gate behind him, and looked over the top. The bull wasn't accustomed to liberty. True, he had a good big field all to himself, but even that had its limitations. The lane was different. He pulled experimentally at the willow-herb and stood for a moment the picture of Big-Hearted Arthur on his day out. Then his head came up, his little eyes widened. You could almost swear he lifted his eyebrows. Round the corner just ahead the rear of the car appeared. A strange animal, thought the bull; he went forward to investigate. What a lark !

In his driving mirror Stan saw the creature approach, and

came to a dead stop. Crime and violence and sudden death he understood, but nothing in his experience had prepared him for bulls. They were something a chap couldn't expect to be armed against. This one came a bit nearer and pressed its beastly forehead against the back window of the car (Stan thought of any animal as " it ") ; its snorting, Stan imagined, could be heard in Piccadilly Circus, and he wished to heaven he was back there himself. He tried to back a bit farther in the hope of frightening the creature off, but he might as well have tried to back through solid rock. True, the bull retreated a few steps, but it still barred his way, tons and tons of prime beef at the top of his form. Stan suddenly sounded the hooter, and the bull stepped sideways, leaning on the wire that made no impression on his sleek hide. Stan continued to back. The bull could now look through the side window ; he licked his big lips, his eyes rolled. " Damn it," thought Stan, almost weeping with apprehension. " It'll trample the bus to death and me with it." The bull's mouth dribbled appreciatively. Stan might not be enjoying this encounter, but the bull was having a high old time. " You never known what the day holds," he might have been saying. " Who'd have thought this would happen ? "

He moved back from the car and leaned on the hedge, which gave before his weight. Stan could have sworn the car tilted. He felt in his pocket. He had a revolver with him, perhaps he could shoot the brute. If the farmer made trouble he could claim self-defence. But—would a bullet from so small a weapon inflict fatal injuries ? And even if it would the car would be drenched in blood, if not crushed by the brute's fall—and he crushed with it. If he could frighten the monster off—he began to make extraordinary noises, sounding the horn again, and backing inch by perilous inch. The bull politely made way for him. Stan's heart lifted. Perhaps it would lose interest. That damned fellow must have opened the gate ; if he could get as far as that he might back the car, and then go full speed ahead for the high road. He didn't know precisely what pace a bull could make, but presumably a car could outdistance it. The bull was enchanted by this development. Now he was in front of the car. He butted experimentally at the windscreen. Too bad, he couldn't quite reach it, all that silly obstruction in front. He picked up a hoof and tested it. Pooh ! The thing wasn't nearly so armour-plated as it looked. Even a playful kick left an appreciable dent. He kicked again and the car rocked in the rutted path. Stan let out a yell. The bull put his head on one side, rolled its eyes, frisked up his tail. He stood there swaying his head from side to side, his tail waving and let out bellow after appreciative bellow. Stan continued to back the car; he remembered being told that if you stared an infuriated beast in the eye it turned tail. He stared. It was difficult, if you hadn't got a squint, to keep one eye on the bull and the other on the driving mirror; the road was so narrow here that a slip would send the car into the ditch and then you'd need a removal gang to extricate it. He wondered if he'd be able to turn it at the gate or if that would give the monster the opportunity for which he was convinced it waited. One thing was clear. Staring wasn't going to deter this bull. It didn't know the rules. Or perhaps it wasn't infuriated enough. It didn't look infuriated as it came mincing after the car, the sun gleaming on the ring in its inquiring nose.

Two farm labourers who had been working at the farther end of the field had been attracted by Geoffrey's yell of " Bull loose " as he loped down the field towards the entrance to the lane. " You'd better get him," Geoffrey continued. " He's a killer."

" 'Im ? " said one of the men, spitting disgustedly. " He'm a young 'un——"

" I don't mean the bull. Of course I could see he was only out for a game. I mean the chap in the car."

They alerted instantly. Chap in a car threatening their Buttercup ? " What's chap in car doin' in lane ? " they demanded.

" I told you, he's a killer. Men, women, bulls, anything."

" Out of a 'sylum like ? " asked one man.

" The police have been warned," shouted Geoffrey, vaulting the low hedge. The men started up the field at a steady run. When Buttercup saw them he let out a bellow of delight. The more the merrier, his attitude said. The men came down to the car, through the gate.

" 'Ere, mister, what you think you're doing to our bull ? "

" Take your damned bull away," bawled Stan. " It's not safe."

One of the men squeezed past the car and reached for the ring in the bull's nose. Buttercup instantly gave an impression of Ferdinand smelling the flowers; his eyes rolled with delight, he put on a meditative air.

" 'Oo let 'im out ? " demanded the older of the two men.

" Some fool," said Stan savagely. " Here, hold on to him. I want to turn the car."

" If you'm do damage you'm pay for it," warned one of the men.

" I pay ? You'll pay for the damage your damned bull's done to my car."

" This yer's private property," retorted the man. " Can't they read Lunnon way ? "

" I haven't done any harm. You'd best keep your mouths shut."

" You'm fritted our Buttercup," said the elder of the two men.

Buttercup opened his mouth and lolled out a huge pinkish-mauve tongue. He lunged experimentally at the car. Now he was being Faithful Fido defending master's property.

" Keep him off," bawled Stan.

" He'm all right," said the younger man contemptuously. " Now then, mister, get going. You'm trespassing."

When they reached the gate Stan found he couldn't turn the car after all, not with the bull and the yokels and the damage the car had sustained. He had to back the whole way to the mouth of the lane, and when he reached it at last he encountered a fresh barrier. Scylla and Charybdis, he might have thought, if he'd ever heard of either. The road seemed alive with chattering, gesticulating, chuckling zanies, all sprung from nowhere. Life is like that. When anything remotely untoward happens, people materialise out of thin air. Anyone who has tried practising a new bicycle in an empty lane will testify to this truth. Run into a tree or a telegraph post or a heap of stones and the road itself opens to disgorge a living host. This one was led by Geoffrey, accompanied by two hikers, an old man with a horse and cart, an enterprising press photographer come to report a local wedding, a man with a milk float, an old woman who from her appearance seemed the original of the one who lived in a shoe, an A.A. man, a village constable on a bicycle and a piebald dog out on his own.

" Clear a path, please," said Stan irritably. He'd never felt such a fool in his life. And here was Geoffrey, the oaf, leaning down and looking through the window, like a second damned bull and even less welcome, chanting " I'm called little Buttercup, dear little Buttercup, though I could never tell why." Then that blasted photographer was flashing his infernal contraption in his eyes, and one of the labourers, the one called Sam, was saying, " Move up, mister, give the bull a show." And Buttercup saw the little dog and bellowed in real earnest, and one of the hikers screamed, and Sam caught the bull by the ring in his nose and gentled him. The photographer said, " Look pleasant, please. Head *up*, sir." While Stan was trying to disentangle himself from the lot of them and get away, to hell if need be, the police-man casually passed the bicycle over to one of the crowd and came to stand before the car.

" Just a minute, sir, if you please," he said. " AMB2803. There's a message out about that car. I'll ask you to move over and we'll go along to the station. I'll want you, too, sir," he added, catching Geoffrey's eye.

" You're making a ridiculous mistake, officer," said Stan trying to recover his lost dignity.

" If I am, sir, they'll let you know at the station."

" I tell you," repeated Stan desperately, getting out to inspect the damage, " nobody's searching for this car."

" That's where you're wrong, old son," said Geoffrey. " George sent the message out—oh, more than two hours ago. Y'see, when I realised you weren't Bill Parsons——"

" What on earth are you talking about ? "

" When you're making a sortie into enemy country you want to make sure you're thoroughly briefed," said Geoffrey in the same gentle voice. " Somebody should have told you that Bill doesn't smoke, and even if he did he wouldn't be carrying a lighter with the initials S.B." He put his hand into his pocket and produced it. The bright surface winked in the sunlight.

" I don't know what this is all about," said the officer stolidly.

" I'll tell you. It's Act Three, Scene One, of the *Lift Murder Case*."

The pressman was suddenly transformed. " What's that ? "

" This," said Geoffrey proudly, " is one of the gang. The rest, including Crook, if I know anything of him, are at Brightstone 1910. If I might make a suggestion, it is that we might join 'em."

" What's going on at B. 1910 ? " asked the enthralled cub reporter. He saw himself making such a scoop as would assure his position on his paper for months, if not years, to come.

Geoffrey proved most accommodating. " My idea is that the police will find Miss Pinnegar there, if they haven't done so already. And if you don't believe me," he added, turning to the perplexed officer, " ring 'em up at that number and learn what's cooking."

" We'll go along to the station," said the policeman, unmoved.

Geoffrey shrugged. " Have it your own way, but first of all . . ." He caught the unsuspecting Stan in a practised grip and before the chap could even protest he had sneaked his revolver out of his pocket. " You might take charge of this," he murmured to the policeman. " I've had the barrel sticking into my ribs—more or less—ever since we started. I'd feel happier if it was in your care."

So, despite Stan's protests and the squeals of the hikers when the gun appeared, they set off for the station.

" Hey, mister," called Sam in outraged tones, " what about the bull ? "

" I'll buy him a wreath that'll make Europa's look like a daisy chain," Geoffrey promised.

The two men looked at one another. Daft. But what could you expect of Londoners ? And wreaths—for their Buttercup !

" This is a real bull, mister," shouted Sam, " not one of they . . ." The car was out of earshot before he could finish the sentence. Buttercup, all this publicity going to his head, made a playful rush at the hikers. The photographer stopped to take a picture of him with his guards, slipped the chaps ten bob apiece, told them they'd find the picture in to-morrow's papers if they were lucky, and went off hell for leather for Brightstone.

CHAPTER XV

As SOON AS she could be moved, which was within a remarkably short time, Miss Pinnegar insisted on returning to her own flat.

" I should appreciate a little privacy for a change," said she with a disdainful sniff. " In hospital one is regarded like a prize pig or a woman with two heads, or some similar monstrosity. And the inspector can visit me there far more easily than in any institution, no matter how well meaning."

Cream agreed at once, but he made the proviso that she shouldn't be entirely alone. Not that he anticipated any further attacks on her life, but he wished to take no unnecessary chances.

" But, of course," beamed Miss Michael, " I shall be only too delighted to do everything possible. It's true I'm not a trained nurse like you, Miss Pinnegar, but I nursed both my dear parents into their graves."

Miss Pinnegar thought she could well believe it. Geoffrey, however, had formed quite an affection for the crazy creature, and Crook said with some severity, " Well, sugar, if it hadn't been for her we should all be taking a collection for a wreath for you. She gave us our first pointer."

" I can see you mean to add to my trials," said Miss Pinnegar rather tartly. " But if you wish to preserve any secrecy about this affair, you will set up an iron curtain between my flat and hers."

" Oh, the time for that was over a long while ago," Crook assured her cosily. " What we want now—at least, what Cream wants—is all the blinding light of publicity he can get. Y'see, a chain's only as strong as its weakest link, and he ain't even got a chain. If enough people start babbling he might get the missing link, and then we can start buildin' the gallows as high as Haman for our pal, Joe Taylor."

" I should have thought there could be no doubt about his fate," exclaimed Miss Pinnegar. " Do you mean to say he is not yet under arrest ? Really, the law seems exceedingly dilatory."

" He's under arrest all right," Crook explained, " on a

charge of attempted murder, jointly with that precious wife
of his. Mind you, it wouldn't surprise me, if he got the
right counsel, if he slipped out of the net like an eel. He
can say he didn't shut you in the garage and that dear Hilda
told him you'd done a bunk."

" Surely no one would believe him."

" Burden of proof's on the police. They've got to prove
he knew you were there, suffocatin' by inches. Likewise,
they can't *prove* he murdered Violet. Yes, I know what
you're goin' to say. Who else had means, motive and
opportunity ? But that ain't good enough for the Law. He
says he wasn't around at the time. When Cream asks where
he was he says he was at home."

" Can anyone prove that he was ? "

" What's more to the point is that no one can prove he
wasn't. We're all dead sure in our minds he sent Violet to
her doom, but until it can be proved the law can't touch him,
not on that count. And Cream's set his heart on seeing him
in the dock on an open-and-shut murder charge."

" What do you suppose happened, Mr. Crook ? " asked
Miss Pinnegar. She was lying up on a meagre sofa, with
Geoffrey on one side and Miss Michael seated at the foot.

" No," Crook had insisted. " I'm not going to talk until
she comes in. She's in the picture, and she might give us
the one hint we're waiting for. That's all we want, just one
scrap of information, one detail we've overlooked or haven't
imagined. If Joe Taylor was here he must have left some
clue, some trace ; of course the police have to play fair,"
he added grudgingly. " It's very hampering for them. They
can't try and trick him as I'd do. Quite a number of chaps
who've been mouldering under quicklime for years 'ud be
walking around to-day if I hadn't tricked 'em into signing
their own death-warrants. And so you want to know how
I think it happened ? I'll tell you. To begin with, I don't
think it was an accident that Violet fell down the shaft. I
think that was part of the original plan. So long as she was
above ground she was a one-way ticket to the Old Bailey
for her pals. The way I see it is this. First of all, along comes
Silver-tongued Sam and puts the comehither on you, honey.
That's, say, half-past four. Round about five Violet comes
in. She has to destroy all trace of drugs in the teacups and
get rid of the coat and hat. She does her act, goes out, clearly

leavin' the door on the latch—you remember (he turned to Miss Michael) you said you hadn't heard it close—and parks the suitcase. That's, say, five-twenty. She puts the ticket for it in the pocket of the mac where Cream found it and sets out on her return journey. In the meantime, Joe has been watching her from some convenient hidey-hole, and as soon as she vanishes into the station he nips up the stairs. The door's open, he goes in. Pretty soon Vi comes back, pulls off your mac, hangs it in the hall, then puts on her coat. At that point there's some interruption. Perhaps she realises Joe's there, perhaps she opens the door and finds he's going through her bag—she wouldn't have taken that noticeable bag to the station—or perhaps she tries to blackmail him. Anyhow, whatever happens, out goes her light and Joe's got the job of getting away. He goes out and reconnoitres; luckily for him, old Ma Thingmajig on the top floor is having a free for all; one half of the people won't know the other half, and I dare say neither Violet nor Joe look any rummer than anyone else."

Miss Pinnegar interrupted. " Had he left the gate open when he brought the lift up ? "

Crook considered that. " Well, sugar," he had to admit, " we shall never really know. My guess 'ud be that he left it ajar and then took the lift up to the top floor. After all, so many people going up there would be a kind of screen for him."

" That pre-supposes murder by intent."

" So it does," acknowledged Crook obligingly. " Mind you, I could be wrong. Maybe he had to chase the lift, bring it back to Floor Five, open the gate and send it up to the floor above. Clearly it was at that floor when Violet took her last (downward) flight. But any road it won't matter to the police if he meant to kill her or he just lost his head and lashed out. The penalty 'ull be the same. Well, he pulls back the gate, pops the corpse into the hole——"

" Bit risky, wasn't it, with all those people going and coming ? " suggested Geoffrey.

" Murder's always risky. But half-past five in the afternoon is as good a time as any. The tenants 'ud either be having their own tea or having it with a buddy at the café over the road. Or maybe they've gone to the pictures. And, as I say, with so many people roaming the stairs Joe's only got to mix with the rest and nobody'll notice him. Where does a wise man hide a leaf ? In the forest. And a stone ? On the beach. Well, part one of the job is done, no one raises the alarm, and back he goes to the flat to take a look round and tie up the odd ends. I suppose the first thing he sees is the bag. He may have forgotten that or he may have kept it deliberately because he's been looking for something, but he's got to send it down after Violet to keep up the pretence of an accidental fall. Out he comes, shuts the door of the flat and—lo and behold—the lift's gone down. That's a pity, but it can't be helped. What he's got to do is nip downstairs, bring the lift up a floor or two, opening one of the gates on the way, run down and chuck the bag into the abyss, close the gate and beat it. It wouldn't take long, you know, and if anyone thinks it's odd a chap carrying a lady's crocodile reticule it'll only be supposed he's been shopping on the top floor. I asked particularly if purchases were wrapped and Her High and Mightiness said ' No,' paper was in short supply, and if people wanted their parcels done up they must bring their own bags. So down he comes (and you know nobody's come forward to say they saw anyone with that bag, and it's pretty strikin'), and then he realises the luck's turned. The last oaf who brought the lift down has jammed it. It can't be moved. Various people, I dare say, are trying, porter's bell is ringing like mad ; he's only got to stand back and watch. I dare say he shoved the bag under his raincoat, it was a poorish sort of day, and most likely he had one. Maybe he even has a shot himself at shifting the thing, but it's no good. He's lost that throw ; all he can do now is get rid of the bag as fast as possible. He takes everything out of it that might prove ownership ; the powder box and lipstick could belong to anyone ; I suppose the gilt initials were too difficult to get out, he daren't take it home in case he meets anyone coming in, but he removes the notes, more, I'd say, to give it a look of a snatched-bag incident than because the money could mean much to him. Latch key ? No, there wouldn't be a latch key. Wonder if she had a railway ticket—the cloakroom ticket for the boxes never turned up—and pitches it on to a bomb-site. Then he goes back, taking care not to be seen. He said in his evidence that he'd been playing the wireless all the afternoon. I wonder if anythin' went wrong with a programme. But even if it did he only has to say he'd gone out to get some cigarettes for a few minutes or post a letter, and, anyway, a chap who can keep the wireless on all the afternoon probably don't listen to half of it. No, there must be something else."

" What have you in mind ? " asked Miss Pinnegar.

" Well, with all those people about someone must have noticed him, coming or going. I did sneak a picture of him up to the top floor and asked the lady if she'd ever seen the chap before and if she'd ask any of her friends if they remembered seeing him."

" Really, Mr. Crook, I hardly see why you should be doing the police's work for them," exclaimed Miss Michael.

" Well, as I said just now, they're handicapped and they've only the evidence to go on. They can believe Joe's guilty till they're blue in the face, and some of 'em 'ud look better that way, but they must have proof. And Cream's got downright bloodthirsty about this."

" Then what do we do now ? " demanded Miss Pinnegar.

" Mark time," said Crook so casually that she could scarcely believe her ears.

" How will that help ? "

" Now, sugar," Crook reproved her, " you know we can't manufacture evidence. Now it's Providence's turn to play a card."

" Why should you expect Providence to intervene ? "

" Don't you believe Providence would go nap on justice ? " asked Crook, sounding rather shocked. " Now, there's no sense you losing any beauty sleep. There's one card that always wins the rubber and that's the invisible witness. We ain't got it in our hand, but Providence has, and we have to wait till Providence chooses to play it. Somewhere," he elaborated, " is someone who'll remember seeing the chap. That's what makes murder so dangerous. You can't get a comprehensive policy."

" The photograph has already been in the papers," objected Miss Pinnegar, sounding almost as bloodthirsty as the sergeant.

" Ah, but our party ain't seen it yet. In hospital maybe, or on a honeymoon, or even in quod. But the wheel comes full circle. You're like me, honey. The hardest command-ment for us to keep is the one that ain't there. Tarry thou the Lord's leisure—likewise, In patience possess your souls."

Crook really did possess the faith that could move mountains and, as usual, it was justified. Soon after this conversation an elderly female, first cousin to Lady Clara Vere de Vere, presented herself at Scotland Yard, accompanied by a friend of Chinese descent, and demanded to see Cream. When an underling tried to explain that he was engaged, she pursed her intolerant old mouth and said it was a bad day for England when the police were too busy to concern themselves with justice. Playing bowls, perhaps ? she suggested. The alarmed constable missed the illusion. The visitor, whose name was Mrs. Leominster, added casually that she had evidence in connection with the lift-shaft murder, which gave the officer an opportunity to inquire why she hadn't said so at once, and he went hell-for-leather for Cream.

" I have evidence," said old Mrs. Leominster. She made Miss Pinnegar look like strawberries and cream. Her aged butler, whose office was still dignified by that outmoded title, said once that if she and Chang Lin, the Pekinese of incredible pedigree who was to prove an essential witness in the affair, went to Moscow they'd have Comrade Stalin rolling on his back with his paws in the air within half an hour.

She now explained to the sergeant that on the day on which the miserable Violet had met her death a monster, whom she identified as Joe Taylor, had kicked her priceless Pekinese. Chang Lin had, naturally, retaliated. The time was about half-past five. If the authorities doubted her word—and her expression said they'd better not—presumably the prison doctor could confirm the fact that the villain bore on one ankle the marks of the peerless champion's teeth.

" What did I tell you, honey ? " exulted Crook, when he heard the news. " Though I ought to have thought of that myself. That boy, Charlie, said there was a bull and cow about some chap who'd complained of being attacked by a Pekinese. And this was the man."

Naturally, the police couldn't take Mrs. Leominster's word for it. She was asked if she could identify this ruffian and she said without hesitation that he was a disgrace to his public school, which was probably Borstal, that any man who wore the rings he wore must be decadent and that Chang Lin never forgot the face of an enemy.

" Must have been wearing his National Health glasses if he could see that far," muttered the disrespectful Mr. Crook. But both witnesses unhesitatingly picked out Joe at a parade, and Joe himself gave the game away by yelling at the little dog to keep off (he was as nervous of him as Stan had been of the bull), he'd bitten him once already and ought to be destroyed. Mrs. Leominster's detailed description of his rings tallied with the police report, and then Joe was faced with the problem so well known to B.B.C. listeners on Tuesday evenings—Talk Yourself Out of This.

Joe did his best, yielding each point only after immense struggle. Yes, he acknowledged, he had been in the neighbourhood on that evening, but he knew nothing about Violet's death. He didn't trust her, and he thought it only a reasonable precaution to hang around to make sure Vi didn't let them down, but declared he had never entered the Mansions. On this point he was pressed without pity. He had simply hung about in the street to make sure that Violet arrived ? Not that. And when he saw her—what then ? Oh, he had watched her emerge with the case and take it over to the station. And had he spoken to her ? No, he hadn't let her see he was there. But he had seen her return to the Mansions ? Yes. Hadn't it surprised him that she should not emerge again ? No, because he hadn't waited.

Once he was sure she had accomplished her mission he had gone into the station and returned home. But suppose Violet had been seen entering the flat—by Miss Michael, say ? Suppose there was trouble ? Didn't he want to be sure she had finished the job ? There was nothing he could do, he insisted. Besides, why should there be trouble ? Then presumably he had rung her up that evening ? How could he, when she was leaving London ? How could he be certain ? Because he'd accompanied her to Charing Cross and seen her dump her baggage. Had she any known destination ? He had no information on that point. You mean, she was involved in a case that was bound to attract a good deal of attention, was wanted by the police as an essential witness, and you had no notion where she was going ? Surely you wanted to keep in touch ?

" I never wanted to see that tramp again," exploded Joe. You say you were deeply anxious that she should leave London. Why ? Because she was dangerous, liable to go to pieces, and then we all knew the police wanted her for the cross-roads crash. And yet, although you were so anxious, you didn't stop to make sure she went ? Didn't want to risk a scene, she was quite daft enough to make one in the middle of the street. Well, then, he was asked, wasn't it more sensible to come to an agreement under cover, i.e., in Miss Pinnegar's flat. You might have made sure if she had a railway ticket. Well, no, she hadn't taken one, not when she put her luggage in.

" But there are travel agencies all over London. She simply had to walk in and get one, and since you didn't speak to her again, you wouldn't know, would you ? "

Joe had to agree that in that case he wouldn't.

" Very likely there was a ticket in her bag before it was ransacked."

" No, there wasn't," insisted Joe, losing his head under this steady rain of questions.

" How do you know ? I thought you hadn't seen the bag ? You said you didn't speak to her when she came out of the station. Come to that, you must have wondered about the ticket for the suitcase. That would be in the bag, of course."

" No, that was in the pocket of the mackintosh."

" How could you be sure ? "

" She—she—oh, it was agreed."

" But she might have forgotten, and since you had made the journey to make sure there were no mistakes, surely you wouldn't go home without making certain everything was in order ? "

Joe hedged and wriggled, but it was no use. A jury of nine men and three women presently found him guilty of wilful murder, and he was brought back to the dock after a remarkably short absence to hear the foreman give the verdict and to see the judge put on the black cap and pronounce sentence of death. It was significant that no attempt was made to get up a reprieve for him. There weren't even grounds for an appeal.

As Crook remarked in his grim fashion, It was curtains for Mr. Taylor.

" So you are one of the elect, Mr. Crook," observed Miss Pinnegar when the result of the trial became public property. " You are justified by faith. I must admit I thought you were very optimistic, but you were proved right."

" How often have you said in your time that God moves in a mysterious way ? " Crook asked her. " And uses the oddest instruments."

He was thinking of Chang Lin, the famous Pekinese, whose picture had been in the papers almost as continuously as Joe's. Miss Pinnegar was thinking of Arthur Crook. She wasn't as surprised as she might have been because she'd had experience of him in the old enthralling Settlement days, but to herself she said that he could give some clergymen points when it came to faith.

" I wonder what Violet's plans really were," speculated Miss Pinnegar. " She was always a fly-by-night, but she can't have anticipated that she wasn't going to need a bed that evening."

" I fancy she never intended to leave London ; not once you were out of the way, sugar. She knew too much, was too dangerous. She saw herself settled for life, for as long as Joe's and Stan's lives went on, that is. And you've told us she regarded the rest of the country as a communal cemetery." (Not that he blamed her for that ; he felt the same himself.) " I think she planned to turn up at Joe's place when the job was done and ask for something on account. You must remember that at that time she didn't know Les had spoken and told the police that it was she who was at the wheel of the stolen car. She knew Joe's hands would be tied, and my guess would be she never thought more than a step ahead. If she had she'd have seen that there was only one thing he could do, which was precisely what he did."

" And the other one—the man who called himself Dr. Weybridge ? What will happen to him ? "

" He won't swing," said Crook thoughtfully, and as it happened, with accuracy. " Y'see, he can say he never guessed his buddy's plans included murder, and there's nothing to prove he did. He can also say, and probably will, that he didn't know you were stiflin' in the garage. He'll play it as a stooge, y'see ; the chap who took orders. ' Call for Miss P. and take her along to Yarmouth Road. We'll do the rest.' And that's just what he did. That may be misdemeanour, but they won't get him for murder. Still, the chap'll be packed away for a nice long time, if that's any satisfaction to you."

Miss Pinnegar lay back on her cushion. She looked very tired. " Oh, I have no desire for revenge," she assured him. " But—what a pitiful waste of a life. When you remember we only have one apiece and there are so many opportunities, I have been so fortunate myself, had such a *good* life, rich, enthralling—to live always on the edge of shameful discovery and then to be locked up. . . . Oh, I don't doubt they deserve whatever they get, Mr. Crook, but imprisonment has always seemed to me a worse fate than death—a new death every day."

" Now, look," said Crook firmly, " that's no way to take it. You think that if it wasn't a new death every day for them (and that's putting it a bit strong, you know) it might be a new death every day for somebody else. Keep your sympathy for that young chap, Carter, if you don't want it on your own account. And now I've got a bit of good news for you," he added. " I've had a word with old Colonel Godalming's man of affairs, and it turns out that the old boy, feeling one of his attacks come on, wrote a letter to the effect that he wanted to leave a legacy to Marcia Pinnegar, née Edwardes, and got two neighbours to witness it, just in case, and that letter's been found among his papers. I'll eat my Sunday go-to-meeting hat if she don't get it in the end." He chuckled. " You should have heard the fellow. Name of Rabbitt. ' The law is not designed to distort justice, but where necessary to enforce it.' " He grinned at Geoffrey. " I told him he should get about more. Coming over for a quick one ? "

Geoffrey was, and the two old maids were left together. " Oh, dear, what exciting lives some people have," said the Goody wistfully. " They say you get the luck you deserve, and perhaps it's true, but—well, no one's ever tried to kidnap me, not even when I was younger. I try not to be envious, I do really, but I do think it's hard."

Miss Pinnegar set her teeth firmly. " If you imagine there is anything pleasurable in being abducted and almost choked to death by noxious fumes you should try it yourself," she remarked.

That, it seemed, was just what Miss Michael yearned to do. " The truth is," she confided, her eyes greener, her hair wilder, her whole aspect madder than ever, " I'm afraid I've been letting my appearance go just a little of late. Sometimes it hardly seems worth while taking a lot of trouble. But this has shown me that it's never too late to hope." She beamed and patted one of Miss Pinnegar's unresponsive hands. " Do you know what I'm going to do now ? I'm going back to my flat and I'm going to write a letter to that droll, fascinating Mr. Crook and ask him to come and have tea with me on Sunday. You can't help feeling, can you, that where there's Crook there's crime, and perhaps it's not too late for something *exciting* to happen even now. Even " —she smiled like someone beholding a beatific vision— " even to me."

>>> If you've enjoyed this book and would like to discover more great vintage crime and thriller titles, as well as the most exciting crime and thriller authors writing today, visit: >>>

The Murder Room
Where Criminal Minds Meet

themurderroom.com

9 781471 909986